ROCK
BOTTOM

Books by Fern Michaels

Sisterhood Novels:

19 Yellow Moon Road
Bitter Pill
Truth and Justice
Cut and Run
Safe and Sound
Need to Know
Crash and Burn
Point Blank
In Plain Sight
Eyes Only
Kiss and Tell
Blindsided
Gotcha!
Home Free
Déjà Vu
Cross Roads
Game Over
Deadly Deals
Vanishing Act
Razor Sharp
Under the Radar

Final Justice
Collateral Damage
Fast Track
Hokus Pokus
Hide and Seek
Free Fall
Lethal Justice
Sweet Revenge
The Jury
Vendetta
Payback
Weekend Warriors

Men of the Sisterhood
Novels:

Hot Shot
Truth or Dare
High Stakes
Fast and Loose
Double Down

FERN MICHAELS
ROCK BOTTOM

KENSINGTON
PUBLISHING CORP.

www.kensingtonbooks.com

KENSINGTON BOOKS are published by

Kensington Publishing Corp.
119 West 40th Street
New York, NY 10018

Copyright © 2023 by Fern Michaels
Fern Michaels is a registered trademark of KAP 5, Inc.

All Kensington titles, imprints and distributed lines are available at special quantity discounts for bulk purchases for sales promotion, premiums, fund-raising, educational or institutional use.

Special book excerpts or customized printings can also be created to fit specific needs. For details, write or phone the office of the Kensington Special Sales Manager: Kensington Publishing Corp., 119 West 40th Street, New York, NY, 10018. Attn. Special Sales Department. Phone: 1-800-221-2647.

The K with book logo Reg US Pat. & TM Off.

Library of Congress Control Number: 2023936110

ISBN-13: 978-1-4967-3712-0
First Kensington Hardcover Edition: September 2023

10 9 8 7 6 5 4 3 2 1

Printed in the United States of America

Prologue

M yra Rutledge was considered one of the most powerful, enigmatic women in business. CEO of a world-fa-
mous candy company, Myra had it all. That was until the day
her pregnant daughter was killed by a hit-and-run driver. The
pain of that loss was almost unbearable, but when the driver
escaped justice due to diplomatic immunity, Myra began a
downward spiral into an emotional abyss. She spent most
days in her nightgown in a semicatatonic state. Not even her
life companion, Charles, could coax any semblance of a
spark from her. He genuinely thought she was going to die of
a broken heart.

One morning, as Myra stared blankly at the television, she
snapped to attention. "Charles! Hand me the remote!" she
shouted. Stunned by this sudden outburst, he ran to her side
and delivered the device. She immediately turned up the volume.

"What is it?" Charles asked with sincere concern.

Myra waved him off. "Shush!" She leaned forward to get
a closer look at what was being broadcast. It was another
story of failed justice, but the real story began when the
mother of the victim shot the perpetrator as he left the court-

room. A puzzled Charles did a double take at the TV but kept himself from asking his question again. He had an idea of what was going through Myra's head and knew she would tell him when she was ready.

Myra then asked for the phone and called her adopted daughter Nikki, a very high-profile lawyer. Nikki was also shocked at the sound of her mother's voice. "Mom! Are you okay?" Nikki didn't know what to make of this resurrection.

"Sweetheart. Have you seen the news?"

"Which part?" Nikki asked.

Myra began to recall what she had just witnessed and ended the explanation with, "I want you to represent that woman."

And so, it began. The Sisterhood.

Over the next few months Myra and Nikki scoured the national news to find other women who'd been failed by the system. One by one, each had her turn at handing out the justice deserved. Now it had become Myra's life's work to use her resources and the many talents of the women she had helped—not to fix a miserably broken system, but to correct its mistakes . . . in her own way.

Charles remained Myra's confidant, husband and bodyguard. He utilized his formidable skills as an ex-MI6 officer surreptitiously. Myra's childhood friend Countess Anna Ryland de Silva was her equal in wealth and spirit. She lived on an estate next door to Myra's home at Pinewood with Fergus, the former head of Scotland Yard. Anna—who went by Annie—also owned the *Post* in Washington, D.C., one of the largest newspapers in the country.

Myra's century-old farm, Pinewood, sat atop several tunnels once used by the Underground Railroad. Charles and Fergus furnished the subterranean hideaway, making it into a well-appointed headquarters, equipping the space with the most elaborate state-of-the-art technology. They referred to it as the "war room," but by any definition it rivaled something used by the Pentagon.

Handpicked by Myra, Nikki, and Anna, the "Sisters" came from a broad range of lifestyles, from an eighteen-wheeler truck driver to a floral designer, a journalist with a nose for a story, and an architect with a talent for computer hacking. While on the surface they had little or nothing in common, they shared the same determination to take control of their lives and right a few wrongs.

When not involved in one of their campaigns, the Sisters continued to lead their own busy, complicated lives complete with the usual family drama, tested relationships, and normal career challenges. They just happened to have a hobby— conspiring and conducting elaborate plans that led to the well-deserved downfall of the people who heinously crossed them and society.

This is their thirty-fifth mission.

Chapter One

Izzie and Yoko

Isabelle "Izzie" Flanders was going over a set blueprints for a new market village. She and Yoko had won the bid on a project being funded by the local commerce commission. It was going to be the centerpiece of this quaint Virginia town, and the project would require tons and tons of commercial materials. Izzie and Yoko had spent months gathering quotes, designing and redesigning the layout. Now they finally had something they knew would be accomplished with the best materials and workmanship.

Izzie was lost in thought when her phone rang. "This is Izzie." Her brow furrowed as she listened. "For how long?" She stood erect. "Do you know when you will have an answer?" She pursed her lips. "I see. Uh-huh." She listened as panic crawled up her spine. "Thank you for letting us know." She set herself and the phone down simultaneously. She shut her eyes and began tapping her fingers on the long plank worktable. The phone call had not been good news.

Yoko glided into the office carrying samples of potted plants. "Izzie. Look at these! I think they will look fantastic in the planters outside the windows." She stopped abruptly when she saw the look on Izzie's face. She quickly set the large box on a side table. "What's wrong?" Yoko could tell by Izzie's expression it was more than getting the wrong coffee at the café.

"I just got a call from the general contractor." Izzie looked up.

"What about?" Yoko took a seat in front of her.

"He said the subcontractor who is going to handle the masonry work is having supply chain issues."

"Seriously? Still?" Yoko shook her head. "It seems like it's been years already."

"There are still a lot of goods in transit. He said in some cases there's a backlog of eighteen months, depending on what country they're coming from." She sighed. "The good news is that when it all arrives, there will be a lot of merchandise in the stores, so there will probably be a lot of things on sale."

Yoko tried to make light of the situation. "Oh yes! They'll have bathing suits on sale at Christmas, and Christmas trees on sale in April."

Izzie snorted. "Swell. Thanks for putting a positive spin on it." Izzie propped herself up on her elbows, her face supported by her fists. "We planned to break ground in a month." She let out a big sigh.

Yoko sat silently for a minute. "There has to be someone else who could do the work, no?"

"I suppose, but they might be having the same issues. Plus, it may cost us a lot more than we put in the budget." Izzie was no shrinking violet, but at that moment she thought she might cry.

Yoko reached for Izzie's hand. "Alright. Let's think about this. Anyone you're still in touch with from engineering school?"

Izzie's face brightened. "Brilliant, Yoko! Yes! Zoe Danfield. She's a VP at REBAR. They're one of the world's largest suppliers of foundation materials."

"Okay. There's a start."

"But I don't know if they would want to take on a small job like ours. They do major commercial construction. Bridges, hotels. Stuff like that."

"Well, it wouldn't hurt to ask if she could at least recommend someone."

"True." Izzie recalled the time after college when she and Zoe had worked for the same firm. Then Izzie had decided to open her own business and Zoe had moved on to corporate America.

Izzie's mood brightened as she scrolled through her contact list. She punched in the number and hit the CALL button. Two rings later a voice answered, "Zoe Danfield."

"Zoe!" Izzie was surprised to hear Zoe's voice on the other end instead of her assistant. "It's Izzie!"

"Hey, Izzie. How are you?" Zoe sounded stressed. Tightly wound.

"I'm doing well. And you?" Izzie gave the phone a strange look.

Zoe's voice was hushed. "Uh, I'm okay. Just a little overworked. You know the feeling."

"I do indeed." Izzie was mustering an upbeat response, but sensed something wasn't right with her friend. "Listen, there's a project Yoko and I are working on, and we are in dire need of masonry work. The company we had originally planned to use is having a shortage of supplies and we are on a very tight deadline."

There was hesitation in Zoe's voice. "I'm not sure how I can be of help."

"I thought you might be able to recommend someone for me."

"That's possible." Zoe hesitated again. "Perhaps I should come down there and look at your plans."

"I can send you a zip-file."

"No, I'd rather review them in person," Zoe said flatly.

Izzie made another odd face at the phone. "Okay. But I know you're busy and I don't want to take up too much of your time."

"I insist." She paused. "For old time's sake." Zoe's office was in New York City, so it would be a three-hour ride on Amtrak to Alexandria.

"That would be fantastic!" Izzie was delighted Zoe could break free from her hectic schedule. "Can you spend the night? We can have a sleepover." Izzie chuckled. "Like we used to!"

"Only if you promise not to cook." Zoe's voice brightened a bit.

"Oh stop. I've become quite a good cook. Myra's husband, Charles, is quite the gourmet and has taught us a few dishes."

"Myra?" Zoe asked.

"Myra Rutledge."

"The candy person?"

"One and the same," Izzie answered, choosing her words carefully. Even though she and Zoe were still in touch, the Sisterhood had never been part of their conversations. She knew she had to clarify a few things, especially if Zoe was coming for a quick visit. "We met at a charity function a few years ago. It was for Animal Care Sanctuary. We discovered we have a few things in common and meet regularly with a small group of other women. That's how I met Yoko, my partner in this project." Izzie realized she had said enough and segued into a more neutral subject by mentioning her husband. "Abner is away on business so we can be loosey-goosey."

"Sounds good." Zoe's voice was a bit steadier. "How's this Friday?"

Izzie checked her desk diary. "Perfect." That would give them the weekend to discuss what needed to be done so they could hit the deck running on Monday.

"Looking forward to seeing you, Izzie." Zoe sounded melancholy.

"Zoe? Is everything alright?" Izzie's intuition was kicking in. Something in Zoe's voice was off.

"Oh, you know. The usual set of daily upheavals." She gave a strained laugh.

"I totally get it." Izzie scribbled a note in her book. "What time will you get in?"

"Noon? Does that work for you?" Zoe asked.

"Absolutely." Izzie circled the word *noon* on the calendar. "I'll pick you up at Union Station."

"I can take a cab," Zoe replied.

"You shall do no such thing," Izzie said with authority. "I'll be waiting outside the station. Silver Lexus SUV."

"Great. Thanks, Izzie."

"I should be thanking you!" Izzie said with a laugh. "See you Friday." She hung up and looked at Yoko. "Something is up with her."

"Marriage problems?" Yoko guessed, not knowing Zoe's situation.

"No. Not married. No kids. No boyfriend that I know of. She travels a lot. Hard to keep something going when you're on the move."

"Family?" Yoko asked casually.

"Kinda normal, as far as I can remember. Parents are in Arizona. She has one brother. Pharmacist. Lives in Boston with his partner." Izzie squinted and cocked her head. "She didn't sound like her usual self."

"Could it be a health issue?" Yoko mused.

"Geez, I hope not." Izzie shook her head. "It's something else." She tapped her pencil against her chin.

"Well, don't go hacking into her email, please." Yoko gave her a wry smile. "I know you when you want information."

"Hey, wait a gosh darn second. I have never spied on anyone. Well, not anyone who deserved *not* to be spied on." She raised her eyebrows. Yoko knew exactly what Izzie meant. Only a mission was cause enough to dive into someone's personal data. Once an individual broke the law or inflicted serious harm to a person or animal, all bets were off. There might as well be a big sign with an arrow pointing at their head: DUMBASS. DO WHAT YOU MUST.

"Fair enough." Yoko nodded. "I'm glad she will be coming in person. People can accomplish much more when there is a dialogue and eye contact in three-dimensional form." She was being philosophical. "I cannot imagine a virtual floral arrangement. I realize they exist, but it's such a flat experience. This NFT thing everyone is raving about. Non-fungible token. What *is* that?"

"It's all smoke and mirrors if you ask me." Izzie was busying herself rearranging things on her desk. "How can something that is only digital be worth anything, unless it's information?" She twisted her mouth. "I don't get it. We live in a three-dimensional world. And yes, we must rely on technology to get a lot of our work done. But the result is something you can touch, smell, see. Too many people depend on illusions for their reality."

Yoko folded her arms. "I completely agree with you, but I think you are on the verge of waxing a bit more philosophical than usual."

Izzie looked up from the pile of papers she had put back in order. "Huh. You are right. I guess it's because we are constantly faced with challenges and I believe if we are calm and thoughtful we can find a solution."

"Again, you are sounding more Zen than usual." Yoko smiled.

"It's your influence on me." Izzie smiled back.

"I think we need to take a few deep breaths and then get something to eat," Yoko suggested.

"But it's only three o'clock." Izzie double-checked the time.

"Ice cream does not work by the clock." Yoko grinned.

"Now that is what I call a splendid idea." Izzie felt much more relaxed knowing there might be a light at the end of the tunnel and it wasn't an oncoming train. She grabbed her cell phone, and they walked the half block to Lickety Split. Izzie ordered salted caramel in a sugar cone and gave it a taste. "We should do this more often."

Yoko nodded as she wiped the dribbling chocolate swirl from her chin.

The two sat on one of the benches under a small grove of trees. Izzie squinted again, a sign she was thinking hard, as if she was trying to see what was in her brain. "They should make it a law that everyone must have at least one ice cream cone a week. I think that would really help in our angst-ridden society." Izzie swirled her tongue around the creamy mixture. "Think about it. When you are eating an ice cream cone, you're really focused on the task at hand. Otherwise, it would be all over you or on the ground. Multitasking is not an option."

Yoko giggled. "You have a good point, great wise one. Now if you would shut up and eat your cone, you would be practicing what you are preaching."

Izzie gave Yoko an elbow tap that knocked her hand into her face, smearing chocolate up her nose.

"Ugh!" Yoko blurted. She grabbed a napkin and removed the excess from her nostrils. Izzie was doubled over laughing.

Once she regrouped, Yoko announced, "You can add, 'sitting six feet away from someone who is eating a cone.' "

Izzie looked at Yoko's face. She still had a mustache of dairy and sprinkles hanging above her lip. Izzie went into a tailspin of hysterics while Yoko continued to clean up her mess. Yoko sneered as she dabbed her face with the balled-up, used napkin. "Yes, there should be an 'eat your ice cream alone' rule."

Izzie jumped up and dashed back into the shop, grabbed a bottle of water and a few more napkins. She plunked down several one-dollar bills. "My friend doesn't know how to use a cone," she joked.

Ruby, the owner, smiled. "If you say so." She gave a wink and gestured toward the front window, where she'd had a bird's-eye view of the incident. While Izzie and Yoko weren't regulars, everyone knew each other in the village green area.

Izzie returned to a sticky Yoko and offered her the cleanup items. As Yoko removed the last of the red and yellow sprinkles, Izzie marched back into the shop and bought another cone for Yoko. "Make it a double." Izzie leaned on the counter and peered over the edge. "Got any towels back there?" she asked jokingly.

Ruby handed her a stack of paper towels. "This should do it." She placed her hands on her hips. "If not, I can't help ya gals." She snickered as Izzie took the cone and carefully returned to her ice-creamed friend.

Izzie held out the cone with one hand and a pile of napkins in the other. "Sorry, Choco-Yoko."

"Funny. Ha. Ha." Yoko swapped the soiled, ice-cream-laden napkins for the clean paper towels and grabbed the cone from Izzie's fist. "You may have redeemed yourself."

They sat in silence for a few minutes, concentrating on their cones, before Izzie spoke. "Depending on who Zoe can recommend, we may need to adjust our budget," she said contemplatively.

"And our profit," Yoko added between licks.

"As long as we don't lose money we should be alright. We have about twenty thousand in reserve, although I'd hate to have to dip into that."

"Agreed." Yoko took another wipe at her chin.

"Well, let's not worry about it until we *must* worry about it. Remember what Annie always says: 'Worry is like paying a debt you don't owe.' "

Yoko gave her a sideways look. "I agree with that concept. Wait until it becomes a problem and then put energy into solving the problem."

"Bingo!" Izzie resisted the temptation to poke Yoko again. One ice cream mess was enough for the day.

When they had finished their treats, they strolled back to Izzie's office. "Let's check out your samples." Izzie looked at the long, white box Yoko had carried in earlier.

Yoko pointed to some of the more unusual plants. "We can do *Achillea millefolium*, also known as white yarrow, for the summer. It has clusters of creamy white flowers. I'll leave room for some exotic annuals." She pulled the sketches of the gardens from her messenger bag. "This will have hydrangeas and boxwood. Then in this corner we'll do a winter mixture of purple moon grass and euonymus." Yoko's passion for plants came through like a giant beam of light. "Then we'll put these in the shaded area," she said, tapping on the photos of the hostas, hellebore, Epimedium and spiderwort. "Together, these varieties should create a tapestry of green."

"Yoko, I think you have outdone yourself. It is going to be magnificent."

Yoko bowed in gratitude. "I want people to really look at the plantings as something artful. Not just a bunch of bushes and flowers."

"I think you have that mastered." Izzie gave her a fist bump. High fives had been the "Sister Salute," but after COVID they'd adopted the fist bump as their new gesture of appreciation and accomplishment. "Floral and landscaping design is an artform for sure."

"That reminds me—do you remember Myra's friend Camille Pierce? From New York?" Yoko asked.

"Vaguely. Involved in the arts? Married to a banker?"

"Yes. Myra told me that Camille introduced her to a woman outside of Ashville, North Carolina. Ellie Stillwell. Ellie built an art center and had the interior and exterior landscaped by a local artist, and it's gone on to win awards."

"I heard about that place. Sounded remarkably interesting."

"Yes. Made me think about expanding my business." Yoko looked at Izzie. "After our project, of course."

"Well, if we can get this masonry issue sorted and we accomplish what we have in mind, you will be in high demand. That much I am certain of."

"I feel as if I need to stretch myself a bit. Don't get me wrong. Our business is doing very well. But I think I would like to create more spaces with the plants that I grow," Yoko said thoughtfully. "I nurture them while they grow, and then I sell them. Once they leave the nursery, I have no control over what happens to them."

Izzie chuckled. "Aw, you sound like a mommy whose kids are all grown up and are leaving home."

"Well, it's not that different." Yoko pouted.

"I know. I know. They are your babies. I get it." Izzie winked. "But I also think you have a very good idea."

"It came to me while I was working on these sketches. Why haven't I been doing this all along?" She gave herself a slight smack on the forehead. "Duh."

"It does not matter how slowly you go, as long as you don't stop," Izzie reminded her friend.

"I think you have been channeling Confucius today." Yoko grinned. "And for my family's sake, let's include *Chansu wa jibun de tsukuru mono*, which means 'You create your own opportunities.' "

"Exactly!" Izzie's mood was improving as the day moved on.

Several years earlier Isabelle Flanders had been an up-and-coming architect, with her own firm and a fiancé. One night she went out with several friends. They were celebrating the promotion of one of their colleagues at a large industrial commercial firm. After hours of many rounds of alcoholic libations, Izzie decided to call it quits. She'd only had two drinks that night, but didn't want to get behind the wheel of her car. One of her colleagues, Rosemary, appeared to be abstaining from the drinks and offered to drive Izzie home.

Thinking her friend was better equipped to make the journey, Izzie had handed her the keys. The women got into the car and started home. A few miles down the road, Rosemary decided to put the pedal to the metal and started zooming down the highway. The car hydroplaned, crashing into another vehicle and knocking Izzie unconscious. When she finally came around, she noticed the strong smell of whiskey on her clothes and a police officer shining a flashlight into her face.

"Have you been drinking, miss?" It was a rhetorical question.

A dazed Izzie looked around and discovered she was the only person in the car. In the driver's seat. "Where is . . ." She was stunned and confused. She did not recall getting behind the wheel.

"Where is what?" the officer asked.

"My . . . my friend," she stuttered.

"There is no one here but you, miss. Do you know where you are?" He pursued his line of questioning.

Izzie tried to stand but her head was spinning.

"Looks like you got yourself banged up there, miss. But

you're in better shape than the rest of them." He eyed her closely.

"Who? What? What are you talking about?" Izzie held up her hand to block the searing light in her eyes.

"The people in the other vehicle," he said bluntly.

"I don't understand."

"I am going to have to ask you to step out of the car."

As the numbness began to fade, Izzie tasted something strong and sour on her lips. Whiskey. She never drank whiskey. Izzie slowly climbed from the driver's seat and steadied herself against the car door.

"License and registration, please."

Izzie blinked several times. "In my purse." She paused for a moment. "Passenger side." She was certain she had been sitting there, but with the lights, sirens, and the smell of alcohol, she wasn't sure if this whole thing wasn't a bad dream. "Officer? I am certain there was someone with me. Someone else was driving. My friend and colleague, Rosemary."

He gave her a stone-faced look. "I can tell you that you are the only person on the scene, except for the three dead bodies being lifted into the coroner's van."

Izzie's legs began to tremble. *What was happening?* She moved toward the hood and leaned against it. *Think. Think!*

The officer pulled Izzie's purse from the right side of the car, rifled through it, and found her wallet. He took her driver's license and opened the glove compartment, where most people keep the registration and insurance documents. They all matched. *Isabelle Flanders*. He walked over to where Izzie was slumped in a crumpled mess.

"Isabelle Flanders, I am placing you under arrest for driving while intoxicated and vehicular homicide."

Izzie turned and retched all over her shoes. The stench of alcohol mixed with vomit was overwhelming. Even *she* would assume she had been on a bender.

"Officer, this is all a big mistake."

"I know. That's what they all say." He brought her to his patrol car and placed his hand on her head as he assisted her into the back.

Finally, Izzie was able to focus on the scene. It was horrific. Two ambulances remained silent. Several police cars had their flashing lights in motion as the medical examiner's van pulled away. The other car was completely crushed like an accordion. From what she could tell, the car had been T-boned and pushed into a guardrail. She peered past the chaos and saw a shadowy figure in the distance. Izzie recognized her. It was Rosemary. Izzie began pounding on the window. "Rosemary! Rosemary!" The woman turned and spotted Izzie, turned again and made a beeline into the darkness. Izzie shouted to the police officer standing closest to the squad car. "Sir! Officer!"

He strolled over to the window. "Yes?"

"There was another person in the car. She was driving. I just saw her in the distance. It was Rosemary!" Izzie insisted. "She ran the other way."

The officer smirked and nodded. "Good story." He glanced in the direction where Izzie was pointing, but there was no one there. He tsked and walked away.

Tears came streaming down Izzie's face. *How could this be happening?* She tried to quiet her nerves, assuring herself everything would be sorted out. She would give them her statement, then they would question Rosemary, and the matter would be cleared up.

But that's not what happened. The following day, when the police questioned Izzie's colleague, she said she knew nothing of the situation. Yes, she and Izzie left the pub around the same time, but Izzie drove off by herself. None of that was true, but Izzie couldn't prove it. Unbeknownst to Izzie, Rosemary carried a flask in her purse to offset the effects of the cocaine she took regularly. The cocaine that had prompted her to drive so fast that night.

When the collision occurred, Izzie had struck her head on the car window, knocking her unconscious. Rosemary saw the opportunity to pull Izzie into the driver's seat and pour the remains of her flask into Izzie's mouth and on her clothes. There was no way Izzie was going to get out of the legal nightmare Rosemary had entrapped her in. And she didn't. Izzie spent a few years in jail. Her former fiancé eventually became betrothed to Rosemary, and her architectural firm fell apart. Her life was in ruins. That was until she met Myra Rutledge.

Chapter Two

Zoe Danfield

Zoe Danfield grew up in the rural town of Point Pleasant, West Virginia. The county seat of Mason County, it sits at the convergence of the Ohio and Kanawha Rivers. The town is designated on the National Registry of Historic Places. Locally, Point Pleasant is celebrated as the "First official battle site of the American Revolutionary War." However, for most people, history does not necessarily come to mind when discussing the area. Two things usually enter the conversation: the Silver Bridge and the legend of Mothman.

In 1967, the Silver Bridge connecting Ohio to West Virginia collapsed, killing forty-six people, the deadliest bridge collapse in U.S. history. Built in 1928, it was known as the "Gateway to the South," allowing for more efficient commerce and commuting. It was also known for its propensity to shake and pitch. Many daily users complained, but to no avail.

Then, on December 15, 1967, a final horrifying shudder began at the Ohio tower, with each link breaking like a string of pop beads. Quickly, the bridge toppled over, pulling thirty-one vehicles and sixty-four people into the forty-four-degree water, causing the deaths of forty-six. The disaster was the impetus for the creation of the National Bridge Inspection Standards.

It was determined that the first link below the Ohio tower had suffered internal stress corrosion. The contractor, American Bridge Company, had settled on a cheaper building material, one susceptible to corrosion. Instead of using cable steel, such as that used for the Golden Gate Bridge and the Brooklyn Bridge, they'd decided on eyebars. The eyebar is a long, flat piece of steel with two round holes at each end that connects to the next eyebar with a pin. And it was an eyebar that collapsed under the weight of rush hour traffic. It was deemed an unforeseeable accident and the engineer and contractors were not assigned blame. Twelve years later a small settlement was reached in the amount of nine hundred and fifty thousand dollars. People were heartbroken, but they carried on.

A strange offshoot of the tragedy was the rise of folklore around the Mothman, described as a humanoid creature—a brown human-bug hybrid. He was said to be six foot seven, with bright red eyes and a wingspan of ten feet. It's said that there were sightings of him starting November 15, 1967, until December 15, 1967, the day of the bridge disaster. Some think he is the harbinger of doom, while others think he is Doom itself, causing horrible disasters. He is a favorite legend of those intrigued by the paranormal, and allegedly haunts an abandoned TNT factory from World War II.

Every year the town celebrates this fabled creature with a Mothman Festival, featuring films, parades, pageants, music, and a variety of events. The townsfolk say it's their biggest tourist attraction, with the Mothman Museum as the centerpiece. The legend was clinched by the publication of John Keel's 1975 book *The Mothman Prophecies*, which was subsequently made into a film starring Richard Gere.

But for Zoe, the idea of the Mothman was just creepy and she avoided discussing him . . . it . . . with anyone. It wasn't that she didn't believe the paranormal existed—just the opposite. When the Mothman movie was released, Zoe was at the impressionable age of fourteen. And who wouldn't believe Richard Gere? The book was even more disturbing to her. It was advertised as a true story of the paranormal experienced by a journalist. Yes, Zoe was aware of the mysterious and mystical, and she preferred to stay as far away from it as possible.

But what truly haunted her was the Silver Bridge disaster. Even though the collapse had occurred two decades before she was born, Zoe was fixated on the tragedy. It was a major part of the town's history and was mentioned on a regular basis. For Zoe, the photo on a shelf at her great-uncle Ralph's was a daily reminder. Zoe's father would occasionally speak about it. He had been five years old at the time. That evening his father came bursting through the kitchen door with the devastating news that his brother had gone into the river.

The history of the tragedy affected her on a deep, cellular level. She sensed the pain her father had felt hearing the news of his uncle's death and seeing his father cry for the first time. It was like having something ripped from your chest. If she let it, it would take the wind out of her. As a child she liked to play with Legos and Tinkertoys, determined to build something unbreakable. Something that wouldn't fall apart and kill innocent people.

It was clear to her family, friends, and teachers that Zoe was bright and curious. Almost obsessive. By the time she was ten she had more building blocks, dowels, joints, and wheels than the entire town combined. Her mother was constantly after Zoe to dismantle her creations so she could vacuum her room. After a lot of pouting and sulking on her part, Zoe's dad rigged a piece of plywood on two sawhorses in the basement, where she would spend hours after school. A few years later, when she began high school, Zoe's parents worried about her lack of interaction with kids her age, until she finally revealed the small village she had created. She entered it in a school contest and won a thousand-dollar prize. At that point, her parents' only concern was how they would pay for a college degree for their kid. She certainly had the brains. And the determination. They knew if Zoe wanted to go to a high-ranking engineering school, it would have to be on scholarship. She studied hard and made few friends. It wasn't because she wasn't personable. Getting into college was her priority. Even dating boys would have to wait.

Ironically, she was also interested in high fashion. She viewed clothing as if it were a building, fascinated by shape, width, height, proportion, color, and texture. And form. It wasn't surprising that her only two magazine subscriptions were *Popular Mechanics* and *Vogue*. She would analyze the structures of the seasonal fashion collections, but also deeply admired Anna Wintour. Wintour was *Vogue*'s editor-in-chief, a position she held for almost thirty-five years. Zoe respected Wintour's climb to success. At age twenty-one Wintour began working as an editorial assistant, forging ahead to become the most powerful woman in the fashion industry. Zoe was impressed with Wintour's reputation for being exacting and her personal taste in clothes. Fortunately for Zoe, she was tall and thin and able to carry off a similar look: bobbed haircut with bangs, and large, black-rimmed glasses. The only thing she did not mimic were Wintour's high-heeled shoes. Zoe was tall enough without them. Maybe if she had a limo like Anna, she might consider it, but only kitten heels. In the meantime, she would have to work her way up to *The Devil Wears Prada* lifestyle.

But Zoe was resourceful and found less expensive ways to achieve a "titan of industry" look. That style helped her gain a position in the male-dominated business of commercial manufacturing. Her civil engineering degree along with her master's degree in business management made her an excellent candidate for upward mobility. And her personal style of dress spelled out "I know what I'm doing" loud and clear. Zoe was somewhat of an enigma. At first glance she was intimidating. Then she would smile and warm the room. Powerful, yet gracious.

It didn't take long for her to rise to the level of Vice President of International Sales at the REBAR Corporation; manufacturer of industrial building materials. Her work in design and development slowly morphed into different responsibilities as the company changed hands. They were consolidating divisions and she could either go in the desired direction or find work elsewhere. Zoe took well to her new position reviewing potential clients' plans, making recommendations, and sealing the deal. She never considered herself a salesperson, but she was quite good at selling. Perhaps it was because she had vast engineering knowledge and could articulate the various options to the clients. In turn the clients felt confident they were in the right hands.

Zoe had been with the company for just over ten years. It was exciting, watching their projects come to fruition. She was able to travel the globe, checking on job sites where her company supplied the foundation materials. Everywhere from São Paulo, Brazil, to Mumbai, India, to Rome, Italy. But now she was having serious misgivings about her job, her future, her ethics, and, most importantly, her life.

Ever since she'd started asking questions about the quality

control department, her life had turned upside down. She was transferred to a different department and a few times she thought someone was following her. Then came the hang-up calls from phones with "Unavailable" as the caller ID. The near-miss on a subway platform had been chilling. She was getting spooked. Only the idea of the Mothman could produce the feeling she was experiencing. She was beginning to think she was on her one last nerve.

Chapter Three

Zoe and Izzie

Zoe and Izzie had met at Tufts University when they were freshmen. Izzie was majoring in architectural engineering and Zoe in civil. It happened in the cafeteria. The room was packed with students and Izzie was craning her neck to find a place to sit. A student was sitting at the end of a crowded table in the corner. It was her severe haircut and black glasses that caught Izzie's eye. The only available seat was across from her. Izzie studied the situation and approached the table.

"Anyone sitting here?" she asked politely.

"No."

"Nope."

"Uh-uh."

Zoe was the only one who looked up at Izzie before answering. She tilted her head toward the available chair. "Please."

Izzie squeezed her way between the crowded tables. She could barely pull out the chair. She set down her tray and wiggled into her seat. "Izzie Flanders," she said. No one else looked in her direction. The others were caught up in conversations of their own.

"Zoe Danfield." The fashionable student was holding her coffee mug with both hands.

"Nice to meet you, Zoe Danfield." Izzie smiled and placed her napkin on her lap.

Zoe smirked. She would bet she and Izzie were the only two people in the entire room who would bother to put their napkins on their laps.

Izzie looked up. "What?"

Zoe set her cup down and pulled the napkin from her lap. She rolled her eyes around the room.

"Ha!" Izzie snorted. She decided at that very moment she wanted to be friends with this mysterious, chic woman who stood out from the rest of the scruffy students.

After they graduated, they both went to work for the City of Boston building department. The pay was decent but the passion and opportunities for them to truly blossom were nonexistent. Each moved on to other jobs: Zoe to a private corporation in New York and Izzie to start her own architectural firm. But after Izzie's tumultuous legal battles, jail time, and a broken heart, she decided a change of scenery was called for and moved to Virginia. The two stayed connected over the years, and Izzie was forever grateful for Zoe's support when she was doing time in the Graybar Hotel.

Friday came quickly and Izzie scrambled to get to Union Station in time to pick up Zoe. She remembered Friday was a busy day at Union Station, with Washington politicians rushing to catch an early train home or the shuttle to the airport. After much honking from other drivers, she found a spot on the other side of the taxi stand, put the car in park, turned on her flashers, got out and leaned against the hood. She kept an eye out for traffic police and the frenzied bicyclists turning in their bike shares before the meter turned over.

The crowds emptied from the station in waves, signaling a train arrival. Izzie stretched her neck and spotted her lanky friend with her signature black, chin-length bob and bold, black-rimmed glasses. She was wearing a chic pantsuit with a long, tailored jacket in hunter green with turquoise and gold trim. The chunky necklace over the ivory silk blouse made her look as if she'd stepped out of the pages of a fashion magazine. Izzie remembered Zoe always had an artsy flair for clothes. "Woo-hoo! Over here!" Izzie shouted.

Zoe gave a quick wave, advanced through the throng, and crossed over the taxi lanes. She gave Izzie a big bear hug.

"I'm so happy to see you!" Izzie exclaimed.

Zoe pulled away from their friendly embrace and looked Izzie straight in the eye. "Me too."

"You're looking smashing as usual." Izzie grabbed Zoe's overnight case and put it in the back seat.

"Thank you, my dear. I found a great seamstress off Seventh Avenue who can make exact replicas of couture. The only rule is we cannot use the same fabrics. Same style, but different colors and patterns."

"Well, you certainly look 'mahvelous,' " Izzie replied as she looked her friend up and down.

They climbed into her SUV and started with the usual small talk about the train ride and how the train couldn't go as fast as possible because of the rickety tracks. "But at least it still got me here in less than three hours," Zoe noted. "I remember the last two times I flew from LaGuardia to National, it took over four hours by the time I got to the airport, schlepped down the concourse, and then sat on the runway for over an hour. The flight was only forty minutes, but we had to circle National for another half hour. Then we landed, schlepped down another concourse, blah, blah, blah. It was so aggravating." Zoe exhaled.

"And you are here now!" Izzie exclaimed.

"Yes, I am." Zoe tilted her head to see the Washington Monument and the Capitol Building pass by.

Izzie treaded carefully with her next question. "So, what's happening in your life?" Izzie noticed how tense Zoe seemed. Almost paranoid, but she didn't want to overstep.

Zoe didn't answer right away. She craned her neck to look over her shoulder. "This is where all the major decisions are made." She shook her head. "My, how government has changed leadership. Or, lack thereof."

Izzie furrowed her brow. "I totally agree. But don't get me started!" She guffawed. She waited a beat, expecting Zoe to say something, but she remained silent. Izzie stepped on the brake and looked Zoe straight in the eye: "Is everything alright? I mean really alright? You seem a bit tense."

Zoe took a deep breath. "I'll tell you about it after we get settled."

"You got it." Izzie drove them the rest of the way to her house with the expectation of unraveling what was happening to her unraveled friend. The drive took about a half hour with Zoe remaining zip-lipped about what was really on her mind. Instead, she asked more banal questions. "How is Abner? Work?" All the usual queries.

Soon Izzie pulled into the large, circular driveway made of gray paving stones. Ahead was the old pickle factory she and Abner had converted into their home. The exterior of the building exactly matched the Virginia bluestone. "We had to cover those hideous green cement walls."

"You did a fabulous job," Zoe said with admiration.

Izzie parked to the side of the meticulously manicured sidewalk leading up to the five bluestone slabs that served as stair treads to the front entry. The custom-made double doors featured frosted glass inserts. Next to one of the doors was a four-by-six-inch box that matched the trim. A door popped open when Izzie tapped the front. Inside the box was a very intricate security alarm. Izzie punched a code into the panel. At the same time, a slight "woof" came from inside. Through the frosted panels Zoe could make out an exceptionally large dog, with noticeably big paws and lots of shaggy hair. The door clicked open and Rufus waited patiently, his tail wagging to the beat of his own drum.

Izzie bent down to cuddle her mutt. "Hello, my pal. Look who I brought home. Say nice to meet you, Zoe!" The dog gave another soft woof and held out his paw.

Zoe squatted to meet the dog face-to-face. "Nice to meet you, too. I guess you feel pretty safe here."

Izzie thought that was an odd comment. "Uh, yes. But I don't think about it. I guess that's because I *do* feel safe." Izzie paused. "Are you going to tell me what the heck is going on or do I have to smack it out of you?" At the word *smack* the dog cringed. Izzie patted Rufus on the head. "It's okay, pal." She looked at Zoe. "Shelter dog." Izzie continued to coddle the big pooch.

Zoe nodded. "He seems like a big mush."

"Come on. I'll show you to your room." Izzie nodded toward the second-floor loft space. The main level was an open floor plan of almost three thousand square feet. The living and dining areas faced a wall of windows. A well-appointed kitchen with a large slate center island divided the space. On the far left, eight-foot sliding doors separated Izzie's and Abner's home offices.

"Your place is beautiful," Zoe said with admiration.

"Thank you. And functional." Izzie grinned, reminding Zoe of one of their professors who had banged the drum about functionality. Izzie led the way up the staircase to the balcony over the main living area. On opposite sides were two large seating areas that overlooked the lower level. They mirrored each other with club chairs, bookcases, and a long table. Adjacent to one lounge area were the two guest bedrooms, each with ensuite baths. On the other side was Izzie and Abner's master suite. Each had its own bathroom and dressing area. It wasn't overdone. Simple, functional, with all the modern amenities including multiple showerheads. Izzie had her Jacuzzi tub, graced with a small Zen garden off to the side. It had taken them a while to complete the renovation, but every detail was all Izzie, with the help of Yoko when it came to the landscaping, both inside and out.

Izzie helped Zoe with her bags. "Put something comfy on and meet me downstairs. I'll fix us some lunch and we can catch up."

"What about the plans?" Zoe asked. She knew Izzie was aware of her angst, but she wasn't sure if she was ready to talk about it.

"We have plenty of time for that," Izzie called over her shoulder as she made her way back to the main level.

Zoe wanted to shake the feeling of dread plaguing her. She was with a good friend. Someone she could trust. She took a few calming breaths. "It's going to be alright," she whispered to herself. She pulled on a pair of soft, cream-colored waffle-knit pants with a matching tank top and duster. Even her nonslip socks matched. A sense of tranquility began to flow over her. Yes, she too felt safe. At least for the moment.

She plugged her phone into the wall socket and left it on the sleek dresser. She didn't want any interruptions, especially if she was about to discuss her concerns with Izzie. Then she reminded herself that was not the purpose of her visit. Helping Izzie with her construction situation came first. If there was time, she'd discuss her angst with Izzie, but then she realized Izzie would not let her get away with avoiding it. She let out a big sigh.

As she unpacked her overnight bag Zoe thought back to the time when she was dating Brian. He worked in an office a few floors below hers. She would see him often on the elevator, and one day they were the only two in the cab. He struck up a conversation with her. Asked her where she worked. How did she like it? The usual small talk. Zoe thought he was nice and agreed to have coffee with him.

After a couple of coffee dates, they elevated it to dinner. He was the consummate gentleman, which made Zoe feel extremely comfortable in his presence. One evening, as they were having dessert, he told her he liked her for her brain. "You have got to be the smartest woman—person—I have ever met."

She was flattered but slightly disappointed. She thought maybe, just maybe she would be, could be, considered attractive. One thing she knew for certain was that he wasn't attracted to her body. She was tall and slim. Just this side of a boyish figure, something she was terribly self-conscious about. Like, forever. She also knew she was not a raving beauty by any means, but she had style, thanks to a keen eye for what was functional and flattering, and was a good seamstress. Yes. She had style *and* brains.

By their third dinner date, just as they got to her apartment Brian put the moves on her. Nothing aggressive. Just a wet, mushy kiss, but it took her by surprise. She truly had little experience with boys or men. If you could call guys in their midtwenties *men*. She didn't quite know how to react. Yes, she'd kissed a few boys in high school, but she had little or no interest in pursuing anything romantic back then. She was a bookworm and she liked it that way. She knew studying would get her the scholarship prize she sought. She had to have that scholarship. It was the only way out of that small town with two things to its name. Neither of which she particularly enjoyed discussing.

She kinda, sorta kissed him back, but without the same zeal he demonstrated. Maybe she would grow to like it. But not at that moment. On the one hand the kiss stroked her ego. It meant he was attracted to her. But on the other hand, it was just meh.

Brian was patient, almost stoic, and their dates became a regular thing. Something you could ink on the calendar. But Zoe wasn't happy. Nor was she unhappy. She was bored. She thought she'd rather be alone reading a book than spending time with a man who had little to say unless it came to the Red Sox or fishing. Was this her future? Was this what having a relationship meant? Sure, she liked Brian, but not enough to imagine spending the rest of her life with him. Then the sex part? Nope. There was nothing about him that made her tingle. It wasn't as if she preferred women; she just wasn't *feelin'* it with him. She'd sought the advice of her friend Izzie, who encouraged her to bail before she got sucked into a long-term thing that was going nowhere.

Instinctively Zoe knew Izzie was right, but she kept seeing Brian until it became a long-term thing. She finally acquiesced to having sex with him. Protected, of course. It didn't rock her boat. As her twenty-fifth birthday was approaching, she knew thirty wasn't far off. Did she want to be with this man five years from now? Ten? Twenty? The thought made her dizzy. The answer was a big *No!* Once again, she'd sought the advice of Izzie and called her. "Before I tell you, promise me you won't say *I told you so!*"

"I would never. What's going on?" Izzie prodded.

Zoe was relieved to divulge her circumstances and her desire to escape. "Brian and I have been seeing each other for almost two years. We have good conversations and enjoy some of the same things."

"But?"

"He's not a bad guy, Izzie."

"No one says he is, but that should *not* be the criteria for a commitment. And you are racking up the years. That spells commitment. Let's just say it's implied. But not a bad guy as in, 'He isn't an axe-murderer'?" Izzie scoffed. "My mother always warned me not to waste my time being unhappy when we have options. We can't make people make us happy. It's up to us. What do *we* want? What do *we* need? We are as important as anyone else." Izzie sighed. "I know we can't expect one person to be everything. But there must be a reason why you're spending precious time with someone simply because he doesn't have a criminal record." Izzie scoffed, stopped, and took a breath. "Listen, you know I love you and I want you to be happy, but clearly you . . . are . . . not."

"Correct." Zoe was introspective. "Do you think it's really possible?"

"What?"

"To be truly happy with one person?"

"You are asking the wrong babe, babe." Izzie laughed. "I don't exactly have a great track record myself. But I will tell you something. If you settle, you will never feel fulfilled. Sometimes we must compromise, but settling, to me, is different. Compromise is give-and-take. Settling is taking what is offered. No negotiation. But that's just how I view it." Izzie paused. "Personally, I think it's important to decide how a person fits into your life. Or how they don't."

Zoe was silent for a moment. "You have a point. And I don't think there is anything to negotiate with Brian. Brian is Brian and I can't say, *Hey, Brian. Would you mind not* being Brian? *Can you be someone else?*" She snickered.

Izzie burst out laughing. "Now that is *the* best breakup line I have ever heard!"

Zoe snorted. "I'm going to write that down in case I need crib notes when I see him tomorrow."

"You are going to break his heart," Izzie teased.

"Hardly. I guarantee you that is not going to happen. The guy has the emotional capacity of tapioca. He may not even notice." Zoe's eyes brightened. She snapped her fingers.

"That's it! He has no passion! He's blah." She paused. "Yes, he can carry on a conversation, but I don't think I've ever seen him get really excited. About anything. Even though he's a Red Sox fan, he still barely musters a cheer. Huh." Another pause. "It's true what they say about stepping back from a situation and looking at the big picture." They both chuckled. "Alright. I am on it. Wish me luck," Zoe said as she ended the call.

And so it went. Zoe gave Brian the old "It's not you, it's me," routine, which he took quite well. They were still cordial when they ran into each other in the building. No one would ever guess they had broken up. Actually, no one would have thought they had ever dated in the first place.

Zoe shook her head, remembering that episode in her dating life, such as it was. Much to her peers' surprise she wasn't concerned about her biological clock. She would respond with "Does an alarm go off? Just checking." It didn't take an engineer to figure out that forcing something that should not be forced could lead to irreparable harm, whether it was a building, a bridge, or a relationship.

Zoe's private reminiscence was interrupted by an exceptionally large, furry dog lumbering up the stairs. He nudged her arm. "Oh, are you my escort?" Rufus gave a soft woof and a downward-dog pose. Zoe scratched his head and his big floppy ears. She called down to Izzie, "Coming! My date just picked me up!"

Zoe checked herself in the mirror. Her face looked relaxed for the first time in weeks. Maybe it was the change in scenery. Maybe it was the dog. Maybe it was being with a good friend. Maybe it was all of the above. Maybe she would be able to put things in perspective.

Zoe bounced down the steps behind Rufus and turned the corner that opened to the kitchen area. A beautiful antipasto platter was sitting on the counter next to a basket filled with an assortment of bread. "This looks lovely." Zoe eyed the delectable tray.

"Just a little something to hold us over until dinner. Yoko invited us to her house. She is going to make something traditional."

"Sounds great."

Izzie stopped. "Oh, but you probably get good Japanese food in the city." She handed Zoe a plate.

"Yes, but it's not homemade." Zoe pulled out a stool from under the island countertop and sat. She automatically placed her napkin on her lap.

Izzie poured some Pellegrino, added lemon wedges, and chuckled. "Glad to see you have maintained your etiquette," she said as she plucked a napkin for herself.

Zoe began to serve herself pieces of prosciutto, salami, and provolone. "Now this is something I could eat every day." She ripped a piece of focaccia bread and dipped it in a dish with olive oil, pepper, and grated cheese. "When did you become the hostess with the mostest?"

Izzie chuckled. "With Abner's and my schedules, we make it a point to create a fine dining experience at home. We try for once a week. We're lucky if we make it once a month."

Zoe stared out the large windows. "Must be nice having someone to share your life with."

"Is that what's on your mind?"

"Who? Me?" Zoe looked surprised. "No. Not really. I mean, occasionally I feel lonely, but only when everyone else is coupled up and I don't have anything on my calendar."

"Really?" Izzie gave her a dubious look.

"Honestly." She was being sincere. "The past few years have been a hustle. I've been traveling all over the world." She took a bite into the sandwich she'd built. Between chews she continued. "But lately they've been keeping me in the

States mostly. And not overly exciting places either. Not that there is anything wrong with West Virginia, but I spent enough time growing up there. I did everything I could to escape a *very* small-town atmosphere." She wiped some crumbs off her chin. "Don't misunderstand me. The people are lovely, but there is little to do in most of those places if you're there on business."

"So, what brings you to the middle of nowhere?" Izzie asked as she assembled her own version of a sandwich.

"Large construction jobs. Mostly bridges." Zoe took a sip of the sparkling water.

"You pretty much grew up in that arena."

"Silver Bridge?" Zoe snorted. "That was exactly what I was trying to get away from. For a while I was working on new construction jobs. Condominiums mostly. In exotic and interesting places." She swallowed. "But then they shifted me over to a different department."

"Didn't they do that to you once before?"

"Yes, but I enjoyed that change. This one? I'm not crazy about."

"Did they give you a reason?" Izzie asked casually.

That's when Zoe froze. She turned to Izzie. Her face was taught. "They didn't say, but I have my suspicions."

"That sounds ominous."

"It just might be." Zoe took another bite.

"Well, you are going to have to explain that to me, tout de suite."

"Please. I am enjoying this lovely lunch my friend prepared." Zoe smirked. "I don't want to get indigestion."

"Okay. But this is the second time you've alluded to something bothering you, so you are going to have to come clean with me or we are not leaving." Izzie was firm but kind.

"Yes. I know." Zoe nodded. "Now let me finish this delicious assortment of gastronomical delights."

Izzie changed the subject back to relationships. She knew Zoe had no problem discussing her lack thereof. "You mean to tell me in all the places you've been you haven't met one interesting man?"

"I didn't say that, now did I?" Zoe gave her a sly smile.

"Oh, you stinker. Do tell." Izzie stopped herself mid-nudge, remembering the ice cream fiasco with Yoko.

"There was one guy in London. Mason Chapman. Quite British," she said with an English accent. "I thought it ironic his name was Mason and I work in masonry. I think that's what got us started. And I'm from the county of Mason."

"That's kind of funny, actually. A bit of synchronicity." Izzie leaned in closer. "So?"

"Geographically undesirable." Zoe pouted between bites.

"What? Now? In this day and age?" Izzie was perplexed.

"Sure, there's Facetime, Zoom, and a bunch of other options for 'staying connected.'" She used air quotes. "But they're two-dimensional. And he's too far away. Boston, maybe. London? Not a good sitch," she replied with the British slang for *situation*.

"Was it serious? Did you like him, as in really-really?" Izzie thought if she could get Zoe to talk about it, Zoe might be a bit less tense. "And why didn't you tell me?"

"Oh, I wasn't sure if it would go anywhere." She shrugged. "He was a good mate." Zoe raised her eyebrows. "I had to spend a month in Old Windsor. Refurbishing a few buildings. He worked at Frogmore House and Gardens. He managed the property. That's how we met." Zoe sipped the sparkling water. "I had to do an evaluation and work with the local authorities. Protocol." She snorted. "They are so *full* of protocol."

"And?" Izzie egged her on.

"And we had several lovely weekends in London." Zoe winked. "But it's a long way from New York." She sighed.

"So, when did all of this happen?"

"A few months ago. I was being very Zen about it. Taking each day and weekend as it came along." Zoe's face softened. "I didn't know what to call it. Label it. I just went with the flow."

Izzie leaned in closer. "And then what happened?"

"And then they took me off the job."

"Do you think it had anything to do with Mason?"

"Doubtful." She took a sip. "It's all quite convoluted. Came from upper management." She took a breath. "Transferred me to a different department. Said the job got sidelined. Canceled. End of story."

Izzie didn't like the sound of that. "Did they blame you for it?"

"Oh no. Not at all." She winced. "At least I don't think so." Zoe's mind went to her suspicions, but she kept the romantic side of the conversation going. "Anyway, it was nice while it lasted."

"Are you still in touch with each other?" Izzie pushed a little harder. "How did it end? Or did it?"

"We email once or twice a week. Jokes. International politics. What we're up to. Pretty banal stuff."

"Well, that shows he wants to maintain the connection."

"I suppose. But you know me. I'm a bit of a loner."

"Only when you're up to your neck in books, blueprints, and cement." Izzie chuckled.

Zoe almost choked on the word *cement*.

"You okay?" Izzie gently tapped Zoe on the back.

"Yes, yes," Zoe responded.

"Anyway, I'm glad you made some kind of human connection." Izzie was relieved to hear Zoe hadn't completely shut down on the idea of a relationship.

"I must admit, I did like him. But, such is life."

Izzie contemplated for a moment. "And life is full of surprises. You never know what can happen."

"True. I never thought I would be attracted to a man." Zoe batted her eyelashes. "Not that I'm into women. But at one point I wondered if I was asexual, especially after Brian. There was nothing ringing my bells. I began to think I had no bells!" She chortled. "But then I met Mason Chapman." She started to blush. "I know this sounds so cliché, but I felt something. Something electrical. And then I had an epiphany."

Izzie looked at her with wide eyes. "Do tell!"

Zoe's threw out her arms and boasted, "I have a libido!"

Izzie laughed so hard the fizz from the Pellegrino shot out of her nose. Zoe was next in line with her own nasal spray. It took several minutes before they could regain their composure.

"Whoo." Zoe fanned her face. "I haven't laughed that hard in a very long time." She thought for a moment. "Not since I last saw Mason." Zoe paused for a minute.

"I think you're still a bit stuck on the lad." Izzie pursed her lips.

"You could be right."

"Don't you have vacation time? Plan a little Anglo-Saxon trek?"

"We'll see." Zoe finished her lunch and brought the plate to the sink.

"Hang on. I'll stick them in the dishwasher." Izzie pushed her chair back and stepped over Rufus. She was giving Zoe a few minutes to gather her thoughts before she pounced on what was really bothering her. "Coffee?" she asked.

"Sure."

"Decaf, regular, espresso?" Izzie asked as she refilled the coffeemaker.

"Oh, espresso. But maybe not. I don't need the jitters."

Izzie wiped her hands on a kitchen towel and turned. "You really need to tell me what is going on."

Zoe looked down at the counter and sighed. "I think something unseemly is happening at my firm."

Izzie stood with the coffee carafe in midair. "What do you mean?"

Zoe began. "You recall that condominium collapse in Florida?"

"Of course."

"And the university pedestrian skywalk over Tamiami Trail?"

"Yes. Incredibly sad." Izzie popped two capsules of decaffeinated into the machine and leaned against the counter.

Zoe was visibly shaken. "Sadly, there are more. In 2004 the roof at the Charles de Gaulle airport collapsed, killing four people." She took a breath. "In the past twenty years over two thousand people have died globally due to the politics of expediency or personal financial gain." She continued. "When buildings and bridges started collapsing in various parts of the world, I found a common thread: inferior foundation materials. Bridges were failing, people were dying. Buildings were crumbling. More people dying."

Izzie furrowed her brow. "That is shocking—not the political or personal gains—but I suppose people don't look at the cumulative statistics." She placed a coffee cup in front of Zoe.

"Exactly." Zoe sat tall. "I decided to do my own little covert investigation and started looking into some of our files." She explained how she'd uncovered a horrendous scheme to save money by manufacturing an inferior product for commercial foundations. "I was concerned that the company I'm working for is one of the suppliers to some of those catastrophes. I called a meeting with Donald Walsh, the quality control manager, and asked a few questions about our manufacturing plant in the Dominican Republic. He implied he had everything under control, and we were compliant. He was also rather defensive and implied I was sticking my nose into places where it didn't belong. He basically told me not to worry my pretty little head . . . in the most condescending manner."

Izzie had a look of horror on her face. "Do you think REBAR is providing subpar materials?"

"It's very possible."

"What happened after your meeting? I know you, and you wouldn't take his answer as truth."

"Exactly. One evening I was in the office after hours, and because of my position in the company, I was able to access the accounts payable and receivables."

"What did you find?"

"Lots. But a few days later my access was denied."

"That sounds rather suspicious."

"You got that right. But I was able to print out some of the invoices before I got shut out. Always better to have a hard copy. I figured I could study them at home without worrying about someone looking over my shoulder."

"True."

"Now I'm paranoid." Zoe sighed.

"You? Never," Izzie said quite confidently.

"Up until now." Zoe gulped. "I think I'm being followed."

"Seriously? Why?" Izzie was stunned.

"Because those invoices don't add up. What we are telling the clients and what we are charging the clients for is vastly different from what we are supplying."

"What do you mean?"

"The invoice states we provide U.S.-grade materials, as per part five hundred and twelve of the *National Engineering Manual*. You know what I'm talking about."

"Yes, of course. The Department of Labor, Office of Federal Contract Compliance Programs."

"Correct." Zoe nodded. "The paper trail leads to the Dominican Republic, but the company listed on the invoice doesn't exist. El Cemento."

"Wait. What you're saying is REBAR is getting materials from an unsupervised offshore company?"

"Seems that way," Zoe said. "And they are falsifying the records."

"Is there anything you can do about it?"

"You mean, like whistleblowing?"

"Well, yeah."

"That's why I think I'm being followed. Someone wants to be sure I *don't* blow the whistle. I think they're using intimidation tactics. And they're working." Zoe took a sip of her coffee. "The other day I was on a very crowded subway platform and someone gave me a serious nudge. I lost my footing. Thankfully, there were two people standing next to me, and they grabbed me and kept me from falling. I was perilously close to hitting the tracks."

"Oh my God! Zoe! That is horrible. No wonder you're all wound up." Izzie placed her arm around her friend. Her first thought was to go to Myra with this information and get her advice. "Listen, I have friends who are familiar with problems such as yours."

"Subpar building supplies?" Zoe looked perplexed.

"No. Ruthless people." Izzie grabbed her cell phone and punched in Myra's phone number.

Myra answered right away. "Izzie, honey. How are you?"

"Hey, Myra. I'm fine. And you?"

"All good at the farm. I'm trying to talk Charles into going to France to take a cooking class with me."

"That could be exciting! Not that he needs any tutorials."

"It would just be for fun, really," Myra added. "Tell me, what's going on in your life? How is the project coming along?"

"We have a little bit of a holdup on the foundation materials."

"Well, that's not good. Have you spoken to Annie? She may know someone."

"Not yet, but one of my friends from college is here now. Do you remember me talking about Zoe Danfield? She is a VP at REBAR."

"Yes, of course."

"She's here visiting and is going to review the plans."

"Sounds like you have it all in hand." But Myra knew there was something else. Izzie didn't call just to chat.

"Not exactly." Izzie cleared her throat. "Do you think I could bring her by at some point? She has an issue you may be able to advise her on."

"Oh?" Myra got the *there's a mission at hand* vibe from Izzie. After thirty-four missions, Izzie and the other Sisters were on each other's radar.

"Yes. I was hoping you could spare a little time later today."

"Let me check with Charles. Do you want me to call Annie?"

"Probably a good idea."

"Hang on a second." Myra started stroking her pearls, a habit she'd developed when something was afoot. She called out, "Charles? Are we all clear for later this afternoon?"

Izzie couldn't hear him, but Myra conveyed his answer. "All clear, my dear. What time?"

"Yoko was planning on making a traditional Japanese dinner for us. She said to come by around seven."

"Not to worry. I'll contact Yoko. She can bring dinner here. Charles will be thrilled to have one of Yoko's meals, and he won't have to do anything!" Myra chuckled. "He and Fergus can argue who will do the cleanup."

"Thanks, Myra. What time should we get to the farm?"

"How about five? That will give us time to chat before dinner. Oh, and bring Rufus. He hasn't had any doggie time with Lady for a while."

"Sounds great." Izzie paused. "Thank you, Myra."

"Izzie, you know we are always here for one another."

"Love you!" Izzie felt a sense of relief for herself and her friend.

"Right back atcha." Myra signed off.

Izzie took the seat next to Zoe. "Myra wants us over at five. Yoko will either bring dinner or cook it at the farm."

Zoe looked very confused. "You're going to have to start at the beginning."

"Can't do that just yet, but once we talk to Myra, we'll be able to come up with a plan."

"A plan for what? The project?"

"That, too." Izzie was careful not to divulge too much information. "Let's just say Myra and her best friend Annie are problem solvers. Hopefully, both yours and mine." She patted Zoe on the back. "How about we take Rufus for a walk?"

Rufus perked up and gave a woof of approval. Izzie put the coffee cups in the dishwasher, then grabbed the dog's leash. "Go put on some shoes."

"Me or the dog?" Zoe chuckled. She was breathing much easier. She wasn't sure exactly why, but she felt safe. Yep. *Safe* was the operative word of the day.

They returned to Izzie's about an hour later. "What should I wear to Myra's?" Zoe asked.

"What you have on is fine," Izzie answered.

"Really? A waffle-knit jogging suit?" Zoe was surprised. They were going to the home of a captain of industry. Surely there was a dress code.

"Really." Izzie nodded. "If anything, you're overdressed." She giggled. "Puh-lease. You were always a geeky fashionista."

"Talk about a mash-up. When I think of geek I think of those nimrods from that show where they're scientists or something?"

"*Big Bang Theory*," Izzie said.

"That's the one. I could never get into that show. Surprising for someone who considers herself somewhat of a geek."

"They were nerds. Big difference, you know," Izzie joked.

"I'm going to freshen up. Give me a few minutes." Zoe went back upstairs. She peered deeply into the bathroom mirror and decided if nothing else, a modest makeup refresh was called for. Just enough to hide the circles under her eyes and brighten her cheeks. She peered at the leather portfolio sitting on the chair in the corner. It contained her incriminating evidence. Even though she suspected someone was following her, she'd decided it was better to bring the invoices with her rather than run the risk of someone breaking into her apartment while she was away. If they were simply trying to scare her, they were doing a good job. But for the moment, she felt secure. She tucked the leather pouch under her arm and headed down the stairs.

Chapter Four

Pinewood

A little after four P.M., Izzie, Zoe, and Rufus climbed into Izzie's SUV. Rufus was unusually excited, with both his tongue and tail wagging. He knew he was either going to the big dog park or to visit his doggie pals. Dogs have an innate sensitivity. They can sense things long before humans can. Izzie looked in the rearview mirror. "Going to see Lady, eh?"

He made a funny sound, as if he were trying to say "yay!"

Zoe and Izzie laughed out loud. "He knows the difference between fun time and work time. When I bring him to the office, he lies flat on the back seat. Almost sulking, like taking a kid to school who'd rather play all day."

"Doesn't he like the office?" Zoe turned to look at the exuberant dog.

"He doesn't dislike it. He's fine with people coming and going, but he isn't in his own space. He can't always take a nap when he wants to or watch his favorite TV show."

Zoe gave Izzie a sideways glance. "He has a favorite TV show?"

Izzie chuckled. "Several. There's *Scooby-Doo* and *Frasier*. He loves Eddie, and Comet from *Full House*. I had to sign up for special subscriptions to get some of those shows. Thank goodness my pal Gail Edwards from *Full House* was able to get me the collection. I spend more money on television for him than Abner and I do for ourselves!"

"That's hilarious. Does he know how to change the channels?"

Izzie bit her lip. "You know Abner is a total computer whizbang genius, right? Well, you may find this hard to believe, but Abner produced three different devices. Each has an individual picture of the dog in the show. The pad on the device is big enough so when Rufus puts his paw on it, the TV will bring up the show he wants to watch." Izzie kept her eyes on the road. "Really. It took a bit of training, but he figured it out. There's a professor of psychology and canine research at the University of British Columbia. His name is Stanley Coren. His team studied over two hundred dogs and discovered most dogs can understand about one hundred fifty words and have the intelligence of a two-year-old child." Zoe exited the highway and drove down a country road. "According to canine research, they found border collies were the smartest, then poodles, German shepherds, Shetlands, and Labradors. And Rufus is half poodle and half Lab so he's in the top five." She glanced into the mirror again. "Right, pal?"

He let out a little yap.

"My cats only know how to turn on the TV." Zoe chuckled. "They haven't mastered the art of changing the channels. But they know how to open the pantry door and the dry food container. I tried to put it up on a shelf, but they climbed their way up and it rained kibble all over my pots and pans. Now the container is back on the pantry floor should they decide it's snack time. You gotta love 'em."

"You've got that right. When I finally got out of jail, the first thing I did was go to the shelter, thanks to Myra's advice."

"You and Myra are really close, aren't you?" Zoe asked. At first, she'd thought Izzie and Myra were simply social friends, but she was beginning to see there was a much deeper connection.

The farther they drove, the thicker the canopy of trees became. They were most certainly in the country. "It's beautiful out here." Zoe gazed out at the bucolic scenery.

"Myra owns a lot of the property on the right. The farmhouse is secluded past that grove of trees." Izzie turned the vehicle onto the gravel driveway that led to the house. The façade of the building was immaculate, as were the grounds. "Hard to believe this place is over a hundred and fifty years old. Myra and Charles try to maintain the historical aspects without making it look like a relic."

"It's quite lovely," Zoe said with admiration. "I feel like I am in the setting of a novel."

"Yoko keeps the landscape in fine order." Izzie pulled the vehicle around to the back where everyone entered through the kitchen.

The whir of a golf cart came whizzing from behind them. "What the—?" Zoe blurted.

"That would be Annie!" Izzie gave a big wave. "Hey there!" She turned back to Zoe. "She's the Mario Andretti of the neighborhood."

Annie bounded out of her golf cart and gave Izzie a great big hug. "Isabel Flanders! I was so happy when Myra told me you were coming over."

Izzie introduced the two. "Annie, this is one of my best college mates and former building department colleague, Zoe Danfield."

Annie quickly offered her hand. "Lovely to meet you, Zoe Danfield."

Izzie continued. "Zoe, this is the legendary Countess Anna Ryland de Silva."

Annie grinned. "I left my tiara on the kitchen table."

Zoe chuckled. "It's a pleasure to meet you, too. Nice wheels." Zoe was admiring the bright orange Plum Quick Bandit cart.

"Don't ya just love it? It can go up to one hundred eighty-eight miles per hour. It's street legal." Annie gave a quick wink. "I'll take you for a little spin later."

Izzie broke in immediately. "Oh, I don't think you want to do that, Zoe. The reason she drives one of these is because they won't let her drive a grown-up car in the county. Said she is a danger to the public." Izzie plunked her hands on her hips.

"Aw, pshaw." Annie waved Izzie off.

Rufus started making sounds of annoyance as if to say, "Hey, what about me?"

Annie quickly bent over and snuggled the complaining pooch. "Hello to you, too, Mr. Rufus. How's about a high five? Or can he fist-bump?"

Rufus sat obediently, lifted a paw, and turned his head in a "take it or leave it" attitude. Annie chuckled. "You are a funny little guy." The dog stood on all fours and then jumped up on Annie, planting his paws on her shoulders. "Okay, so you're not so little." She gave him another nuzzle that seemed to satisfy him. He politely pulled himself back to a normal standing position.

"Smart and agile," Zoe remarked.

"Is Fergus coming?" Izzie asked as they all linked arms and walked toward the kitchen door.

"He'll be here a little later. Now that Yoko is providing dinner, he doesn't have to hover over Charles."

"Ha. He loves it. They're like peas and carrots in a shepherd's pie," Izzie said.

Annie hooted. "You've got that right!"

They could hear dogs barking and yapping inside the

house. Rufus chimed in. It was a bark-a-thon. Myra tried to shush her pups, but to no avail. Everyone got excited when the Sisters arrived, whether it was with a dog or another friend. Myra trusted her band of Sisters with her life. Literally. They'd all been in peril at one time or another, and it was always the Sisters who saved them or the people they loved.

Myra swung the door open. "Izzie!" She gave Izzie a big hug. "Zoe, please come in. Come in." She stepped aside and waved them on as the women piled in, Rufus in tow.

The dogs needed no introduction. Lady immediately brought her ball to Rufus, who happily chomped at it and made his way into the atrium, where Lady's other pups were lazily soaking up the sun.

"Charles is in the study watching a football game, or as we Americans call it, soccer. He has a bet with Fergus and they've been on the phone every time someone scores. They've been taunting each other for two hours. I don't know why they're not watching it together." Myra shook her head in confusion.

"Who's playing?" Zoe asked. She'd watched a couple of soccer matches when she was in England.

"Manchester City and Chelsea. Or is it Liverpool? I don't remember. It's all the same to me. Men running around, kicking a ball. Why they subject their heads to that is beyond my comprehension." Myra shrugged.

"I agree. But men will be boys. Rowdy boys," Annie added. "But when they are good, they are very, very good." She chuckled.

They heard a shout from Charles, accompanied by a few expletives. His cell rang immediately, and he had a few foul words for Fergus. "Oh bollocks! And I don't mean Sandra!" he shouted into the phone.

Zoe didn't know what to make of it. He certainly sounded

angry. Myra chuckled. "They've been doing this for years. Long before we ever met." She ushered them into the atrium, where the dogs had taken over a good part of the floor. "Just step over them." Lady lifted her head and gave the other dogs a look that said, "Let's get out of here before someone steps on us." In less than a minute all six dogs meandered into the big, bright kitchen. It would be at least another ninety minutes before the kitchen started bustling.

A long, simple oak sideboard buffet was against one wall. On top were a teapot, cups, and a plate of scones. Myra gestured. "A little snack."

Zoe snickered. "I am going to gain ten pounds before I leave."

"Is that a complaint or a promise?" Izzie teased.

Zoe turned toward Izzie. "You served a delectable charcuterie when we got to your place. I never eat like that. It's been a salad at my desk since they gave me my new position." Zoe rolled her eyes.

"Yes, that's why I phoned," Izzie said. "Zoe has a situation on her hands. Quite dangerous, possibly deadly."

Myra encouraged the women to have a cuppa and, if they preferred, half of a scone. "You'll only gain five pounds that way."

Annie claimed the chaise lounge. She lay back, laced her fingers together and placed them behind her head, then crossed her ankles. She was ready. Ready for whatever Zoe wanted to share.

Zoe and Izzie sat in the club chairs while Myra remained standing, leaning against one of the floor-to-ceiling bookcases. She fidgeted with her pearls.

Zoe opened the leather portfolio she'd brought with her and pulled out the paperwork. She held it with great distress. She began by reviewing the construction disasters she'd discussed with Izzie. "I know you are familiar with most of these tragedies. Something wasn't sitting right with me. Just weeks after these incidents, the stories were swept to the back of the news."

Annie cleared her throat and raised her hand. "Guilty. With all the political nonsense over the past several years, it's been tough to prioritize. People want the most up-to-date information so they can make sound decisions." She paused. "At least that's what my paper hopes to provide."

Zoe looked at Annie. "Oh, I totally get it. I'm not blaming the media. Well, at least not all of it. We've come to a very grim period in the human race. Mass shootings, war, bombs, storms, floods, wildfires. All of it has become daily news. It's heartbreaking. It's a matter of which disaster do you want to be depressed about today? Whether it's people, politics, or the climate. No wonder so many people are on antianxiety medication." Zoe took a sip of her tea. "For the most part, the public was never made aware of any of the investigations. And I suspect some of those investigations were put in a box, on a shelf, in the back of a closet in a basement somewhere. Swept it under the rug. Ambition above safety.

"The most recent condo collapse in Florida hit close to home. Old family friends had a condominium in that building. Fortunately, they made it out alive. A few broken bones. But they lost their neighbors. Their friends. So, I started looking into the public information on file. As you're probably aware, they discovered there was an inspection three years before citing cracks in the poolside part of the foundation. Nothing was done even though the residents kept complaining. Water was seeping into the garage area. After the tragedy, they discovered insufficient reinforcement steel and possible political corruption. Meaning inspections were not thorough or not done at all." She paused. "It's an international crisis replete with corruption, yet there is no central organization investigating these events."

Everyone remained silent, absorbing what Zoe was saying. It was apparent where she was going with this. "Minneapolis, 2007. Total failure of the gussets on the Missouri River Bridge. Thirteen people died.

"Argentina, 2014. Faulty concrete. Thirty people. 2019. Hard Rock in New Orleans. Three people. 2011. Indiana State Fair. Seven people. The pedestrian bridge in Miami. Six people. Faulty design. Morandi Bridge, Genoa, Italy. 2018. Forty-three people. Faulty construction in the sound barrier. One major difference is three people were arrested that time. Through a wiretap the authorities discovered the construction company used a type of glue used by schoolkids. The judge cited them with 'grave criminal conduct linked to entrepreneurial policies.' But that is rare. Companies are putting people in potential danger for bigger profits." She stopped to let the information sink in. It didn't take long.

Myra leaned forward. "You suspect your company is involved in similar practices? Ethical failures?"

"Indeed, I do." Zoe organized the paperwork and handed it to Myra.

Myra gave it a cursory glance and passed it on to Annie, who whipped out her rhinestone glasses and began to read aloud. "El Cemento?" She looked up.

"That's the company where the checks are going. But I can't find a record of their business certificates anywhere."

Annie read on. "The Dominican Republic is where the REBAR plant is located. Not terribly surprising. There is a lot of corruption going on down there."

"As of now, I can't link any recent disasters to REBAR, but looking at the paper trail, my big concern is that REBAR *will* be responsible for certain disasters if they are supplying subpar materials for major construction projects," Zoe explained. "And we are busy."

"Do you think the clients are aware they are buying sub-par materials?" Myra asked. "Trying to save money?"

"That much I do not know. I have no idea how deep or how far this goes."

Izzie cut in. "Tell them about your own experiences lately. The job change. The subway."

Myra got up and took a bottle of brandy off the sidebar. She poured a little of it into Zoe's cup. Zoe looked up into Myra's sympathetic eyes. "Thanks. I am a bit rattled."

"No doubt." Annie sat straight up. "So tell us, what has been happening with you?"

"I was in London working on a project and got pulled off. They said the job got canceled. When I got back to the States, and after my chat with Donald Walsh, I found myself in the oversight department. My job is to go to different projects and check that all the plans, invoices, and permits are up-to-date. Once I give the green light, we deliver our products to the job site. By the time the materials arrive, I'm on to the next one. It was not what I signed up for. And I don't think it's a coincidence my transfer happened after I spoke to Mr. Jackass Walsh."

Annie snapped her fingers. "Yes, I am a conspiracy person from time to time, and to me this sounds like one. They wanted to get you out of the home office for one thing. For another, should anything happen in the future, you'd be the one to take the fall because you signed off on the job."

Zoe nodded. "Pretty much. And there are at least a dozen international jobs where I signed the contracts. If REBAR provides subpar materials, I am screwed all over the place." She took a sip of her spiked tea and winced.

"You get used to it." Myra gave her a devilish smile.

Zoe went on. "I let the subject and Mr. Walsh drop while I was making the transition from one job to the other, plus all the traveling. I hadn't had much time to think.

"But after one of my recent trips, while I was on the way back from the airport, I decided to stop by the office to update my files. It was around seven P.M. The place was empty. I flipped through my inbox. The one on my desk. There were a few newspapers and as I was separating them for recycling, I noticed an article about the anniversary of Hurricane Katrina, and how the loss of human life was due to a systemic failure. The politics of speediness. Eighteen hundred people died. That's when something clicked in my head and I decided to check out a few things. Invoices and such." She pointed to the pile of papers sitting on Annie's lap. "A few days later my access to the financial systems was denied. I'm being shut out. I went from Vice President of International Sales to project inspector."

"Do you think they did this to force you out?" Myra asked.

"Firing me would not fly well. My employment record is impeccable, and I am a woman. Very touchy subject these days. So, give me a job they know I'll hate and maybe I'll quit." Zoe sighed.

"Sure sounds like it." Annie nodded.

"Yeah, well, I won't. Not yet." Zoe let out a big sigh. "What creeps me out is cutting off my access to the financials. As far as I know my title is still Vice President. At least they let me keep that."

A deep English baritone voice carried across the room. "Obviously someone is monitoring log-in information. For security purposes, I would presume," Charles proclaimed as he entered the atrium.

Myra turned. "Hello, love. Good game?"

"Most definitely. Can't wait to collect my winnings from Fergus." He rubbed his hands together, insinuating a big payday.

Annie rolled her eyes. "How much this time?"

"Five quid." Charles grinned. His bets with Fergus were never more than five dollars.

Charles approached Zoe and extended his hand. "Charles Martin."

Zoe got up and shook his very large, very strong, smooth hand. "Zoe Danfield."

"Excuse my interruption, but I couldn't help overhearing the last bit of your conversation," Charles apologized.

Myra rested her hand on Zoe's shoulder. "He's part of the team."

Zoe still wasn't sure what kind of team she was about to become a part of.

"Please, sit." Charles gestured to the chair. He stood next to Myra.

"Tell them about the subway thing," Izzie urged.

Zoe took a deep breath, recalling her harrowing experience. "Last week I was standing on a crowded subway platform. As a train was pulling into the station, someone nudged me. I really can't say I was shoved, but luckily for me two people grabbed my jacket before I fell to the ground, or onto the tracks. It all happened very fast."

Myra eyed Annie. They could almost read each other's minds. Annie nodded. Myra fidgeted with her pearls and began to address the small group. She smiled. "Now, Zoe. Here's what's going to happen. After dinner we are going to have a meeting."

Zoe looked confused. "A meeting? What kind of meeting?"

Izzie chimed in. "The kind we have when something needs to be handled."

"But . . . what? Handled? How?" Zoe asked. Her eyes blinked.

Annie stood and patted Zoe on the shoulder. "Don't you worry your pretty little head." The rest of the group laughed out loud at her reference to Mr. Walsh's snide remark. With that the dogs began to bark and charged through from the kitchen.

"Alright, everyone. Settle down." Myra spoke with an even tone. They immediately sat at attention. "That's my girls. And Rufus."

"I'll get them sorted with their dinner. You carry on and catch me up when Fergus gets here," said Charles.

Izzie peered at Zoe, who looked like a deer in the headlights. "You'll get used to it. Us. All of it."

Annie continued to look through the invoices. "It appears we have a two-fold situation. From what you gathered from your research, one is the plethora of disasters due to criminal behavior, white collar or otherwise, and the other is how to stop REBAR from becoming the next member of the League of Ethical Failures." She pursed her lips. "That would be a good subject for an article. I should bring Maggie in." Annie explained to Zoe that Maggie was her top investigative reporter. "And she is one of us." Annie made a circle with her finger indicating Myra and Izzie, and Charles in the other room.

Myra followed Charles into the kitchen and picked up the receiver of an old-school yellow landline wall phone with push buttons. The features were modern, but it had that nostalgic look. Myra hit the pound sign and the speed dial number assigned to Maggie's cell phone. Maggie answered within two rings.

"Myra! What's up?" Maggie's almost-always-perky voice answered.

"Izzie is here with a longtime friend. We have a situation. Annie would like you to join us." Myra stroked her pearls again.

"Sure. When?"

Myra could hear Maggie chomping on something crunchy. "As soon as you finish whatever you're eating."

"Ha." Maggie tilted her head back and dumped the remaining bits of pretzel and salt into her mouth. "Done! I'll be there in about forty minutes."

"Wonderful. See you in a bit." Myra hung up and returned to the atrium. "She'll be here shortly. I should phone Yoko and let her know there will be a few more of us tonight."

"Maggie counts for at least two," Annie joked. Maggie was petite and skinny, but she could eat enough for two people. Everyone marveled at the amount she consumed, though it surely didn't show on her body.

"What about Kathryn?" Izzie asked.

"I believe she is still in Atlanta." Myra checked the wall calendar where she kept track of everyone's whereabouts. She said it was a lot easier to look at one page than scroll through a bunch of electronic pages. First you had to turn on the phone. Then you had to find the right app. Then you had to search via the person's name or find the calendar. "One page. Simple." No one could argue with that logic. "She's not due back until next week."

"Alexis?" Annie asked.

"She just finished a case so she may be available. Nikki and Jack are vacationing in Toronto at a film festival."

"Okay. Let's go over the situation completely after we have dinner and then we can decide who we need to pull in," Annie said. "I assume there will be some travel involved so I'll be sure the jet is ready."

Zoe still couldn't figure out what was going on. *Jet?* She then realized who she was talking to. Two of the richest women in the country, one of whom was a countess. Of course, she would have a jet, right? But she found Annie very much down-to-earth. *Maybe she'd give off more of a royalty vibe if she was wearing her tiara?* Zoe thought to herself.

"Like I said, you'll get used to it," Izzie said in response to

Zoe's puzzled expression. She pulled Zoe up from the deep-seated chair and walked her into the kitchen area.

Barking dogs signaled an approaching vehicle. It was Fergus, driving the slower of the two golf carts. The sound of gravel under the tires came to a halt and Fergus jumped out. Annie was waiting at the door. He gave her a peck on the cheek. "'Allo, lovey." Fergus had a distinct Londoner accent. Slightly different from Charles's. Over the years Charles had modified his pattern of speech and enunciation to get him farther away from his rough-and-tumble childhood and adolescence.

"Gambling again, I hear?" Annie pretended to scold him as they made their way into the kitchen.

"Afraid so." He frowned and pulled out a five-dollar bill from his wallet.

Charles snapped it from Fergus's fingers. "I love nothing more than besting you."

"It's not as if you were out there breaking a sweat. Running in your knickers," Fergus argued.

"And *you* were?" Charles bantered back. Then they gave each other a slap on the back. "Good to see you, mate. How long's it been? One? Two days?" Charles wasn't kidding. Fergus and Annie lived on the other side of the property. They were in each other's company constantly.

"Not long enough," Fergus joked. "I hear we are getting a treat from Yoko this evening?" At the word *treat* all the dogs lined up. Fergus never entered the house without a pocketful of them for the dogs. "Here ya go." He gave each of them a dog biscuit.

"Yes, Yoko is on the case," Izzie said. "Fergus, this is my good friend Zoe. She's from New York but we met in college and worked together for a couple of years."

"Ay. Nice to meet you, Zoe. In the engineering game, are ya?" he asked.

"Yes. At least for now," Zoe answered.

Izzie gave Fergus the ten-second version of Zoe's job and title.

Charles gave Fergus a look. Both men were typically suspicious of most large corporations, especially the international sort. "I don't mean to belittle you, but given your experience and education, wouldn't your current job title appear to be a demotion?"

Zoe raised her eyebrows. Izzie continued. "Not on paper, but certainly in scope of accountability. But it gets a little convoluted."

Myra began. "What we know is Zoe works for a large manufacturing company. REBAR. They have a very large global reach in both steel and masonry. Zoe wanted reassurance from their quality control director, but he brushed her off."

"Men don't like to be questioned," Charles said in a friendly way. He didn't want to spook Zoe, so he kept it a bit light. "Fergus and myself, well, we're a bit more educated in that arena, wouldn't you say, old mate?"

Fergus chuckled. "You've met Annie, eh?" A few chuckles circled the room.

"Please continue," Charles urged.

"A week or so after my conversation with Donald Walsh, I got abruptly reassigned, and my executive clearance for the database has been declined," Zoe explained.

"Yes, that's when I walked into the conversation. Rather than put our guest through another round of explanations, shall we wait until everyone else arrives?" Charles asked.

"Brilliant," Fergus agreed. "How soon will Yoko be here? Haven't had a good teriyaki in a dog's age." A disapproving snort came from Rufus. Fergus tossed him another treat.

"Any minute," Myra said. Lady's tail concurred as the sound of vehicles crunching the gravel reached them.

The first one out of her car was Maggie, her curly red hair bouncing in rhythm with each step. Right behind was Yoko's van.

"Let me help you." Maggie started toward Yoko.

Yoko put her hand up. "Stop right there. You have to promise you will not eat anything on the way from here to the kitchen."

"Oh geez. Yes. I promise. Girl Scout's honor." She held up her three fingers.

Yoko grinned. "Think you can trick me? Turn your hand the other way."

Maggie indeed was holding her hand in the opposite direction. "Dang. I can't put anything past you."

Yoko handed Maggie a small wax-paper bag. "Here. Just for you."

Maggie ripped the bag open like a little kid who just got a surprise. "Dumplings!" She popped one in her mouth. "Yum!"

"They're called gyoza. Show some respect, please," Yoko teased. She handed Maggie a large basket.

"Yikes. What's in here?" Maggie grunted.

"A few pounds of chicken. Some beef. Some shrimp."

"Geez, you'd think you were feeding an army."

Yoko stopped in her tracks and eyed Maggie up and down.

"Alright. Alright." Maggie lugged the basket to the back door.

Charles greeted them. There was a yapping of approval from the dogs as well. "Let's have that." He took the basket from Maggie. Yoko followed with another. The clanking of bottles was the tip-off that there was sake in their future.

There were lots of hugs and a cacophony of remarks and questions: "So good to see you!" "What's happening?" "How's Abner?" "Harry?"

Then came a multitude of answers.

"Harry is at a training camp for the next six weeks," Yoko offered her husband's whereabouts to the group.

"Abner is at a geek convention. Oops, sorry, Zoe," said Izzie.

"Nikki and Jack are in Toronto, Kathryn in Atlanta," Myra explained.

Charles addressed Yoko. "Let me help you with all of that." The two of them began unpacking the food.

Fergus handled the sake. "Very nice." He held up a bottle of Shichida Junmai Ginjo. "From the southern part of Japan."

"It is!" Yoko exclaimed. "And it should be served cold."

"Most definitely," Charles agreed.

"Most people drink it warm, but that's really used to disguise cheaper grades," Yoko added.

"This one is clearly not a cheaper grade, dear girl," Fergus said with approval. "I'll pop them in the fridge in the butler's pantry."

"No taste testing, old chum," Charles admonished.

Yoko took the marinated packages of chicken, steak, and shrimp from the insulated basket as Charles set an oversized grill across the six-burner stove.

"Smells divine," Charles said as the aromas of ginger, garlic, scallions, and soy sauce wafted from the containers.

"Old family recipe," Yoko said. "I brought skewers to make it easier."

Lady gave a soft woof, followed by her pups and Rufus signaling another car was about to pull into the driveway.

"Must be Alexis," Myra said. Her dogs had an individual bark for each of the Sisters. It was far superior to a Ring doorbell. Myra and Annie stood in the large opening of the twelve-foot-wide French doors that separated the atrium from the kitchen, surrounded by Maggie, Izzie, and Zoe. A tall, stunning African-American woman stepped over the threshold. She resembled the model Iman.

More hugs, kisses, questions, greetings, and a little barking filled the space.

"Just in time to set the table," Annie said. The women began the routine of setting the table, as Maggie explained Zoe's role as napkin folder. Zoe fell into rhythm as if she had done it before. The aroma of teriyaki on the grill permeated the air.

"Oh, my goodness gracious!" Maggie squealed with delight. "Wait till you taste the dump—I mean gyozas!"

Yoko opened the insulated bag where she was keeping the dumplings warm. She placed them on trays and handed them to Izzie and Alexis. She nodded in Maggie's direction. "I don't trust that one." She snickered.

"Why is everyone always picking on me? So I like food. Does that make me a bad person?" she whined.

Izzie laughed and addressed Zoe. "We go through this at almost every meal."

Maggie pouted. "They're so mean."

Zoe scoffed. "I don't think so."

"Oh swell. You're on their side and you just met me."

"Your reputation precedes you." Zoe was in on the jokes now.

Maggie shook her head, feigning annoyance. Then she scurried past Annie and grabbed two dumplings from the tray Izzie was holding.

Izzie looked at Zoe. "Need I say more?"

Maggie stuck out her tongue and then popped another dumpling into her mouth.

Myra began to herd the crowd. "Come on, everyone. Let's go sit in the atrium and enjoy these luscious-looking gyozas."

Annie addressed Fergus. "Let's crack open one of those bottles of sake and grab the *ochoko* cups." She was referring to the short, rounded cups used to serve sake. She brought over a small stack of plates and paper napkins.

Everyone settled into a chair or ottoman, or leaned against something. Fergus did the honors of pouring the Japanese rice wine, then added, "I should probably go check on Charles and Yoko." He thought he'd give the Sisters a chance to catch up before the serious stuff started later.

In the kitchen, Charles shooed Yoko toward the atrium. "You've done all the hard work. All we need to do now is to cook it up." He checked the steamer basket filled with slightly aromatic rice. "All good here." Charles grinned. "Fergus and I will get this sorted."

Before Yoko went to sit with the others, she returned to her van and retrieved the beautiful white peonies she had been growing for Myra. She could barely get her arms around the bundle.

She entered the house to a chorus of oohs and aahs.

Ordinarily, peonies were available for only a very short time in the spring. With all the other flowers available, most florists didn't try to keep them throughout the year, but Yoko was masterful. And she did it for Myra.

"Oh, Yoko, they are glorious!" Myra jumped out of her seat. She was over the moon.

"Myra, you stay put. We'll take care of this." Yoko and Alexis walked through the atrium and along one side of the kitchen to the entry area at the back door.

Straight ahead was a large utility room. There was a professional-size washer and dryer, two tankless water heaters, a large laundry folding table, a double utility sink, a wall-hung ironing board, and floor-to-ceiling cabinets on the far end. To the left was a very old wooden door that led to an equally old set of steps. These were the stairs that led to their "war room."

Yoko gave the stems one more quick cut while Alexis filled a clear, large, wide-mouthed vase. "Had you met Zoe before?" Alexis asked Yoko.

"Not in person. But Izzie often spoke about her. When she had to go into the city, they'd get together. Drinks. Dinner. Lunch. Whatever they could fit into their schedule. Zoe traveled internationally for several years." Yoko paused and looked at Alexis. "There seems to be something going on with the company she works for."

Alexis furrowed her brow. "Didn't Izzie call Zoe about *your* job?"

"Yes, that's why she's here. I mean that's the reason she came down. To look at the plans."

"So, what happened?"

"Izzie felt some serious tension coming from Zoe. Izzie said Zoe seemed tightly wound. Not at all like herself, Izzie said. But you know Izzie—she is almost as relentless as Maggie and she coaxed it out of her."

"Izzie has a little more patience than Maggie." Alexis chuckled. "What did Zoe tell her?"

"It all started when she read some articles about structural failures. So she did some research and discovered dozens upon dozens of buildings collapsing. Bridges falling over." Yoko continued fussing with the flowers. "You know she grew up in the town where the Silver Bridge collapsed?"

"But that was years before she was born." Alexis calculated the two decades in her head.

"True, but her father's uncle was one of the people who died. Her dad was around five years old at the time."

"That's terrible. No wonder she had an interest in building failures."

"And, get this—in almost every incident it was due to a faulty design or substandard materials. Politics and greed. Just to reassure herself, she asked the head of quality control of her company how things were going. Compliance. All that." Yoko shaved the end of the last flower with her florist knife.

"That doesn't seem like an unreasonable query." Alexis began to put the stems in the water.

"No. But almost immediately she got transferred to a different department. Almost like a demotion. They let her keep her title, but it seems like they're pushing her out." Yoko ruffled the leaves. "Apparently she was looking into some invoices and two days later her access to the database was denied."

"That's one too many coincidences." Alexis stood back and admired the lovely bouquet. "Stunning."

"Yes. But there's more. She got shoved on a subway platform last week."

Alexis stopped in her tracks. "So, Zoe may have stumbled upon something that other people don't want her to know about."

"Correct." Yoko nodded. "Here, take these into the atrium. I should check on what they are doing with my chicken." Yoko made a quick dash into the kitchen just as Maggie was shoveling more gyozas onto a platter. "Weren't you taught to share?" Yoko playfully tapped Maggie's hand.

Maggie rolled her eyes. "These are for everyone." She pouted. "Will it ever stop?"

"Never!" Annie, Myra, Alexis, and Izzie shouted from the other room.

Maggie begrudgingly handed the platter over to Annie, who picked one up with her chopsticks. "This is how you do it."

"Yeah, yeah." Maggie was licking her fingers.

"You didn't touch anything, did you?" Izzie asked.

"I switched hands." Maggie smirked and the others chuckled.

For the next half hour, the women chatted about their latest projects. From there they went on to a discussion about film, television, art, and music.

Zoe added her perspective. "What I enjoyed about traveling the globe was discovering different cultures and their artistic development."

Maggie chimed in. "I don't think we've had our renaissance in this country yet unless you call *Real Housewives*, *The Bachelorette*, and the remake of old game shows artistic development. One network bragged how they had the most game shows on television."

Annie looked over at Zoe. "Maggie thinks we're experiencing a cultural calamity. Can't say I disagree."

Murmurs of agreement passed through the room.

"Well, enough of that nonsense." Charles stepped into the room. "Dinner is served."

Alexis collected the sake cups and Izzie picked the last gyoza off the platter.

The group assembled around the massive oak kitchen table. It was large enough to seat twelve people comfortably. The dining room table could accommodate up to twenty when they had a special occasion. That usually took place after a mission was complete. And accomplished.

Everyone took their usual chair, and Myra indicated the one next to her for Zoe.

Once everyone was settled, they held hands as Myra said grace. "Thank you for this food. Thank you for our friends. Thank you for all the blessings in our lives." A resounding "Amen!" ensued.

Myra handed the platter of skewered teriyaki to their guests while sounds of anticipation filled the room.

"Yoko, you outdid yourself tonight," Alexis exclaimed as she dished some of the rice onto her plate.

Yoko bowed her head in appreciation. "Thank you. As I mentioned to Charles, the gyozas are an old family recipe."

Everyone's eyes went to Maggie. "What? I didn't eat all of them!" Laughs and giggles from the others followed.

There was lots of lively chatter and more banter about Maggie's voracious appetite. She kept trying to change the subject. "I don't want to bring anyone down, but I've been working on an article about the increase in gun violence. It's horrifying."

"And there doesn't seem to be any end in sight," Annie acknowledged as she plucked a few more skewers onto her plate. "The news is horrifying. We're trying to keep it top of mind at the paper, but there is so much other static filling the air."

"And it's become commonplace. Last weekend there were four mass shootings in the country, and I'll bet most people couldn't even tell you where they were. There are just way too many."

"You are so right, Maggie. But can we please change the subject to something more pleasant?"

"Of course. I was just trying to distract everyone from my eating habits!" She carefully balanced a gyoza on her chopstick. "See? I can do it!" There was a light round of applause.

To be sure the conversation wouldn't turn dark again, Myra spoke. "Tell me, Zoe, what is your favorite place to visit?"

Zoe smiled and looked around the table. "This is beginning to become one of them."

"You are too kind," Charles said.

Fergus broke into the conversation. "I understand you spent some time in our old stomping grounds."

"Yes. I was recently in London for a month. Old Windsor, actually. I was looking into some of the buildings there that need renovation."

"Lovely place," Charles said with a tone of nostalgia.

"Indeed." Zoe paused. "But then the company pulled me out and sent me back to New York."

"Any particular reason?" Fergus asked.

"They said the job was canceled."

"Doesn't surprise me." Charles fiddled with one of the skewers. "They can't seem to make up their mind what to do with some of those older buildings. The royal buildings have been well maintained over the years, but since the war, funds have been redistributed and many of the non-royal establishments are in dire need. With the Queen now gone, it shall be interesting to see what King Charles has in store. There are several royal residences and fewer people to occupy them. "It's been a long debate. I doubt we will see any changes in our lifetime, though," Charles said wryly.

"The royals don't pay taxes and haven't really had much to say about governing ever since Parliament was formed," Fergus said. "It is quite remarkable, the never-ending obsession people have with the royals. Although I agree with Charles, with the passing of the Queen, there may be a waning of interest in England's celebrities."

Alexis spoke up. "Please don't get me started with celebrity culture, although those two words do not belong in the same sentence. We just finished a case where a star athlete put an elderly gentleman in the hospital. You could see the admiration in the jury's eyes. Flashbacks of O. J. Simpson."

Maggie shuddered. "And I get to report on all of these atrocities!"

Zoe instinctively steered the conversation back to England. She hadn't realized how much she longed to return. Her life had been rather wonky lately and she hadn't had time to dwell on matters outside of work. She looked at both Fergus and Charles. "Do either of you miss it?"

Charles let out a guffaw. "Certainly, some of it. But it probably misses me even less than I do it."

"Ditto, here," Fergus chimed in.

"I suppose the thing I miss is the countryside. South of Kent, East Sussex, the villages, old churches. And the south-west with the rolling hills and farms in Devonshire, the Cotswolds, and the farmland in Dorset county." Charles took a moment to remember. "I think that's why I like it here so much. Here, at the farm." He reached over and patted Myra's hand. "Right, lovey?"

"I think you miss the pubs the most," Myra joked.

"That goes without saying." Charles guffawed. "Speaking of pubs, would you mind if I switched over to a mild brown ale?"

"Count me in, mate!" Fergus exclaimed. "Don't get me wrong, Yoko. I thoroughly enjoyed the sake, but it's time for a heartier libation."

Yoko smiled. "No offense taken. You should drink whatever you want."

Charles got up from the table, went into the pantry and brought back two pints of room-temperature beer.

Maggie winced. "I could never understand why Brits drink warm beer."

"Because one cannot appreciate the taste if it's cold," Fergus informed her.

"Blech." Maggie made a face.

Charles tried to hand her his mug. "Here, give it a try."

"Ew, no thank you." Maggie pushed the mug away from her.

"She'll eat almost anything, but is quite fussy about her beverages," Izzie noted.

"Ha. Ha. Hand over the sake."

Zoe returned to the few things she'd experienced in England during her short time there. One weekend she and Mason had driven from Windsor to Cornwall. "It was beyond my expectations. When you see the countryside in a film or on television you simply cannot get the full effect."

"Sounds like someone is a bit smitten with the Commonwealth." Fergus grinned.

"I'd been to London a few times, but never long enough to

really see England. And when I was there, it was all business. Even dinners, lunches. I prayed for room service!" She snickered.

"I'm pleased you got to see more of it than the inside of a hotel or office building. The Greater London metropolitan area has been catapulted into the twenty-first century."

"But not without a whole lot of kickin' and screamin'." Fergus laughed. "I think the Thirty Saint Mary Axe building was the kicker."

Zoe chortled. "Yes, the Gherkin building."

Izzie gave a shudder. "I'm all for modernization. But I think it's hideous, especially among all the other buildings. Frank Lloyd Wright would have been apoplectic." Izzie fondly referred to the brilliant work of the man whose architectural philosophy was about joining harmony with humanity and the environment. "A far cry from his vision of organic architecture."

"Isn't the Gherkin a pickle? Doesn't that make it organic?" Maggie wisecracked.

"See? Everything always goes back to food with that one," Izzie joked.

As dinner began to wind down, Myra spoke directly to Zoe. "We have a special group of women here. A few are unavailable, but I can promise you we will do whatever it takes to fix the problems you've uncovered."

Izzie, Alexis, Maggie, and Annie shouted, "Whatever it takes!" Their robust enthusiasm startled Zoe. Myra placed her hand on Zoe's shoulder. "After Fergus and Charles clean up the kitchen, we are going to have a meeting and discuss everything."

With that, everyone got up from the table and proceeded single file to scrape their plates, making sure the wooden skewers were securely disposed of so as not to get the dogs into a dicey situation. Lady, her pups, and Rufus were extremely well-behaved dogs, but better to be safe than sorry, and keep temptation at bay. Izzie wrapped the wooden sticks in foil, placed them in a brown paper bag, tied it in plastic and took it immediately outside to the large trash container secreted behind wooden panels. She checked to be sure the lid was on tight. She brushed her hands and said out loud to no one, "Don't any of you critters get any ideas."

Once the kitchen looked as if no one had set foot in it, Annie put bowls on the kitchen table for their after-meeting ice cream treats. *Spoons. Check. Napkins. Check. Two for Maggie. Make it three. Check.*

Myra took Zoe by the elbow and shuttled her toward the rear entry area. Fergus and Charles got in front and opened the big wooden door leading down a very precarious set of stone steps stained with over a hundred years of who-knows-what. "Mind your head," Fergus said over his shoulder.

"And your feet," Charles added.

"It's not as bad as it looks," Annie said, noting the perplexed expression on Zoe's face. "Not quite a dungeon." She chuckled.

The hanging bare lightbulb may have suggested the opposite. "Myra, we really should have a proper light fixture here." Charles looked up at the light.

"And ruin the mood? Don't be ridiculous." Myra chuckled.

As they made their way to the basement, Myra explained how the farm was once part of the Underground Railroad and a few of the tunnels were still intact. "Annie and I stumbled upon them when we were kids. Our friend Charlotte lived here on the farm. Her father was one of the caretakers. We would meet her out by the back buildings and play. Then one day Annie discovered a wooden hatch under a pile of old hay. The three of us could barely lift it." She chuckled. "After a lot of heaving we pulled it open, sending all three of us backward. There was a very old, and I do mean old, ladder leading to the level below. We weren't sure what to make of it. We were excited and scared witless at the same time. Of course Annie wanted to climb down immediately, but her good sense kicked in." They were halfway down the stone steps as Myra related the rest of the story. "We sat around the edge and concocted stories. Over the years we'd heard rumors about the railroad and the property, but it had been over one hundred years and no one had been below. Or, so it seemed.

"When I got back home, I asked my father about it. The Underground Railroad, that is. I told him we were reading about it in school. Which wasn't a lie. But I didn't want to tell him about the hatch. I thought we might get into trouble. And whenever Annie is around, well, trouble seems to find her."

"Oh, you shush, now," Annie admonished her friend.

Myra gave her a loving smile. "That is part of your charm, my dear." She continued her story. "The next day we went back to visit our new discovery only to find Rigby, Charlotte's father's helper, nailing the hatch shut."

"How did he know?" Zoe asked.

"We were very bright young girls, but the operative word is 'young.' We hadn't covered our tracks very well." Myra shot Annie a confident look. "That won't ever happen again, I can assure you."

"You've got that right, my friend." Annie raised her eyebrows in acknowledgment.

"When I inherited the farm, I had the tunnels inspected and repaired. Not all of them. Just enough of them." She had a sly twinkle in her eye.

When they reached the lower level, another wooden door could be seen on the left and a very shadowy corridor lay ahead. It appeared to disappear into the darkness. Zoe didn't ask any more questions.

As old as the door looked, it featured a very modern, intricate electronic lock that required a fingerprint and a secret code. Zoe remained silent, taking in as much as she could, her leather portfolio tightly tucked under her arm. This was all beginning to feel quite surreal. Izzie inched closer to Zoe and whispered, "Just follow my lead."

At the entrance to the room a statue of Lady Justice stood boldly. As each of them entered, they saluted the symbol of justice. Zoe quickly caught on and followed suit. Charles hit a few switches and the room lit up like NASA's Mission Operation Control Room. Zoe was in disbelief. She sure wasn't in Kansas anymore. Or West Virginia. She resisted the temptation to ask. All she could do was gawk. There were a dozen monitors of various sizes lit with a logo she didn't recognize. All she could make out were the letters W. I. T. in a beautiful script. Soon she would come to know it stood for "Whatever It Takes." It was the Sisterhood's very own motto. There were two ten-by-eight-foot walls that appeared to be made of plexiglass but were actually video screens where the Sisters could download maps. Maps from anywhere in the world. Zoe was dazed and very confused.

Alexis, Izzie, Maggie, and Yoko pulled out their chairs at the large conference table. In front of each seat was a monitor embedded in the table. Myra indicated where Zoe should sit while Fergus and Charles stationed themselves on the other side of the room, fiddling with something electronic. Annie stood at the head of the table and addressed the assembly.

"Zoe, you may have guessed by now that we are a very unusual group of people."

Zoe nodded slowly as her eyes circled the table of friendly faces set in the most highly technological room she had ever seen. The running joke was it could make the Pentagon blush.

"All of us have a backstory," Myra continued. "A story that brought lives to the brink of ruin, and in one case death." A moment of silence fell across the room as they remembered their fallen sister Julia, who had died of AIDS she contracted from her philandering, politically ambitious husband. "We can't fix every injustice in the world, nor can we fix the broken system that perpetrates these injustices. We can, however, fix one at a time." Annie paused to give Zoe an opportunity to comprehend the magnitude of this secret organization.

"Each of the women who sits before you experienced great loss and anguish at the hands of others. Offenders who slipped through the system or were quickly released, even praised. You may recall Izzie's horrific experience when her colleague framed her."

Zoe nodded. "I do."

Izzie was the next to speak. "I have everyone in this room to thank, and a few others who were unavailable tonight, for the reconstruction of my life." She stopped and giggled. "Sorry. No pun intended. It's these people"—Izzie motioned to the group—"to whom I owe my deepest gratitude."

Annie spoke next. "It's because of your relationship with Izzie, and her concern for your well-being, that we are gathered here tonight."

Charles and Fergus had their backs to the rest of the group as they huddled over their computers. Charles turned. "Excuse me. REBAR, ya say?"

Zoe nodded her head. "Yes."

"Offices in New York, San Francisco, London, São Paulo, and Rome?"

"Yes. Those are mostly sales offices. That's where I went when I was still traveling for the company."

Charles turned back to whatever he and Fergus were doing.

Annie went on. "Each of us has a specialty or two. Once we are made aware of the problem, we arrange for the solution. At that time the appropriate people will be assigned a task. Or two. Or more. It depends on how complicated the problem is, how internationally it spreads, and how ruthless the perpetrators are."

Myra took over at that point. "Izzie tells me you have some documents with you?"

Zoe opened the portfolio. "I wanted to check the progress of my jobs and see what stage they were in and if everything was going according to the timeline I laid out."

Fergus spun around in his chair. "According to what we found, REBAR is a multinational company, with offices in the aforementioned cities. They do, however, have accounts at banks in several other countries." He cleared his throat. "That in itself isn't unusual to facilitate financial transactions, but ultimately the money trail should lead to the main accounts associated with the various divisions."

"Correct," Zoe said. "But?"

"But it appears there could be a few detours."

Zoe pursed her lips. "I had a feeling about that." She began to explain what she suspected. "As you know, REBAR has two divisions—steel and masonry. Our clients are major commercial contractors building hotels, condominiums, and bridges. The contractors would send us their plans and then I would review them and give them a bid, using the highest standards of safety. It could take weeks to compile the information, and then I would meet with the client and discuss the specifications, per codes and ordinances."

"That all sounds like it was on the up-and-up," Charles said.

"As far as I knew it had always been that way."

"When did things start to get dodgy? Or, I should say, when did you notice?" Fergus asked.

"It was the beginning of this year. When I was in London and got pulled off the job. Something didn't seem right. A colleague of mine, Mason Chapman, is the executive director of Frogmore House. He told me our company had pulled out of the bidding for another job. A job I knew nothing about."

"And that other job was something you should have known about?" Annie asked.

"Correct. I thought he might be mistaken so I pushed him on the issue, and he said while there was no official memo, several of the directors of historical buildings were cautioned."

"By your company?" Charles furrowed his brow.

"Unofficially. But all bids for renovations would be put on hold." She paused. "And I was *officially* sent back to New York."

"And that's when you started doing some digging?" Alexis asked.

"Not right away. I was simply filing paperwork and discovered some discrepancies in the timelines. Then there was that article about structural failure. I suppose you could say it was a confluence of things."

"Synchronicity, perhaps?" Annie asked slyly.

Zoe's eyes widened.

"Divine intervention?" Myra added.

"All of it." Zoe raised both her hands. "I don't discount anything."

"Please continue," Myra urged.

"When I was looking through some of the documents, I discovered we purchased supplies from a different company than we normally do. It's not that unusual, especially with all the supply chain issues we've had over the past several years, but I'd never heard of them before. And they're in the Dominican Republic. Again, not unusual; however, when I tried to find information about the company, it didn't exist. I checked to see if an LLC or a division of some other company existed, but came up blank. Nothing." Zoe pulled out one of the pages from her file and handed it to Annie, who passed it over to Fergus.

Charles leaned over his shoulder as both read the information. Charles was the first to speak. "Let me see if I have this right. El Cemento was hired by your company to manufacture cinder blocks for a job you were working on. The job got canceled but El Cemento still got paid. The accounts payable log has the date and time the money was released, and it was to a bank in the Cayman Islands."

"A wire transfer. We do that for most of our accounts. Large sums of money are exchanged and it's the easiest way to follow them. But the Caymans? That's the black hole of hidden money."

"To your knowledge, no one in your accounting department found this unusual?" Fergus asked.

"Everything is done via email. They get an invoice, check with the account executive, the account executive checks to be sure the inventory was received. Buttons get pushed; money gets shuffled. No one has the time or the enthusiasm to care where it ends up. They did their job." She looked up at the two Brits. "And Bob's our uncle."

Charles and Fergus busted out laughing over Zoe's use of a common British phrase meaning "and there you have it."

Charles regained his composure and continued. "But you said the job was canceled."

"That's what I was told." Zoe sighed.

"What do you suppose is going on?" Annie was trying to get a handle on this complicated problem.

"My take? Donald Walsh has a scheme to buy subpar materials and mixes them in with our compliant ones. He gets to stretch the goods. I wouldn't be surprised if Walsh was the head of El Cemento and is pocketing a big chunk of change."

"How does this implicate you?" Myra asked.

"If my suspicions are correct, he is using the substandard materials for jobs where he'll lower the price and get a kickback. Meanwhile, other jobs are also getting garbage. Jobs that were mine."

"This is where we need to start. Do you have a list of the jobs you oversaw that are still under construction?" Myra inquired.

"Yes. I keep everything on a flash drive."

"Splendid," Fergus said.

Annie began to make her lists. "We'll send two of you to each of those sites. You'll either be official or unofficial. Whatever it takes to get samples of the masonry."

"Fergus, Charles, do a background check on REBAR and all its executives. Who has come and gone in the past eighteen months. Any severance packages. And this Donald Walsh person.

"Next is tracking down this mysterious company in the Dominican Republic with an account in the Caymans. Fergus? You think you can hand that off to Avery Snowden?" Annie was referring to one of their colleagues who was a master of surveillance, among other talents.

"Let me ring him up," Fergus replied.

Zoe's head was spinning. Was this really happening? Had she slipped into another dimension and landed in the middle of a James Bond movie? She looked at Charles. He resembled Patrick Stewart more than Daniel Craig, but Stewart could have pulled off playing 007. Fergus reminded her of Colin Firth. *Was he in any spy movies? Yes! He was part of a group who fed the Nazis false information in the movie* Operation Mincemeat. She remembered that it was based on a true story, and one of the characters was named Ian Fleming. *Ha!*

"Zoe?" Annie asked with concern. "Are you alright?"

Izzie poured a glass of water and handed it to Zoe.

Zoe slowly scanned the room. Then her eyes darted across the table.

"Sister shock." Maggie chuckled. "Hey, kiddo." She reached for Zoe's hand. "It's okay. We are all friends here."

Myra placed her arm around Zoe's shoulders. "Yes. Sister shock. I guess we should have prepared you better, but there really isn't any other way. 'You're either on the bus, or under the bus.'" Myra looked around. "I know, it's supposed to be 'off the bus,' but let's be honest. That is what we do."

Maggie was the first one to throw her arm up in the air. "Woo-hoo!"

"Easy, girl," Annie said. "There's plenty of time for the rootin' tootin' stuff."

Maggie pouted. "Geez, you guys have been brutal to me since I got here."

Annie approached Maggie and held her arms out. "Need a hug?" Maggie got up and wrapped her arms around her dear friend and mentor, who also happened to be her boss. Annie winked at the other women, who threw their arms into an air fist-bump, and "Woo-hoo!" bounced off the walls.

"Okay then. What's next on the list?" Yoko asked.

Izzie looked up. "What about Yoko and I?"

"For now, get your project on track. I've got it covered. One of my associates, Danny Lodge, is going to get in touch with you to arrange for the construction of your foundation while we take care of the other construction items. We'll probably deploy everyone in about a week or so. When Charles and Fergus can put a few construction sites on the map, we'll decide which ones to target first."

"Avery is good to go," Fergus called over his shoulder.

Annie continued to add to her list. "Maggie, I want you to research all major structural failures over the past ten years. But start backwards, beginning with last year. If there's a pattern, we'll see it sooner than waiting for history to catch up.

"Zoe, we need you to go back to work so you can keep an

eye on the office. Act like you are getting used to the new job. I know it'll be hard, but I am sure you can fake it. You can't quit now. Otherwise, it would look very suspicious."

Myra added, "Fergus, ask Avery to have Zoe shadowed. Sasha would be the best choice. She knows the city inside and out." Myra looked at Zoe again and placed her hand on Zoe's shoulder. "Sasha is one of the best people when it comes to tracking, following, shadowing . . . basically stalking." She chuckled. "She will be on your tail whenever you leave your apartment. Not only will she be a good source of protection, but she will also find out who is following you. I promise, you will be in excellent hands."

She turned to Alexis. "Can you work with Maggie to find out if any lawsuits were filed after the disasters?"

"Absolutely."

"Everybody good with this?" Annie asked.

In unison they shouted, "Whatever it takes!" This time fist bumps were happily shared.

Myra nodded at Izzie. It was time to bring Zoe back into the kitchen and soothe her nerves with some of her home-made ice cream. "We'll be up shortly."

Izzie linked her arm through Zoe's, and they saluted Lady Justice as they exited the room. When they entered the kitchen, a line of dogs sat waiting for their people friends, their tails slapping against the floor. Izzie and Zoe made sure each of the pooches got a pat, scratch, and tickle on the head.

"Take a seat," Izzie suggested to Zoe. "You must have a zillion questions."

"No. Just one." Zoe let out a big whoosh of air. "Where the heck am I?"

Izzie couldn't help but burst out laughing. "You are at Pinewood, and yes, the technology is off the charts. You've heard of the 'dark web'? Well, we can navigate black holes on the web!"

Zoe shook her head back and forth. "I feel like I got

dropped into the middle of a movie set. But which one?" She was clearly disoriented. "*Alice in Wonderland* or *North by Northwest*?"

"I can say with great confidence it is not *Mission: Impossible*," Izzie joked. "I can totally relate to your confusion right now. When I was in jail a woman came to visit me. I didn't know where she came from or who sent her, but in a relatively short matter of time, I was exonerated and ultimately started to get my life back."

"Did you ever find out who it was?" Zoe asked.

"You met them. At least some of them. I owe them everything."

"Kind of a secret society?" Zoe asked nervously.

"Yes. Of sorts." Izzie heard footsteps coming from below and began to dish out the ice cream. "I'll fill you in when we get back to my place. For now, relax and know the Sisterhood is on the case."

Maggie was the first one in the kitchen. She immediately went into the pantry and pulled out several packages of cookies and set them on a plate. In typical Maggie fashion, she had one in her mouth as she walked toward the table, stepping carefully over the mass of canine pals. "Oh, shut it," she said between bites, anticipating a wisecrack from Izzie.

"I didn't say a word." Izzie was scooping out the ice cream and handing the bowls over to Zoe to place in front of each chair.

Myra was next to arrive in the kitchen. "Lady, why don't you bring your party into the atrium so we don't all end up on top of you?" As if Lady understood every word out of Myra's mouth, she stood up but waited. She knew Fergus would have an incentive in his pocket.

Right on schedule Fergus came around the corner into the kitchen and was blocked by a line of dogs. " 'Ere ye go, ya little rascals." He dug into his pockets and pulled out a handful of treats. Once the dogs were satisfied, they meandered into the atrium one at a time.

Zoe watched with delight. "Myra, I've never seen so many well-behaved dogs in one place!"

Myra smiled like a proud mother. "I can't take all the credit. Charles and Fergus spent a lot of time with Lady and her babies." She watched the golden retriever doggie parade move into the other room with Rufus falling in behind them. "They're not such babies anymore!" Each of the dogs had to stand at least twenty-four inches tall and weigh around fifty pounds. "And if Fergus keeps giving them treats, they are going to have to go on a diet."

Lady stopped in her tracks and tilted her head toward Myra.

"Just kidding." Myra gave her a reassuring look and turned to Zoe. "Yes, they have a very large vocabulary. Unfortunately, I used the word 'd-i-e-t' for so many years, Lady picked up on it. Now I don't use that word at all when it comes to my eating habits. Food is good. Good food is even better."

Charles entered the conversation. "Myra didn't always have the best 'd-i-e-t,' which is understandable coming from a candy empire. But I started experimenting in the kitchen and now I've become quite good at it." He gave Myra a peck on the cheek. "Wouldn't you say, lovey?"

She returned the peck. "Indeed. It's truly amazing I am not as big as a whale."

"That's because I cook wholesome food." Charles gave her a pat on her fanny.

Everyone took a seat and devoured the frozen treat. Sounds of delight enveloped the table. Alexis was the first to finish and began gathering up the empty bowls.

"I think I should take this woman back to my house."

Izzie put her arm around Zoe. It was clear Zoe was spent. She was exhausted and exhilarated at the same time. Knowing people had her back was a huge relief. But not knowing what was ahead was terrifying. "Yoko, why don't you come by for breakfast and we can show Zoe our plans. I know Annie has someone lined up, but I'd like Zoe's take on everything."

"Sounds like a very good idea." Yoko nodded.

Zoe profusely thanked Myra, Annie, Charles, and Fergus for their hospitality and their support. "I cannot tell you how much I appreciate this. Whatever the outcome, it was worth meeting all of you."

Myra gave her a motherly hug. "Don't you fret. Annie and I, the Sisters, Charles, Fergus, and our associates will be all over this situation."

Annie placed her arm around Zoe. "It may seem a little cloak and dagger, but it will also be fun. Fun knowing certain people will get their comeuppance and maybe we'll save a few lives in the process."

The group walked them to Izzie's car. Rufus reluctantly jumped in the back seat and Izzie latched him into his harness. "Seat belts for everyone!" she proclaimed. The SUV kicked up a few stones as they made their way down the driveway.

The rest of the group said their goodnights with hugs and kisses. Yoko picked up the empty food hampers and Maggie helped her carry them out to her van. "This certainly was not what I was expecting for this evening," she said to Maggie. "But I'm happy we are going to help Zoe."

"Me too," Maggie agreed. "And thanks for dinner. It was a real treat."

Yoko chuckled. "Anything that goes into your mouth is a treat." She gave Maggie a big bear hug and got into the van.

"I really do have discerning taste. I taste it. I like it!" Maggie hooted and waved as Yoko started the engine.

As Alexis, Myra, Annie, Fergus, and Charles reentered the house, they were already discussing their next moves. "Alexis, time to pull out the old wardrobe. We're going to need a few disguises," said Myra.

Much later that evening

It was close to midnight. Charles and Fergus returned to the war room and fired up their equipment. There was no time to waste. They had to get the ball rolling if Zoe was returning to work on Monday.

There was a new message on one of the consoles. Charles read it out loud: "*Avery confirmed Sasha will be shadowing Zoe. I'll send Sasha Zoe's dossier. We'll let Zoe know Sasha will start on Monday. She'll meet her at a coffee shop, but they will not acknowledge each other. Sasha will get behind Zoe and pretend she is looking for something in her messenger bag. She'll casually drop a few pieces of paper on the floor. Zoe will help her pick them up and then Sasha is to drop an envelope into Zoe's bag. It will contain the usual device and contact info.*"

Charles picked up the intercom phone. "Myra, we are getting Sasha set up for Zoe. Sasha is going to shadow her first thing. As soon as Zoe leaves her apartment, Sasha will follow her and hand off contact information. We just need to let Zoe know that the woman who will be standing behind her at the coffee shop is her contact."

"Good idea. We want Zoe to be aware of who we have tailing her," Myra said. "She doesn't need any additional paranoia."

"Meanwhile, Sasha will keep enough distance between them to see who else might be following Zoe," Charles added.

"I'll go over to Izzie's tomorrow morning with a photo of Sasha and explain what is going to happen."

"Splendid," Charles concurred. "Fergus and I have a bit of rifling to do. We'll probably be down here for a few hours."

"Annie and I can watch a movie. Let me know if you need us."

"We always need you." Charles never missed an opportunity to flirt with his wife.

Fergus turned on the gigantic plexiglass map and marked the locations of REBAR's offices and manufacturing plants. He pulled down the menu for the company's executives and marked their spots on the map. "This chap, Donald Walsh, is not listed as an executive."

"Zoe said he was the head of quality control. You'd think that would come with a few letters—VP, COO, CEO, COB, no?" Charles asked.

"Maybe he's not well favored with some of the bigwigs, but he serves a purpose," Fergus offered.

"And maybe that's why he has a little side game going on." Charles nodded. "We're going to have to get payroll information so we can see how much he earns, and how much he actually has."

"It's those Cayman Islands again." Fergus scowled.

"We've done a workaround before." Charles had a twinkle in his eye. "Remember the last mission when that plonker tried to get money out of the bank?"

Fergus chuckled. "Ah, that Annie of mine."

"With a bit of luck the funds will be at Cayman National."

"Right-o," Fergus agreed. "That would make it a little easier."

"That would also mean Myra and Annie will have to go down there together." Charles laughed.

"That is always risky business." Fergus guffawed. But then his laughing stopped abruptly as he read some new information. "This is interesting. Malcolm Fielder. Been with the company about a year. He's head of manufacturing in the Caribbean."

"So does that mean our boy Donald Walsh works for him?" Charles rolled his Branch ergonomic chair closer to where Fergus was sitting.

"Seems likely," Fergus answered. "But look where Fielder worked before REBAR. FREDO in Santo Domingo."

"The Dominican Republic. But that's not too big of a stretch," Charles said.

"Ah, yes, but he was part of a small group that resigned."

"Reorganization, perhaps?"

Fergus opened another browser and looked up FREDO. "Ha. About a year ago the government shut them down for two weeks. Safety inspections."

"Was the company fined?"

"No, but three people, Mr. Fielder included, 'left the company,' according to this article."

"Did they give a reason?" Charles stood and began to read over Fergus's shoulder.

"You got it, old chap. Reorganization."

"I find that curious. And coincidental. Looks like the company was given a clean bill, and the press release says they had taken precautionary measures to assure they were compliant."

"Sounds a bit dodgy. Can we get into the financials of the company?"

"I'm working on it, but it's going to take a bit. There's a tremendous amount of deep diving through a lot of firewalls before we can get close to their mainframe."

"Alright. Let me know if we need to bring Izzie into this. Maybe Abner."

"Let's not forget about Libby. She was a tremendous help with her computer and technical experience during our last mission when Nikki was injured in the car bomb explosion."

"Right." Fergus yawned.

"I think we should call it a night. Give our noggins a rest. We've got to find out what REBAR and FREDO have in common, if anything. Need to start with a clear head."

Fergus began to shut down most of the monitors, leaving one search program to run overnight.

They saluted Lady Justice as they left the room, locked the door and climbed the stone steps. In the atrium they found all the dogs and two women, dozing in various positions.

Lady lifted her head and immediately put it back down. She, too, was too tuckered out to care about a treat.

Chapter Five

Donald Walsh

D onald Walsh was the third generation of his family to
work in masonry. Donald's grandfather began the family business right after World War II in Waretown, New
Jersey, and took advantage of the burgeoning housing market and the G.I. Bill. As a kid, Donald heard about the
Freemasons and asked his grandfather about them, but his
grandfather never wanted to discuss it. At first Donald thought
that was because it was a secret society, but their tenets were
familiar: brotherly love, truth, relief. Donald suspected it was
the lack of "brotherly love" in his own family that kept them
out of the larger fraternity. There was always bickering
among the adult brothers—and the sisters-in-law weren't
much better. The rivalry and jealously was palpable. Like a
lot of families, holiday dinners were often tense. But as he got
older, Donald discovered truth was yet another tenet they
lacked.

Sometime around Donald's fifteenth birthday his father instructed him to take a ride with him and his two uncles,
Tommy and Jimmy. Starting then, every Friday night the
three men and Donald climbed into their Buick Century and

headed into town, arriving just as the stores were closing. The first time Donald got fidgety, thinking the stores would be shuttered before they got there. By the third or fourth stop, Donald realized he was their lookout while the others collected their weekly "vig." They called it "protection money." Protection from the Walshes and their pack. They got away with it for a very long time.

No one would have suspected they were a criminal family. They certainly didn't *look* like gangsters. And Donald's father, George Walsh, was no Vito Corleone. The older Donald got, the more he discovered that racketeers come in all shapes and sizes: flannel or cashmere; bolo or four-in-hand silk tie; Gucci loafers or Timberland work boots. You didn't need to wear a black suit with a black overcoat and a fedora with a cigar hanging out of your mouth to be a criminal.

In the light of day, the Walsh family looked like a typical, blue-collar, middle-class family with a family-owned business. The three brothers were married with children, lived in typical modest ranch houses, and attended church regularly. At least the women did. The men would show up for the holidays or special occasions. The brothers belonged to a bowling league and the wives tended to the kids while holding part-time, even full-time, jobs.

It was the 1980s. New York City was rife with crime. The rate of violence had doubled in less than two decades. Even though their little town was over an hour away from the pit of chaos, the Walshes preyed on people's fears. It didn't take much to convince the local merchants that they needed protection. Fear was what the Walshes counted on. Truth be told, the only regular crime in Waretown was someone stealing the newspaper off someone's front lawn, or the occasional shoplifter. But it only took one staged mugging to convince the townspeople they needed their own godfather. The brothers weren't necessarily greedy. They didn't want to wipe out the local businesses. But they knew a skim off the top of the cash the storekeepers weren't declaring on their taxes wouldn't do that much harm.

George Walsh didn't have the brains of a Corleone, fictional or otherwise. His racket looked easy enough and lasted almost a decade. The Walshes' plan was to invest the money in a casino in Atlantic City. In the beginning, the casino owner kept telling them the casino wasn't making money, and it normally took five years before they could expect a profit. But within those five years, the developer declared bankruptcy and all their illicit gains were gone. Stupidity or karma? Maybe a bit of both.

As the big-box stores began to spring up in the towns along the Long Island Expressway, the mom-and-pop shops closed, were sold, or the owners retired. The days of pilfering the locals were over. The Walshes were forced to live within their means and lick their financial wounds.

By the time Donald finished high school, he knew his future was in concrete. Provided it wasn't cement shoes. Donald was not a stellar student; nor was he a dolt. At the very best, he was average. Not that there was anything wrong with average, except where his father was concerned. George took his own failings out on his son, telling him the only thing that mattered was money and power. Get one, you got both. "And ya got neither, boy! Make something of yourself!" Those words were drummed into Donald's head until his father's last, booze-soaked breath. Yes, George was bitter. Everything he and his brothers had built was in shambles. But who was to blame? No one took responsibility, so he just took it out on his own kid.

After the family business folded and his father passed, Donald went to work for a competitor. Over the course of five years, he rose in middle management and developed a good network of contractors in Long Island. As luck would have it, one of the biggest manufacturers of masonry products was looking for a plant manager and Donald had exactly the right credentials for the job. For the next thirty years Donald would continue to work for REBAR, but climbing the corporate ladder was not in the cards. He didn't have the finesse. What he did have was experience, and a little bit of intimidation—something in his family's DNA.

The roller-coaster ride that was his family's business had made Donald wary of almost everyone he met. He was somewhat of a loner apart from his bowling league. Now, at fifty-five, he was still single with no prospects. Not that he cared. Like the rest of his coworkers, he was just going through the motions. Retirement wasn't too far off on the horizon when an opportunity presented itself. And it came from someone he least expected: Malcolm Fielder, head of manufacturing in the Caribbean.

Late one afternoon when Donald was making the final rounds for the day, Fielder approached him. "Walsh, is it?"

Donald was surprised the man knew him by name. "Yes. I'm Donald Walsh." He reserved the comeback "Who wants to know?" The custom-tailored suit and polished shoes indicated this man was a very high-ranking official, so he'd wait for an introduction.

Fielder held out his hand. "Malcolm Fielder. VP of manufacturing in the Caribbean."

Donald shook the man's hand. It was very unusual for executives to visit the plant unannounced. Once a year, around the holidays, the bigwigs would parade about the plant offering holiday greetings as they handed out paltry bonuses. "Been a rough year. The economy and all," was the usual excuse. But everyone knew the bonuses were drawn from a pool and the executives divvied it up, keeping the lion's share for themselves. The employees would smile and offer their gratitude, secretly knowing they were being duped. But it was a job and came with benefits. For most of them that was enough. But Donald was still on the fence about accepting his lot in life.

"Nice to meet you, Mr. Fielder. What can I do for you?"

Fielder put his arm around Walsh's shoulder. "Perhaps there is something we can do for each other."

And so it began.

Walsh was given a small office in the corporate building in Midtown Manhattan. Because he wasn't considered an executive, he wasn't required to wear a suit. Instead he stuck with a blazer, trousers, button-down shirt and tie. He went to a thrift shop in Great Neck where they carried the castoffs from rich families who only wore what was trending for the current season. Women had much more to choose from amid the discarded clothing, but rest assured the rich housewives of Long Island weren't going to allow their husbands to be seen in last year's Burberry, so there was also a modest selection for men. Walsh was fortunate that he was of average build and he managed to find three blazers that had been barely worn. The sleeves on one were a bit short, but he didn't care. No one was going to call the fashion police on him. He stopped at a Target store on the way home and also purchased six ties and five shirts. He managed to pull it all off by rotating shirts, jackets and his six ties. He thought he was rather clever about the ties. He wouldn't be seen wearing the same one within the same week. He had two pairs of shoes. One he wore to and from work, the other when he was in the office or on the rare occasion of a seasonal dinner with the bowling league. Each day he carried his laptop and his good shoes in a nylon bag with him to work.

The new gig suited Donald, but things began to change when Fielder sent him on his first fateful trip to Santo Domingo.

Chapter Six

Izzie/Zoe/Yoko

When Zoe and Izzie returned to Izzie's, hot toddies were in order. The two sat curled up on the long sofa facing the fireplace with their drinks. "I know this is a lot to process," Izzie said, and she began to explain in as much detail as she could without compromising confidential information. "As you noticed, Myra, Annie, Charles, and Fergus have a very elaborate operation. They rescued me and many others like me."

"Yes, I got that part," Zoe said steadily.

"All I can tell you is that they are the most trustworthy and loyal people you will ever meet. While it's not mandatory, you may be called upon at a later date to help another woman in jeopardy." Izzie peered at Zoe, trying to read her thoughts. "Yes, kind of like the mafia but . . ." Izzie stopped short. She was going to say, "but not as ruthless," which would have been a lie. "But we don't use guns." Then she giggled, trying to lighten the mood.

"Well, that's a relief." Zoe snickered as well.

"Seriously, this is what it seems. We are a secret group of justice-seekers. Our range is far and wide thanks to our leadership and resources. If I were asked for a suitable description, I'd say we're not very different from *Charlie's Angels.* The difference is there are more of us, and we know who Charlie is." Izzie chuckled and gave Zoe a little more background about the women. "Kathryn drives an eighteen-wheeler cross country. When her husband was wheelchair-bound she took up his route while he accompanied her as a passenger. One night when they were at a truck stop, three men on motorcycles decided it would be fun to rape Kathryn while her husband helplessly watched."

"Oh my God! That is awful," Zoe said with dismay.

"Unfortunately, Kathryn's husband passed away not long after. Myra and Annie became aware of this horrendous situation and through their connections they were able to track down the perpetrators. Turned out they were well-heeled businessmen out on a weekend joyride. I can't say how they got their comeuppance, but I can assure you it was justified." Izzie's eyes sparkled as she remembered the incident.

Zoe was transfixed. "How long have you known Myra and Annie?"

"Several years," Izzie replied. "They also helped me when I discovered a little boy was being abused by his stepmother. She would beat him with her shoes."

"Really?" Zoe's eyes widened.

"Yep. Let's just say the wicked stepmother will never be able to wear Charles Jourdan pumps again." Zoe winked as she took a sip of their nighttime beverage.

"Wow." Zoe was dumbfounded.

"There's plenty more. One of Myra's childhood friends got hoodwinked into some youth preservation and restoration program run by three doctors. They had offices in Aspen, New York, and London. Called it 'Live, Life, Long.' They preyed on rich widows and were handing out uppers saying they were nutraceuticals and bioceuticals. The women would be high and therefore would think they were rejuvenated. Then they would crash and go back for an injection at five thousand a pop!"

Zoe shook her head. "People can be really horrible."

"That's why there are people like us. The Sisters." Izzie smiled and looked at the clock. It was almost one A.M. "I think it's time we hit the sheets."

Zoe stretched and yawned. "This was certainly not the day I had imagined." She paused. "Izzie, I don't know how to thank you. I feel such a sense of relief."

Izzie gave her a big hug. "Get some rest. We'll pick this up in the morning." The women parted on the second-floor landing, each going to her own private quarters with Rufus settling in with Izzie.

Zoe was asleep as soon as her head hit the pillow. Izzie, on the other hand, wanted to give Abner the heads-up on what was about to happen. Another mission.

The next morning Zoe followed Rufus to the kitchen, where Izzie was already making coffee, heating scones, and dishing out fresh fruit. "What time is it?" asked Zoe, still only half awake.

"Almost ten. How did you sleep?"

"Like I haven't in weeks. That was some powerful toddy." She snickered. "Oh, and all the other stuff that came before."

Izzie grinned as she set a mug of coffee in front of Zoe. "Yoko should be here in about an hour."

Zoe looked up from her mug. "I didn't ask last night. There was so much stuff spinning in my head. But what's Yoko's background?"

"She specializes in martial arts. When she's not running the nursery."

"I see." Zoe nodded. "And Alexis?"

"She got pinned for a stock scam she knew nothing about.

After her release Myra helped her get into law school. Now she works for Nikki's all-female firm." Izzie paused. "She is also a master of disguise." She winked.

"This sounds like a British mystery caper."

"We certainly have all the right characters for one, including Charles and Fergus."

"What's their story?" Zoe asked.

"I'd rather not say, but as you could tell, they hail from very high security backgrounds."

"Sounds like MI6."

Izzie spit out her coffee. Before she had a chance to respond, the doorbell rang and Rufus ran to greet their visitor. "Must be Yoko." Izzie pressed the communication button on the intercom. "Good morning."

"Hey. It's Yoko."

Izzie hit the release button for the front door. Yoko was hidden behind a large bouquet of dazzling blue flowers. It was an assortment of periwinkle hydrangeas, love-in-a-mist, and grape hyacinth. Her face finally appeared after she handed the flowers to Izzie as she said her good-mornings.

"These are gorgeous! Yoko, you are a true artist," Izzie proclaimed. She opened one of the massive pantry doors and reached for a vase. Yoko gave the stems a clean cut as Izzie placed them one at a time in water. The blue monochromatic colors were striking against the kitchen's gray slate backsplash.

"Coffee?" Izzie asked Yoko.

"Please. Can you make me a cappuccino?"

"With just a push of the button." Izzie placed a cup under one of the spigots of the professional-grade coffeemaker. Then she steamed the milk. She eyed Yoko and then glanced at Zoe.

"Have you recovered from last evening?" Yoko asked Zoe.

"I'm not sure. That was a lot to absorb, especially since I

was supposed to be here to help both of you initially. I had no idea it was going to become such a . . . such a, what?" Zoe's eyes grew wide again.

"Big commotion?" Yoko interjected.

"Hubbub?" Izzie countered.

"I don't know what to call it!" Zoe screwed up her mouth.

"Let's just say it was an intervention," Izzie offered.

Zoe laughed out loud. "That's a good one! I guess I needed it. I was getting terribly paranoid."

"Sounds justified," Yoko said just before she took a sip of her frothy beverage.

The phone rang, causing everyone to jump. Then they broke out in laughter. "See?" Zoe smirked.

Izzie answered the phone. "Good morning, Annie." Izzie listened for a moment. "Yes, Zoe is doing fine. She got a good night's sleep." More listening, then came a chuckle. "Yes, I did make one of my special toddies for her." Izzie grabbed a pad and pen and started writing something down. "Got it. I'll let her know. Thanks, Annie. Talk later." Izzie ended the call. She leaned on the counter, facing the two other women. "Zoe, tomorrow you may notice someone following you as soon as you leave your apartment. Though odds are you would never spot her. She's *that* good. But if you get a creeped-out feeling, not to worry. That will be Sasha. She'll be on a silver and black Brompton bicycle wearing bike shorts and a helmet. She'll have a messenger bag over her shoulder." Rufus sensed another visitor and gave a bark. "That must be Myra. She is dropping off a photo of Sasha." Izzie clicked the video camera on and buzzed Myra in. "I know most people would expect a text but we haven't set up your private network yet, and we don't want to leave an electronic trail."

"Understood." Zoe nodded and turned toward the door. Myra bounced across the room, wearing a pair of navy jogging pants and a matching hoodie, high-top sneakers, and of course, her pearls. She looked years younger than her passport stated.

Morning greetings and hugs went around the kitchen island. "I was explaining the logistics for tomorrow when you arrived," said Izzie.

Myra pulled out a stool as Yoko fixed everyone a fresh cup of coffee. "Carry on."

"You are to stop at the Peet's coffee shop on Thirty-Seventh," Izzie said to Zoe. "Sasha will get behind you in line. Make sure your tote bag is unzipped. She'll pull out a file from her bag and a few papers will fall out. You'll turn to help her while she slips a beige envelope into *your* bag. Don't open the envelope until you know you have total privacy. The envelope will contain a watch. A Fitbit kind of thing. It has a red emergency button. When activated it will send a signal to Sasha, her boss, Avery, and Charles. It is also a two-way radio. If you get into trouble, push the white button and you'll be able to tell us what the problem is." Izzie could sense that what she was saying was overwhelming to Zoe. "Don't worry. You should have no reason to use it. It's there just in case, and to make you feel safe."

There's that word again, thought Zoe. "I feel so much better already." She let out a huge sigh.

Izzie continued. "There will also be a burner phone for you to use when you need to speak to any of us. Untraceable, but we'll know it's you."

Yoko placed both her hands on top of Zoe's trembling fingers. "It's going to be okay. Promise."

"Is this real? I don't mean are you for real. I mean, am I having a waking kind of dream?" Zoe asked.

"I know it's a lot to take in, especially since you haven't even been here a whole twenty-four hours," Izzie comforted her friend.

Yoko turned Zoe's swivel stool so they faced each other. "Why don't we take a look at the plans now? We can come back to our"—Yoko cleared her throat—"mission . . . later."

Zoe let out another big sigh. "Sounds good." Izzie placed everyone's coffee on a tray and carried it to the office area on the other side of the loft.

Izzie's desk was made from an old oak door, fixed on triangular posts. It was the perfect space for blueprints. She unrolled the plans and began to discuss her and Yoko's ideas.

"We're responsible for the entire project, but the café will be our own space. We have some friends from Ashville, North Carolina, who will help with the fixtures and setup. But for now we need to focus on the entire project from below ground on up."

Zoe perused the plans. "Looks like you have the right specs for the job. What are your concerns?"

"We want to make sure we're compliant. I know we are, according to the ordinances, but we want to be sure we're above reproach."

Yoko echoed Izzie's concern.

"Even if you use the specs you already have, you should be way beyond the requirements." Zoe took a closer look. "Really. You get your foundation constructed according to these and you should be absolutely fine."

"Good to know," Izzie responded. "And Annie has someone lined up who can meet these specs."

"Then we should be okay, especially if Annie is recommending someone. You know how she is. The best or nothing," Yoko added.

Myra peered over Yoko's shoulder. "I haven't seen these plans yet. The complex looks fantastic. It will be such a wonderful addition to the town center. Very exciting."

"Well, if there is anything else you need me to do, please

let me know," Zoe offered. "By the looks of it, you have everything under control."

"Can we call on you if we need an assessment while we're under construction?" Yoko asked. "I'm still working out the exterior landscaping design."

"Of course you can!" Zoe replied. "And I would be delighted to confer on the conifers. We are here to help one another."

Izzie held up her hand in the Sisterhood fist bump. "Whatever it takes!"

Zoe jumped in. "Whatever it takes!"

They all laughed, hugged, and finished up their java. Izzie and Zoe then walked Myra and Yoko to the door, Rufus leading the parade. Myra put her hands on Zoe's shoulders and looked her straight in the eye. "I don't want you to spend any more energy worrying. I want you to stay focused. You are our boots on the ground. Once you get the devices from Sasha, we will also arrange for you to get a tablet so you will be able to share information on an encrypted site."

Zoe finally had a look of confidence on her face. She was assured that Myra and company had everything in hand. She was confident she could take an active role in her very own caper.

As soon as Izzie's two guests left, she checked the clock. "What time is your train?"

"Three o'clock," Zoe replied. "Should get me in by six."

Izzie scrunched up her face. "Let me see if Sasha can meet you earlier than planned, at Penn Station. Just to be safe. Hang on." Izzie pulled out her cell phone and dialed Charles's number.

"What can we do for you, Izzie?" Charles said by way of greeting. He often used the word *we* because most action involved all of them.

"Hey, Charles. Do you think Sasha might be available to

escort Zoe from Penn Station? I'm sure she'll be fine, but the last time Zoe was in New York and near train tracks, she got a good scare."

"What time?"

"Her train gets in at six."

"Hang on," Charles said as he sent a text to Avery. Within a few seconds he got a reply and returned his attention to Izzie. "Right. Sasha will be waiting at the platform. Tell Zoe to exit the train at the front of the café car. She needn't look about. Sasha will spot her. What will Zoe be wearing?"

"Zoe can't be missed." Izzie grinned at her stylish friend. "A blue plaid duster. Tell Sasha she resembles Anna Wintour."

"Indeed she does have that look about her." Charles smiled into the phone. "I'll convey that to Avery. Mind how you go."

"Roger that." Izzie ended the call and spoke to Zoe. "Sasha will be on the platform when your train arrives. Get off at the front of the café car. Don't look around. She'll find you and shadow you."

Zoe gave Izzie the biggest hug she could muster. "I'm all atwitter!"

"As you should be. We're taking down the bad guys."

Izzie helped Zoe with her overnight bag as Rufus looked on. "So nice to meet you," Zoe said as she bent down to give him a hug. He gave a woof in return.

"I'll drive you past the site and then we can grab a bite at Doris's Diner," said Izzie.

"Sounds good to me!"

Rufus gave Izzie a sad look. "Okay, you can come along. It's nice enough so we can sit outside." Rufus's tail went crazy wagging, thumping a rhythm on the floor.

Izzie punched in the code for the alarm and they piled into the SUV. Zoe rested her head against the SUV window as they pulled out of the driveway. "I'm glad your contractor couldn't do the work." She turned to Izzie. "Otherwise, I wouldn't have come down here."

"Well, it really had been much too long since we got together. I know people always say, 'Let's make a plan' and they either never get around to it, or the plans get canceled and never rescheduled."

"You are so right. Why is that?"

"I dunno. Maybe they just make plans in case nothing better comes along."

"I also believe people assume they're connected because there is always the internet, phones, and social media. But it's an illusion. Mea culpa. I, too, should make more real plans to see people."

Izzie looked over at Zoe and raised her eyebrows. "Any particular person you have in mind?"

Zoe folded her arms and smirked. "Maybe."

Izzie drove for about twenty minutes until they came upon the large parcel of land soon to be the centerpiece of the town. The backhoes were already on-site.

"Going by your drawings, it should be spectacular," Zoe commented.

"Thanks. It's a great space in a great location. We didn't remove any trees. Just relocated them where necessary. It was a hefty bill, but the town agreed to share the expense, which made all of us happy."

"Don't you just hate it when people come along and raze everything to the ground? When I lived in Brooklyn, I had neighbors who were building a new house. They removed every stick, branch and trunk. Another neighbor made a comment about the yard going bald, and the contractor building the house, who was also the owner, told us he had a permit to remove the trees. Neither of us wanted to question him. That would not have been the neighborly thing to do.

Why would he lie? Turned out the guy *was* a big, fat, lying jackass. You should see what he did to the property. Surrounded it with a cheap, white plastic fence. Then he put up a half dozen signs stating there was twenty-four-hour surveillance. Such an ass. It's probably the safest neighborhood in the borough. Then he installed motion-detector lights that shined onto everyone's property. So glad I moved away from him. He was totally unhinged."

"And now? How are your neighbors in the big city?" Izzie asked.

"Funny thing. I live in a pre-war, twelve-story building, and I can count on one hand the people I know by name. I think it's a New York thing."

Izzie chuckled. "I am so happy to be surrounded by woods. When Abner and I bought the pickle factory, we ripped up all the asphalt and planted all those evergreens."

"You did an amazing job. No one would ever know what came before."

"Oh my gosh! I just realized I have the *real* gherkin building!" Izzie howled with delight.

They walked over to Doris's Diner and sat at a table on the sidewalk as Rufus wiggled his way underneath. The jolly, pink-cheeked owner came out and greeted the two women and the dog. Doris pulled a piece of ham from her apron. Izzie shook her head. "You are going to spoil him."

"I think someone beat me to it." Doris handed Rufus the usual treat he got when he visited.

"Doris, this is my friend Zoe. We went to school together. She's consulting on our project."

"Nice to meet you, Zoe. Welcome to my humble establishment. Coffee?"

Izzie and Zoe groaned. "I think we've consumed more than our share of caffeine today," Izzie explained.

"Tea, then?" asked Doris.

"Chamomile?" Izzie queried.

"Sure thing. Zoe?"

"Yes, please."

After lunch, Izzie drove Zoe to the train station. Izzie gave her friend a few more words of encouragement before they parted. "You got this, girl."

"*We've* got this," Zoe replied, feeling completely connected to this group of wonderful people she'd met by chance. Or was it? She thought of the words *divine intervention* as she descended the escalator to the awaiting Acela.

Chapter Seven

Malcolm Fielder

Considered one of the most eligible bachelors in Miami, Florida, Malcolm Fielder was living the high life in South Beach. In the early 1950s his grandfather, Herbert Watson, was one of the first to declare South Florida the new frontier. He opened a bottle-and-keg shop on A1A just below Key Biscayne near Coral Gables. The Gables was one of the wealthiest communities in the country and the nearby university proved a great source of underage drinkers with fake IDs. But Herbert was quite careful and scrutinized those customers who looked like they'd barely begun to grow facial hair. With the influx of "snowbirds," business flourished and Herbert opened several more liquor stores, always on the fringe of future property developments.

By the mid-1960s he had over two dozen stores and decided it would be worth his efforts to open his own distribution center, which eventually became the largest in the Southeast. Not only was he making a huge margin on his retail establishments, he was also making tremendous profits across the state as towns, golf courses, hotels, motels, and condominiums filled their need for alcoholic beverages. Truly being in the right place at the right time was a boon for Herbert. By the time he was thirty-five, he was one of the richest men in Florida. His keen business acumen not only made him the libation king, but he also parlayed much of his money into real estate, purchasing penthouse apartments on Miami Beach and leasing them for the winter crowd in search of sun and sand.

Herbert was not a flashy dresser, nor was he a bon vivant. He considered himself a simple man with good business sense. Despite his wealth, Herbert and his wife Marsha lived in a modest home in Coral Gables where they raised their two children in a beautiful, banyan-tree-filled neighborhood. They sent their children to top-notch schools. Rather than join the family business, Herbert's daughter Andrea wanted to become a college professor with a degree in international studies. Her sister, Lisa, moved to Bar Harbor, Maine, where the family spent their summer vacations. She met her husband there and put down roots. After Andrea got her PhD, she married Raymond Fielder, also a college professor in the engineering department.

Andrea had two children, Malcolm and Daisy. Malcolm was Herbert's hope for continuing the family legacy. Because of Raymond's and Andrea's tenure at the university, Malcolm's tuition was free of charge and his grandfather encouraged him to study business management. After graduation, Malcolm took a year off to travel abroad, spending a lot of his time in the South of France, learning about wine, and spending his trust fund as if it was a bottomless pit. His father constantly reminded him that "one hundred thousand a year doesn't go very far."

Malcolm learned that lesson quickly and soon returned to his roots. It took little effort to convince him that he would be an asset to the family business, especially with his first-hand knowledge of wine. His grandfather was overjoyed that a member of the family would finally be involved. Malcolm took his role seriously, believing he would be the heir apparent to the family fortune. Not that he expected to inherit *all* of the family money, but if he could parlay his way into running the company, he would surely have a sizeable fortune. The first two years proved fruitful, and the distribution center soon became known for its vast wine collection.

When Herbert celebrated his seventieth birthday, he decided it was time to elevate his grandson's position and made him Vice President of Wine Imports. It was an excellent promotion for the twenty-seven-year-old Malcolm, but it still wasn't enough. He'd discovered his father's old adage of "one hundred thousand a year doesn't go very far" proved true, even with his six-figure salary.

Malcolm figured that with the company's annual volume of business, a few nicked cases of Caymus and Opus One wouldn't be missed. While the wines were on the higher end of the price spectrum, they weren't in the stratosphere. No one would notice. Malcolm was able to pull off the skimming for another two years while he continued to justify it to himself. *It was his money, too.* But when Herbert passed away suddenly, there was a whole lot of commotion, with everyone wanting their fair share of the financial pie. Malcolm was one of three grandchildren. Even though the other two were removed from the business, they were all heirs and were all entitled to their portion. To assure an honest accounting, there was an extensive audit of the business inventory, accounts payable and accounts receivable.

When the paperwork didn't match up to the reality, there was a lot of finger-pointing. Warehouse personnel, delivery drivers, and store clerks were all accused in turn. No one would have believed that it was Malcolm—but his own mother had her suspicions. She knew her son was living well beyond his means with his penthouse in South Beach, his Maserati, and his Louboutin shoes. Raymond thought Malcolm's wealth came from investing his money thanks to his business background. Besides, Raymond would never believe his son was capable of malfeasance. And Andrea was not about to have her sticky-fingered son come between her and her husband. Instead, she took Malcolm out for a lavish lunch at a rooftop restaurant. The view included Malcolm's condo building.

"Beautiful view," Andrea noted as she looked around for local celebrities. "Isn't that your place right there?" she asked, knowing very well it was.

"Of course, Mother." Malcolm sensed something big was about to be revealed. Maybe another promotion? Maybe a windfall from his granddad's estate?

Andrea peered over her champagne cocktail at her son. "Tell me. How are you getting on?"

"What do you mean?" he asked with a silly grin.

"Your investments," she said calmly.

"What about them?" He was starting to get a little nervous at this line of questioning.

"You appear to be doing quite well, and I know it cannot be the cumulative effect of your salary and trust fund. Your condominium alone is worth over a million dollars."

Malcolm almost choked on his pinot noir. He paused before he spoke. "Yes, but I bought it at half that." He set his glass down. "Mother, what are you getting at?"

"I think you know." Andrea swirled the bubbles in her glass.

Malcolm still pretended the conversation was going to go in a different direction. But it didn't.

"I want you to apply for a job at FREDO," Andrea stated.

"What?" Malcolm's voice was loud enough to draw attention to their table.

"Keep your voice down." She looked him squarely in the eye. "Do not lie to me. It is not a coincidence that tens of thousands of company profits are unaccounted for. In the wine department."

Malcolm thought he would choke.

"I do not want to hear any more about this." She pulled a business card from her Valentino purse. "You will call Alonso Alvarez tomorrow. I've already spoken to him."

Malcolm looked dazedly at the card printed with the masonry company's name. "How do you even know him?"

"Remember that I was a professor of international studies. We went to school together."

"What am I supposed to tell him?" Malcolm asked as he broke out into a sweat.

"Tell him you are calling about a job in the Dominican Republic."

"What?" Again heads turned in their direction.

"Please keep your voice down. Unless you want this to blow up in your face, and it could, you need to make yourself invisible."

"But what am I supposed to tell people?"

"You tell them you have a wonderful opportunity that you simply cannot pass up."

"But what about the family business?" He was almost apoplectic.

"We are selling everything. Your father wants to move to a more temperate climate. Someplace with less humidity. And I am in complete agreement."

Malcolm was devastated. "What does Dad think about me moving to the Caribbean?"

"He'll think you're finally putting your college education

to good use instead of just your palate." Andrea waved her fork toward his fifty-dollar glass of wine, and the one-hundred-and-eighty-dollar Kobe beef tartare.

Malcolm could not believe what he was hearing. He hung his head in disbelief.

"End of discussion, dear," Andrea said. Then she raised her glass. "Cheers!"

Chapter Eight

New York City

Zoe spent most of the train ride scrolling through email on her tablet. If someone was keeping track of her digital footprint, it would be quite normal for her to be working on a Sunday. Or any day. Anytime. In fact, if she hadn't accessed her company email account in longer than twenty-hours hours, someone would question why. For all intents and purposes Zoe was a workaholic. Her one exception was Mason Chapman. He was the only distraction she had allowed herself in recent years. She'd thought about visiting him. Many times. But she wanted to keep her fantasies alive, rather than quash them with the reality that he had lost interest. She heard Izzie's voice in her head: *Don't be a jerk. You don't want to live with any regrets.* Izzie had said this the night before as they were sharing their hot toddies.

Zoe blinked several times. It hadn't even been twenty-four hours ago and yet it seemed like ages. As they began to enter the tunnel, the conductor announced, "Next stop: New York, Penn Station. New York, Penn Station. Next stop. Please remember to take all your belongings. New York."

Zoe gathered her overnight bag and tote and put on her

identifying coat. She moved toward the café car and stood behind the anxious travelers waiting to disembark. As she stepped off the train, she purposely did not look around. *Act normal*, she told herself. She moved with the throng of people along the platform, careful not to get too close to the tracks. The group slowed as they approached the stairs, while people fumbled with their suitcases, baby carriages, and shopping bags from an assortment of retailers. Zoe tried to avoid touching the handrails—something she'd never thought about before COVID. When you lived in the city, you tended to ignore the grime. It was the least of your worries. Now, pretty much everything invoked angst.

Zoe caught a glimpse of a woman about her own age and height moving with agility. She wondered if that was Sasha. She resisted the temptation to look again, but then the woman caught Zoe's eye. It was a fleeting moment, but Zoe immediately understood the woman to be Sasha. How? She wasn't sure. Was she merely imagining the communication? One thing was certain—she felt confident. She knew a group of people had her back.

When she exited the station she stood in the taxi queue. Zoe noticed the woman she had spotted a few minutes before walking toward a private car, but she paused before she got inside. When it was Zoe's turn for the next taxi, the other woman got into the private car, which pulled out and got behind Zoe's cab. The town car followed the taxi to Zoe's apartment and pulled over a few feet ahead of them. Zoe noticed the rear passenger window roll down as the woman pulled out a mirror and pretended to reapply lipstick. The woman continued to watch Zoe in her mirror until she entered her apartment building.

Zoe got a thrill knowing she was being covered. She was greeted by the doorman who had been charged with feeding her cats.

"Hello, Carlton. How's it going? How are my babies?"

"Good evening, Ms. Danfield. All's well around here. Your fur babies are just fine. Fed them about an hour ago."

"Thanks very much." Zoe handed him a fifty-dollar bill.

"You are too kind," the elderly gentleman responded.

"You are worth every penny." Zoe smiled, thinking Carlton must have been guarding that building for decades.

As Zoe thanked her doorman, from her half-hidden position across the street, Sasha sent an update to Avery, who relayed it to Charles: **Unknown Woman in black town car NY Plate LIB122 followed mark from Penn to apt.**

Charles read the message from Sasha and then relayed it to Myra. "Right. Sasha is on the job and confirmed that someone else is also following Zoe."

"But how did that other woman know Zoe's arrival time?" Myra mused.

"Perhaps her itinerary was somewhere that was easily found?" Charles pondered.

"I'll call Izzie and have her call Zoe. Until Zoe gets the burner phone, conversations are going to be cryptic," Myra said. She picked up the landline and pushed the speed dial button for Izzie.

"Myra? Everything okay?" Izzie asked with a bit of trepidation.

"Not exactly. Sasha spotted the other person who has been tailing Zoe. But the question is, Who knew Zoe's schedule and which train she would be on?"

"Good question." Izzie's brow furrowed. "I'll call her and have a casual conversation. Stand by." Izzie immediately ended her call with Myra and dialed Zoe's number.

"Izzie! I was just about to call you! Thanks so much for your great hospitality," Zoe said into the phone.

"A pleasure." Before Zoe left, Izzie had instructed her to

be careful about what she said on her phone. It could be tapped. Their cue word for being secretive was *Rufus*. "Rufus and I were just sitting around, and I thought I'd check to see how your train ride was," Izzie said carefully.

"No issues. Right on time." Zoe cringed a bit, wondering what Izzie was about to communicate.

"I was thinking about hiring a personal assistant. Tell me, does yours do all your travel arrangements?"

"Yes. Kyle is right on top of things."

"He keeps a copy of everything?" Izzie treaded carefully.

"He does. Right on his desk. Just in case anyone else needs to find me." Then it hit her. Her life really was an open book—right out there for anyone to see.

"Well, that can come in handy." Izzie chuckled, keeping the conversation light.

"Yes, I suppose it can." Zoe wasn't on the verge of panic, but concern began to flow through her mind. She made a mental note to speak to Kyle in the morning. *He couldn't be in on REBAR's scheme, or could he?* At this point she knew the only people she could trust were the Sisters.

Izzie decided to switch topics. "And the kitties? Did they miss you?"

"Of course they gave me the cold shoulder when I got home, but it didn't take long for them to sniff out your doggie and climb in my bag." Zoe nudged Buster and Betty off her clothes.

"Ya gotta love 'em. I'll let you settle in. We'll chat more tomorrow. Sweet dreams," Izzie said, hoping it would be true.

Zoe was a little unnerved by their conversation. She could only surmise her whereabouts were now public knowledge. But she wondered exactly how much was known. Had someone followed her to Washington? To Izzie's? To Pinewood? Probably not without getting noticed. She was confident Pinewood, at least, was highly guarded. And Izzie's place also had the highest technology as far as security was concerned. She grabbed her two kitties and gave them hugs. "I guess we're going to have to wait until tomorrow to see how all of this plays out." Buster concurred by rubbing his head on Zoe's leg. Betty rolled over in agreement.

The following morning Zoe went through her usual routine as she got ready for work. Coffee. English muffin. Feed the cats. Change the litter. Take a shower. Hair. Makeup. Get dressed. As she was leaving her apartment and locking the dead bolt, she realized she didn't have an alarm system. When she thought about it, she was hard-pressed to recall if anyone on her floor had one. She snickered to herself. *Doorman building.* Now there was a false sense of security. Frankly, anyone could get into the building if they really wanted to. She made another mental note to call a security company when she got her burner phone. If anyone was listening in, she didn't want them to know her plans.

When she walked out onto the sidewalk she noticed a woman on a black Brompton bicycle a few yards ahead across the street. A different woman from the one she'd noticed following her back from the train station the day before. A chill ran down Zoe's spine. This woman's clothes exactly matched the description Izzie had provided. *So who was the woman yesterday, if not Sasha?* Zoe wondered. It was a crisp day and so Zoe walked the fifteen blocks to Peet's Coffee in an effort to ease her mind. The woman on the bicycle stayed a good distance away, but still within her line of sight.

As expected, the woman on the bicycle followed her into the coffee shop and stood behind her. Just as planned, Sasha dropped her papers and slipped the envelope into Zoe's bag. Zoe went along as if they had practiced this stunt before. Relief washed over her. Mission accomplished. At least this part of it. The rest remained to be seen.

By the time Zoe got her coffee, Sasha was nowhere to be seen. Zoe walked to her office, checked in with the security guard and took the elevator upstairs. Again, she thought about the word *security* and how it was very easy to have a false sense of it just because someone nearby was wearing a uniform and a badge.

Zoe was greeted by the two receptionists in the foyer of the company offices. She walked at her normal pace even though she wanted to run to her desk and lock her office door behind her. "Good morning, Kyle. How was your weekend?"

"Good. Went to the High Line with some friends. And yours? How was D.C.?"

"Nice. It was good to get away and catch up with my friend." She surreptitiously glanced at Kyle's desk. Sure enough, there was Zoe's itinerary for all the world to see. "I have to say that the Acela is a great way to travel." She lifted her coffee cup in a salute and then went into her office. Normally she kept the door open, but today was different. She stuck her head out and said, "Listen, I have a bit of a headache so I am going to keep my door shut until the caffeine kicks in."

"Gotcha." Kyle nodded without looking up.

Zoe hurried to the credenza behind her desk and removed the contents of her tote. She gingerly handled the envelope Sasha had deposited. Just as they'd said, inside was a burner phone and more instructions: *Bloomingdale's. Six P.M. Dolce & Gabbana handbags. You will be picking up a black leather tote. Already paid for by Annie de Silva.* The "already paid for" was a relief. Zoe knew the price tag on that particular item was a hefty two thousand dollars. She slipped the phone into her own bag, zipped the bag shut and put it in the bottom drawer of her desk. She exhaled. Had she been holding her breath for the past hour?

She powered up her computer and began to go through the various jobs and their timelines. Everything was on schedule. She checked to see when she would have to go back to West Virginia. As she scrolled through the spreadsheet, she noted a change in the delivery of the foundation materials. Also the vendor, which was now El Cemento. A chill went up and down her spine. Her first reaction was to call Malcolm Fielder, VP of Manufacturing, but then she thought better of it. Now was not the time to bring attention to herself. If he was involved in the corruption, she didn't want him to have any clue that she was suspicious. She would tell Izzie when she was back at her apartment. It occurred to her that her apartment might be bugged. She knew she was taking a big risk, but she opened the desk drawer where she had secreted her bag and pulled out the burner phone. Phone numbers had already been programed. "They are good," she whispered to herself. She quickly sent off a text to Izzie: **Apartment bugged?**

An instant later she received a response: **Will check.**

Within the hour Zoe received a phone call from Carlton, her doorman. "Sorry to bother you, Ms. Danfield, but there is a gentleman here who said you called about your cable?"

Her first reaction was to say no, but then she remembered whom she was dealing with.

"Hey, Carlton, can you hold on for a moment? I'm on another line." She immediately sent another text to Izzie: **Cable guy?**

Answer: **Yes. Checking for bugs.**

She got back on the phone with Carlton. "Sorry about that. I should have mentioned it. Yes, I need an adjustment. You know me. Not too techie."

"The problem is, I can't leave the desk right now." Carlton sounded a bit put out.

"That's alright. Give him the spare keys and you can send him up. Just tell him to mind the cats so that they don't run out."

"Ya sure about this?" Carlton was always concerned about bending the co-op rules.

"Yes, it's fine. Besides, the cats will probably be sleeping. When I spoke with the dispatcher this morning, I mentioned the cats and gave them my cell number." Zoe raised an eyebrow. Lying was coming naturally to her.

"Okay. I'll let you know when he's done."

"Thanks, Carlton. Again, sorry for not telling you in advance. I know how persnickety you are." She chuckled.

"No worries, miss."

After hanging up, Zoe sat silently and stared across the room. It was one espionage episode after another. She went back to the spreadsheets to check if any more of her jobs were going sideways. Only the one in Toledo. So far.

Avery Snowden had been working with the Sisters for several years. He was the master of surveillance, whether it was audio, video, or in-person. He would often send one of his employees to check for bugs, but he had also been instructed to install a security system and a new lock in Zoe's apartment. He knew he could do the job quickly and without drawing any suspicion. He maintained a vast wardrobe that included a variety of service uniforms. Manhattan Cable happened to be one of them. He also packed a locksmith jumpsuit into his work kit so he could change into it before installing the lock. Then he'd change back into the cable uniform and exit the building.

Now Avery frowned at the old locks on Zoe's door. It was a newly renovated apartment in a pre-war building that should have had a more secure lock and dead bolt. He looked up and down the hallway. All of the doors and locks looked the same. Avery wondered if it was a co-op rule. They had so many. He entered the apartment and sent a quick text to Charles.

Check with Zoe. Co-op rules for locks?

While he was waiting for a reply he began to unpack his tools. First was the SpyBust detector. It was calibrated with active laser scanning, detection for bugs, GPS trackers, cameras, wiretaps, and pretty much anything else invasive and hidden. Then came the items for the security system. One for the front door, and one for each of the large windows that looked over Gramercy Park. By New York standards it was a large two-bedroom apartment. A short hallway with built-in closets led to the open living room/dining room space. New York apartments were also known for very small kitchens, with very small appliances. This was no exception, but with Zoe's background, she had been able to convince the co-op board to allow her to remove the wall between the kitchen and living area and replace it with a light gray slate peninsular counter with base cabinets. The twelve-foot-high ceilings, white painted walls, and large windows gave the thousand-square-foot apartment the appearance of being larger than it really was. The high-gloss wooden floors allowed a good amount of reflection from the windows, which were flanked by traveler's palm trees. The mid-century furnishings gave it a chic and well-designed look. No one would guess the building had been erected in the 1930s.

Avery began his search for any kind of listening, recording, or video devices. He checked the intercom phone, the landline, the cable boxes, and the microwave first, then did a sweep of the bathroom, bedrooms, and the living area. So far nothing. Then he began installing the sensors on the windows. He placed one on the bottom for when the window was completely closed, and then another six inches higher than the ledge in case Zoe wanted to open them. That would allow her to have fresh air and safety at the same time. There were heavy screens and cat-proof panels on the lower half of the windowsill. In all his years of experience Avery had yet to meet a thief, burglar, or intruder who could fit through six inches. He was confident no human was getting in, and no feline was getting out. Thinking about felines, Avery wondered where they were. Then he spotted a ball of fur curled up in a luxurious cat bed bathed in sunshine. He squatted down to speak to the kitty. "Hey, which one are you? Buster or Betty?" By the look the cat gave him, she clearly said, "I am Betty." He could have sworn she shook her head in disgust before she stretched and resumed her position.

"Pardon me, miss. Sorry to disturb you, but is your buddy Buster around?" Again, she gave him a look of disdain, then stared toward the kitchen. Avery grinned. Sure enough, Buster must have come out of hiding because he was now sitting on the countertop. Avery wasn't going to judge. He knew a writer who let her cat live on her dining room table. Cats were interesting creatures. Sometimes more interesting than people.

Avery continued turning Zoe's apartment into a high-tech flat. He installed the operating panel near the front door and another in the bedroom. Both had panic switches for the police and EMS. She could activate and deactivate the alarm from either post. It had been almost an hour and he hadn't heard back from Charles about the lock for the door when his phone pinged.

Good to go.

Avery slipped the locksmith jumpsuit on and opened the Schlage Touch keyless electronic dead bolt package. It only engaged the knob after you entered the proper code on the keypad. He favored it because it complicated any attempt to pick or drill through it. The bolt and the alarm system would be sufficient safety measures. Should someone break in, the

alarm system would signal the police. Just as Avery was finishing installing the lock in the hallway, an elderly woman
poked her head out of her apartment. Avery moved swiftly in
an attempt to evade any questions, slipping back into the
apartment and closing the door behind him. However the
words, "Young man? Young man?" echoed through the hall.
He decided he should speak to her so as not to draw suspicion. He pulled down the jumpsuit and zipped up the cable
jacket, swapped baseball caps and slowly opened the door.
He kept his head at a level where she couldn't get a good
view of his face.

"Ey? Can I help you?" Avery used one of his international
accents. This time it was Canadian.

"Oh, I thought you were a locksmith?" The confused
woman furrowed her brow.

"Not this feller. Just the cable guy fer sure."

The woman blinked several times and, without a word, returned to her apartment.

That was a lot closer call than he'd expected. He gathered
his tools in a hurry, set the lock with the name of one of Zoe's
cats, and headed toward the stairwell. If the woman decided
to come out again, he figured she wouldn't follow him down
the twelve flights of stairs.

By the time he reached the eighth-floor landing, Avery figured it was safe to take the elevator to the lobby. Much to his
shock the elderly woman was on the elevator. He thought he
might be in a *Seinfeld* episode. The one when Jerry stole a
babka from a lady in New York and then she turned up at his
parents' condo in Florida. The woman looked up at him.
"Busy day you're having?"

Was she being facetious? "Ey. Every day." He touched the
tip of his cap and got off on the next floor.

*Why did these things only happen when it was a Sister-
hood caper?* Silly question.

* * *

For Zoe, the day moved at a snail's pace. By lunchtime she was ready to climb the walls. Waiting until she could leave for the day was torture. Then, around two, Kyle buzzed her. "Mr. Fielder wants to have a meeting."

"Zoom?" Zoe knew Fielder spent most of his time in the Caribbean or Miami.

"No, he's in the office today. I think all week."

Zoe thought she would throw up in her mouth. "Oh. Okay. Big conference room?"

"Nope. His office," Kyle replied.

That, too, was unusual. Malcolm liked to have an audience and usually held forth in the conference room. Zoe's radar told her something was awry. "Did he say what it was about? I'd like to be prepared." Now *that* wasn't a lie.

"No, but Donald Walsh is going to be there, too."

Zoe felt the bile climb up her throat. "Okay. Thanks, Kyle."

She quickly sent off a text to Izzie:

VP called meeting with me and Walsh

Izzie replied:

Pretend you are fine with Walsh's assessment and that you weren't questioning him or his role. Play innocent.

Zoe was getting used to the idea that her second job was now acting. At two she walked toward the big corner office that remained empty most of the time. Along the way she stopped in the ladies' room to splash water on her face. She took off her large black glasses and peered into the mirror. "You can do this," she told her reflection. Then she jumped when another colleague exited one of the stalls.

"Talking to yourself?" Blaire teased.

"I'm the only one who listens to me," Zoe joked.

"I hear ya." Blaire moved toward the sink. "So, Malcolm is in town. What do you think that's all about?"

"I don't know, but I am about to find out." Zoe replaced her glasses, dried her hands and moved on.

She arrived at the suite of offices where the CEO, CFO, and Senior VP held court. Even though Zoe was a VP, she didn't have "executive" or "senior" attached to her title. The buxom blonde assistant with a vacuous look greeted her.

"Hey. He's expecting you." She tilted her head in the direction of Fielder's open door.

Fielder was a very good-looking man just over the age of forty. He had a permanent tan and an excellent golf swing and was always impeccably dressed for every occasion. As Zoe approached the doorway, he got up from his chair.

"Zoe. Good to see you. Please have a seat." He gestured to the large gray leather Luxley club chairs. "Donald should be here shortly." He sat back down, fingers interlaced across his chest.

"I didn't realize you were going to be in town. I'm sure your dance card is full, but if you're available, we should have drinks." Zoe thought, *Am I being too forward?*

"I'll only be here for a few days." Malcolm smiled at her. "Perhaps next time?"

"That would be lovely." She heard Walsh's familiar voice greeting the bubblehead sitting outside.

Malcolm got to his feet again. "Donald. Donald, come in. Please, shut the door."

Zoe didn't know if she was going to faint or puke. *Relax. Act blasé.* She sat tall in her seat and greeted him with a pleasant "Hello, Donald."

"Zoe." He gave her the customary nod.

Again, Fielder motioned to the chairs. "Please sit." He then started the conversation. "Zoe, Donald tells me you're concerned about our quality control. May I ask why?" He leaned back in his seat with his hands clasped behind his head.

Zoe feigned surprise, then looked straight at Walsh. "No, not at all." She turned to Fielder. "I was simply asking because it's a very sensitive subject with me. You may not know this, but I grew up in West Virginia. Point Pleasant. My father's uncle was killed when the Silver Bridge collapsed. It's haunted my family ever since. Including me. That was the main reason I became an engineer." She paused. So far almost everything she'd said was true. It was only the first bit that wasn't. "After the South Florida incident there were several articles about structural failures. Globally. I simply wanted to ease my mind." She turned again to Walsh. "Donald, I was in no way accusing you of anything. And if you thought so, I truly apologize." She was making herself sick with all this smarmy talk.

Malcolm sat upright. "See, Donald? I told you not to worry." He looked at Zoe. "You've been in the sales department for several years, correct?"

"Yes. But recently I was transferred to overseeing job sites." She tried to hide her anger and frustration.

"That's a very important function, as you know." Malcolm was being patronizing and Zoe knew it.

"Yes, of course. But I must admit I miss working with clients." She had to get that in.

"I am sure you do. And as soon as we reorganize, I am sure you will be moved back to your post." Now Malcolm was the smarmy one.

"Reorganizing?" Zoe asked with curiosity instead of incredulity. This would be the third time in less than two years.

"Yes, we have to shift a few things around. The supply chain issue has pretty much choked us financially and some people will be asked to take on additional or different responsibilities. We appreciate your being willing to utilize your skills and talents where they are needed."

Not necessarily wanted, she thought to herself. "I've been with the company for a long time, and I want to continue to work here. It's important for the company to not only survive but to thrive." She thought she was going to vomit. Then she remembered the Sisterhood's motto: *Whatever it takes.*

Malcolm leaned forward and put his palms on his desk. "Glad to hear it, Zoe. You are a valuable member of the team."

Zoe could see Walsh was seething. He didn't believe her for one minute, just as Zoe didn't believe all the bull that was being tossed about.

"Thank you, Malcolm." She waited.

"Well then. I guess we're finished here." Malcolm stood up.

Zoe got up from her chair, expecting Donald to do the same. But he didn't. She received the message loud and clear. Walsh and Fielder were going to have their own private meeting as soon as she left the room.

She smiled at both men. "Thanks. Enjoy the rest of the day." As she exited, bubblehead was playing some gambling game on her computer. So much for the #MeToo movement. As long as there were television shows where women were objectified, and women who would gladly go along with it, nothing was really going to change all that much. Zoe had quickly learned there was no glass ceiling. Glass implied it could be broken. When she was made VP of International Sales she'd thought she'd earned that elusive place at the conference table. But as long as there were men willing to do anything for money and power, she would remain an underling. Title or no title. She tried not to feel as if she'd just had her hand slapped, so she shoved those emotions out of her mind. *Karma will win at this game.*

When she got back to her own office, she busied herself with email. She thought about Mason Chapman. Now *there* was a decent man. True, she hadn't known him for any great length of time, but she could tell he was a man of integrity. Not only did his employers expect it, so did his community. She thought about her conversation with Izzie and knew Izzie would approve, so she began to write him an email suggesting that she might plan a visit to London. Then she stopped. *What if he doesn't want to see me?* She shook her head and fell back on her usual noncommittal approach. She began to type:

> *Hey Mason,*
> *Hope this finds you well. Anything interesting happening on your side of the pond? Warmly,*
> *Zoe*

There. That was easy enough. Zoe checked the time. It was almost four o'clock. That would be ten P.M. in England. She wasn't going to obsess over it. It was simply a friendly hello.

She began to pack her tote bag and ready herself for the next clandestine operation. The Dolce & Gabbana counter at Bloomingdale's. She was about to switch off her computer when the "new mail" ting sounded on her computer. One more email to answer shouldn't keep her from her appointed rounds. She clicked on her inbox and much to her joy, there was an email from Mason:

> *Hello, my friend. Happy to hear from you. Nothing to report here. Lots of grockles: 'hop-ons and hop-offs.' Hope all is well.*
> *Fondly,*
> *Mason*

Fondly? Now there was a word that could imply many things. She decided to interpret it as a good thing. She smiled at his British slang for tourists. As he had explained to her, "The tour buses go from one historic building to another, and the tourists hop on and hop off the bus."

Her fingers immediately hit the keyboard and then she stopped herself abruptly. Instead of responding, she thought it best not to seem too needy. Even though she *was* feeling needy. For now she was on a mission and must get to the famous department store. She unlocked the drawer of her desk, removed the brown envelope and placed it in her bag.

Kyle was still at his desk. "Go home. Or go do whatever young people do after work," she teased.

"Having drinks with friends at six. Thought I'd get some of the approvals out."

"Well, don't be late for your friends. They are an important commodity in life."

As she exited the building, she spotted the woman on the bicycle, who then slowly followed her toward the East Side. It was a crisp day and the walk was invigorating. Or was it the mysterious gift that was waiting for her? In either case, Zoe felt things were moving in the right direction. The meeting with Fielder seemed to have allayed his paranoia about her concerns with Walsh's department. She hoped it would get whoever was on her tail, off it. But, then again, she shouldn't take things for granted. She was encouraged by Fielder saying she would return to sales. When? That remained to be seen, but it was something to hope for. The emails to and from Mason? Those were surely a reason to be light on her feet. Having Sasha shadowing her was also a big part of her good mood.

Bloomingdale's was the Disney World of shoppers. The air was filled with the scent of fine perfume, leather, and luxury, as representatives from fragrance companies tried to spritz her as she entered the store. A smiling face asked, "Would you like to try Acqua Di Giò by Armani?" She gave a pleasant "No, thank you" until the next one asked, "Would you like to try Sacred Wood by Kilian?" There was a perfume assault at every turn. Zoe continued to smile and politely refuse. She finally made it to the posh handbag counter.

A woman in her sixties with perfectly coiffed hair and makeup and wearing a navy-blue suit greeted her. "Good evening. How may I help you?"

Zoe smiled at the woman, who was giving her the once-over. Zoe's look and taste blended in well with the usual patrons of the high-end store. "Good evening. I am here to pick up a tote bag. Purchased by Annie de Silva?"

The woman became animated. "Of course! Countess de Silva personally called this morning. I shall fetch it for you."

Zoe tried not to roll her eyes. Within a few minutes the woman returned with the iconic Bloomingdale's shopping bag. Inside was a neatly wrapped tote within a dust bag. "Here you are, Miss Danfield."

Zoe was surprised the woman hadn't asked her for her name or identification. She guessed that's how the incredibly rich operated. No questions asked.

"Special occasion?" Now the woman was getting nosy.

"Just friendship." Zoe smiled at her. "Thank you very much." She scurried out of the store. The woman on the bicycle was still in the same place. Zoe hailed a cab and the bicyclist followed at a comfortable distance. Zoe opened the shopping bag and looked inside. It was a gorgeous black leather tote with large DG initials embossed on the side. She opened the leather bag and found a note and a tablet inside. The note read: *B-U-S-T-E-R. Combination.* It immediately clicked. It must be the combination to her new door lock.

Once Zoe got out of the cab, the cyclist watched and waited for her to enter the building. Sasha knew the apartment had been personally handled by Avery. No bugs, a new security alarm, and a new, high-tech lock.

"Hello, Carlton," Zoe called out as she entered the lobby.

"Good evening, miss."

"All good here?" she asked.

"Yes. The gentleman from the cable company finished up. No escapees." He chuckled.

"Thanks for handling it, Carlton. I appreciate it."

"Well, I didn't do much except give him the keys. Against my will. Just for the record." He winked.

"No worries. Thanks again." When she arrived at her door, she saw the new apparatus. She punched in the letters as instructed and—voilà! Open sesame. She shut the door behind her and secured the lock. Buster and Betty slowly ambled down the hallway, yawned, and stretched.

"Hello, my lovies!" She bent down to rub their soft fur.

Buster rolled over onto his back, requesting a belly rub. Betty waited her turn. After paying tribute to the cats, Zoe quickly hung up her jacket and changed into soft flannel lounge pants with a matching hoodie. She opened the small wall safe that was fitted inside the bathroom closet and removed the manila folders where she kept copies of the invoices.

The night she'd discovered the bogus invoices, no one else had been on the floor. She knew paper was easier to hide than electronic fingerprints. She'd hit the print icon on her computer and sent the data to the printer that everyone shared. She printed two sets and had given one to Charles before she left Pinewood.

Now Zoe tucked the folder under her arm and went back to her light oak kitchen table. She set everything in front of her: the burner phone, the watch, the tablet, and the gorgeous Dolce & Gabbana bag. She wondered if they would let her keep it. Then she gave herself a tsk-tsk. *Aren't they doing enough for you?*

"I wonder how they managed to smuggle this into that?" She tapped her finger on each item in turn. "What do you think?" she asked her furry friends. They blinked in response. "You're no help." She powered up the tablet. There was a message waiting for her:

> *Hello, Zoe. This tablet operates via a special encrypted private server only accessible to the Sisters & associates. We will have a face-to-face consultation later this evening. Nine PM. See you then. Mind as you go —*
> *Fergus*

The intrigue alone was invigorating. Zoe checked the fridge for anything that she could turn into a meal. *Leftover Chinese food? Why do I always save it?* Not once did she ever eat it. She tossed the soy-soaked containers into the trash. "Pizza anyone?" she asked the cats.

By the time the pie was delivered, devoured, and the remaining pieces wrapped in foil, it was close to nine. Zoe took her position at the table and powered up her new tech toy. She stared at it, thinking she had no idea how to log on, or whatever the procedure might be. She had lots and lots of questions. *Had they found any hidden audio devices in the apartment? What should I do next?* Naturally she would apprise them of her meeting with Fielder and Walsh. *That Walsh guy. What a tattletale.*

At the stroke of nine the sound of a piano playing a crescendo burst from the tablet's speaker. One by one faces popped up in little boxes on the screen: Annie. Myra. Charles. Fergus. Izzie. Yoko. Alexis. "Hellos" went around the block of boxes as if it was a game show. Zoe giggled.

Annie grinned. "I see you got the D and G bag."

"Yes," Zoe said and promised herself she wouldn't get attached to the beautifully constructed tote.

Before she could take another breath, Annie chimed in, "It's yours, honey."

"Oh my goodness!" Zoe squealed. "Thank you so much!" She picked it up and put it close to her face, inhaling the rich smell of leather.

"You are most welcome." Annie smiled at the boxes of faces.

"What's the latest at the office?" Myra asked Zoe.

"Malcolm called a private meeting with Donald Walsh and me. He questioned my questioning Walsh. I apologized and told them about where I grew up and how I have an inordinate amount of concern when it comes to safety. PTSD."

"Brilliant," Charles responded.

Zoe continued. "Malcolm said I would eventually get my previous responsibilities back, but the company is going to go through another reorg. That would make three in less than five years."

"No surprise," Fergus broke in. "The financials of the company are all over the place. Some places more difficult to track than others, but we will carry on."

"What about Walsh?" Zoe asked. "Any monkey business going on there?"

"He's not the sharpest tool in the shed, I might say," Charles said. "From what we can tell, he has two accounts at the same bank. Savings and checking. The savings account has quite a sum in it, considering his salary."

"Do tell!" Annie said.

"The man makes a hundred and thirty-five thousand quid a year, yet he has over fifty thousand dollars in a savings account he opened within the past year. All deposited via small amounts under three thousand dollars. All cash."

"So as not to draw attention from the gov," Fergus added.

"There is no indication he inherited the money, nor did we

find any history of gambling. At least not online. We still need to learn his routine," Charles finished.

"That is a lot of new information for just one day!" Zoe exclaimed. Everyone else burst out laughing.

"I said you'd get used to it, so start getting used to it," Izzie teased.

"You have the name of the job site where the latest materials are going?" Charles asked Zoe.

"No, but I have the name of the contractor. It's Costruttori Internazionale. They are in Italy. We provide them with the materials, according to the specs." Zoe scrutinized the hard copy of the spreadsheet she'd printed out earlier. "Oh, geez."

"What is it?" Myra asked.

"It's for a school in Abruzzo."

"They're sending subpar materials to build a school?" Myra was horrified.

"Looks that way," Zoe said.

"Do you think Construttori is involved in it? Or do you think they are being duped?" Charles asked.

"I've dealt with Construttori before. They were always concerned about meeting the proper requirements. Ever since the bridge collapsed in Genoa, the Italian government has put contractors under considerable scrutiny." Zoe paused. "My guess is that El Cemento is making a cheap version of the materials and we are shipping it without the contractor's knowledge. It would be too risky for Construttori to try and do a bait and switch."

"We're going to have a look at Construttori. See if they've been involved in anything dodgy," Fergus said.

"We need to get someone down to the Dominican Republic to snoop around," Myra agreed.

Alexis was the first to offer. "I'll go."

"Okay, but not alone," Myra said.

Maggie chimed in next. "Once I finish my research, I

should be good to go in about two days." She crinkled her freckled nose. "Plus, snooping is my specialty."

"Besides eating." Annie chuckled.

Maggie rolled her eyes. "It never ends."

"Then it's settled," Annie said. "Maggie and Alexis, you two will be leaving for Santo Domingo in two days. Alexis, how is your Spanish?"

"*Muy bueno*," she answered.

"Good. You will go to REBAR's factory and pretend you are applying for a job. Zoe, give Alexis a list of positions she could apply for."

"I'll check the job posting board for a list of positions. I know there are a few after the island was slammed by two hurricanes. A lot of the management team left the country. Two hurricanes two years in a row was all they could stand," Zoe said. "I can get that to you first thing."

"Maggie, I know how much you hate stakeouts, but I want you to check out the factory. See who comes and goes," Myra ordered.

"Got it."

"I think you're going to need a disguise. Your curly red hair will make you look out of place in the Caribbean."

"Fine with me. I trust Alexis will transform me into someone who can blend in."

"Blend in?" Annie snorted. "That will never happen. The best we can hope for is that you don't stand out like a red lollipop."

Myra had a look of concern. "I don't think Maggie should be doing this alone. I know Alexis will be close by, but not necessarily close enough, and Maggie is in uncharted territory." She continued. "Charles, see if Eileen from Avery's group is available. She would be a good partner for Maggie."

"Right," Charles replied. "I'll ring him up now."

"Alexis, when you go for the job interview, ask for a tour

of the facility. Check for opportunities to access the building after hours," Fergus said.

"Now, what about the bank?" Charles asked.

"I think Myra and I should fly down there ourselves. I'll phone Mac, the manager at Cayman National, and invite him to lunch," Annie said.

"How do you suppose you'll get him to divulge confidential information?" Charles asked.

Fergus guffawed. "It's Annie, remember?"

Myra folded her arms. "After all this time, you gentlemen still underestimate us?"

Fergus and Charles threw up their hands. "Oh no, love!" Charles backpedaled and Fergus murmured his agreement.

"That's better." Myra gave them an expressionless stare.

Annie assembled the list of each person's respective assignment:

1. Maggie: research building failures for last ten years
2. Zoe: get list of job postings and send to Alexis; we'll doctor up her résumé to fit one of the positions
3. Alexis: get disguises ready
4. Charles & Fergus: keep digging into financials of Fielder and REBAR; see if Eileen is available
5. Maggie & Alexis: off to Santo Domingo
6. Annie & Myra: get the Gulfstream ready, make hotel arrangements, contact Mac at Cayman National. Then off to Grand Cayman in two days.

"Is this all doable?" Izzie asked.

The women and two men looked at one another in their boxes on the screen.

Alexis was the first to answer. "I don't see why not."

Charles and Fergus nodded; they were already on their assignment. Maggie had also started her research earlier that day.

"I don't want to use my laptop to do my part," Zoe said. "If they are shadowing me, I don't want a job search coming up at this hour. So I'll get into the office early tomorrow and use my assistant Kyle's computer instead."

"Very good thinking," Charles said.

"All good, everyone?" Annie asked.

"All good!" was returned in unison.

"Tomorrow night, then. Same time, same station!" Annie said. They said their goodnights and signed off.

Zoe leaned back in her chair. It occurred to her that she truly had been living a solitary life up until now. It had been nothing but work, work, work. Which wasn't unusual for an upwardly mobile corporate executive. That's how she'd gotten to where she was. But where was she, exactly? The more she thought about it, the more she realized she had bonded more deeply with this new handful of strangers than with anyone else over the past ten years living in the city. It was so odd. New York was the biggest, liveliest city in the country, probably the world, yet most people remained strangers. Who did she socialize with? People from work when required. Where did she vacation? Vacation—what was that? She was in her late thirties and what did she have to show for herself outside of her career? She looked over at her two cats lounging on the sofa. "You two! You are the reason I live!" She smiled and wiggled herself between the two furry creatures. "Am I becoming a crazy cat lady?" She rubbed her face in their fur. "Who cares?"

Then there was Mason. He had caught her attention, and it felt good. A rush of warmth poured through her. Maybe there was something there, and maybe she would pursue it. Her gut was telling her that her days at REBAR were probably numbered. If there was a scandal, the company would go down like the *Titanic*. One way or another she knew there was going to be a big change coming. But what kind? Zoe felt confident the future would be better than what was going on in her life now—which wasn't much. She was ready to take down Donald Walsh and his puppet master. She was certain Malcolm Fielder was the one pulling the strings. Now to prove it. After what she'd experienced in less than forty-eight hours, she was confident that if anyone could succeed, it would be the Sisters with their tight network of associates.

The government should run this well.

Zoe checked the clock on the far wall and saw it was eleven fifteen. She was shocked at how quickly the past two hours had gone by. She nudged her companions. "Come on, guys. Time for nighty-night." She powered down the tablet, switched off the lights and checked the alarm system. ARMED glowed red on the small box in the hallway. The same message appeared on the box in her bedroom. She pulled down the comforter and Buster and Betty commandeered their usual spots at the foot of the bed. As soon as her head hit the pillow she was out like a light.

She was almost comatose when a loud beeping came from her alarm panel. She sprang up in horror as sweat poured from her neck. Someone was trying to break into her apartment. Zoe dashed to the panel, ready to press the red emergency button when she heard footsteps hurry away from her door. She peered through the peep hole, but the hall was empty Her pulse was racing almost as fast as her thoughts. She took several deep breaths and thanked her lucky stars Avery had been there earlier that day and installed a highly sensitive system that could detect any hint of intrusion. But another brush with danger was putting Zoe's nerves on edge. She sent a text to Izzie, who promised Charles would check the security footage from Zoe's building. Hacking into that system was a walk in the park for Charles and Fergus.

The following day the only thing the security footage showed was a man of average height, a bit thick in the waist, wearing brown trousers, a flannel jacket and a cap. Zoe suspected it could be Walsh, but there was no way to prove it. She took great measures to tread carefully around him. Trying to become his pal was out of the question, but being nice to him was a possibility, as much as the idea made her skin crawl. What would he have done to her if he'd managed to break into her apartment?

Chapter Nine

Preparation

Maggie reached the newspaper office at the crack of dawn. She wanted to review the list she'd begun the day before and get it to Charles and Fergus as quickly as possible so she could have the rest of the day to get ready. The skeleton crew on the night shift was wrapping up and leaving the building as she arrived.

"You're early," the metropolitan night editor grunted at her.

"Catching the worm . . ." Her voice trailed off. She knew a lot of her coworkers were envious of her relationship to Annie, the big boss. *Too bad. So sad. Boo-hoo.* That wasn't to say Annie wouldn't go all out for any one of her employees. It just so happened that Maggie had a special connection with Annie.

Maggie powered up her computer and accessed the archives she'd saved from the day before. She categorized them by type: bridges, buildings, and so on. Then she sorted them by year. Hundreds of articles appeared on the screen. She started with the bridge failures. At least fifty came up, with the most recent on top: a bridge in Pittsburg. Then Katihar, in Bihar, India, where a bridge collapsed while still under construction. One official blamed "negligence" and another called it "collusion." A few years back there was another bridge in India, this one crossing the Anjarakandi River. Farther back there was a pedestrian bridge that spanned a street near Florida International University, then the infamous bridge collapse in Genoa, Italy. Maggie read on. Fifty-nine people were facing various charges. She let out a low whistle. "Well, at least someone is being held accountable," she said to herself. The list went as far back as the 1800s. Many were railroad bridges. She also noted the high rate of failures in countries like Cambodia, India, and China. It was making her sick to her stomach, something Maggie rarely experienced.

She switched to the file she'd made for buildings. First up was the building failure in South Florida, where a condominium collapsed, killing ninety-four people. Maggie made a note to see if the two South Florida incidents had anything in common besides political corruption and incompetence. She also discovered there was a one-billion-dollar settlement pending within the year. Someone wanted to get it out of the way, pronto, with no indictments or accountability.

Maggie shook her head as she read on. There were so many more disasters. Some of the incidents resulted in no injuries, while others resulted in hundreds of deaths. Then add the eighteen hundred people who'd died due to the levee failure in New Orleans during Hurricane Katrina in 2005. It was one thing to hear someone talk about it. It was another to read about it all in great detail.

Maggie culled the information from the past ten years and sorted it so Charles could cross reference to see if there were any similarities, such as contractors and materials. She copied the file to a flash drive and then emailed Charles the info with a note: *Not a pretty picture.* By the time she was finished, the rest of the staff had begun trickling in for the workday. It was time for donuts and coffee.

Zoe left her apartment at six thirty that morning. She had sent a text to Sasha the night before alerting her to the earlier-than-usual departure. As Zoe stepped out of her building, Sasha was already waiting across the street, ready to roll. Zoe walked to the corner of Twenty-First and Park Avenue and hailed a taxi for the ride to her Midtown office. Every so often she would glance into the sideview mirror to see Sasha keeping up with the early morning traffic. When they arrived at the sleek office building on Fifty-Third and Madison, Sasha pulled over, gave Zoe a nod and pointed to her wrist. It was a reminder for Zoe to alert Sasha via her wrist device if she was going to leave the building.

Once inside, Zoe checked the halls for any other colleagues. Empty. She scooted over to Kyle's desk and logged on to his computer. She knew his password was *LADY-GAGA* and hoped he hadn't changed it after their recent webinar about cybersecurity. She quickly typed in *LADY-GAGA*. Red letters appeared: *Incorrect password*. Dang! She thought for a moment and began to go through all of Kyle's favorite Broadway plays. *KINKYBOOTS*. Nope. She knew she only had one more shot before she got locked out. She looked up at the cubicle wall. There was a ticket stub from *The Music Man*. Of course! Kyle couldn't stop talking about it. She gave it one more try. She resisted the temptation to start humming "Seventy-Six Trombones."

Zoe realized her palms were sweaty, as was her forehead. She was not the type of person to do anything underhanded, so being a sneak was not a comfortable activity for her. She opened the browser in Private Mode. Theoretically that allowed the user to surf the web undetected, with no tracking. *Theoretically*. She went to the company's homepage and then to the Human Resources tab. She scrolled down to the Job Postings, and then to the Dominican Republic. Just as she'd expected, the list of job openings was quite long, particularly in the factory division. Obviously those would not be appropriate for Alexis. She checked under the Management tab: Assistant Office Manager, Inventory Management, Legal Associate. Perfect! She copied the last link and sent it to Alexis and Charles, then clicked the tab to Erase History, just in case . . . although nothing was ever really, truly erased, even if you thought you were in stealth mode. It would just make tracking her a tad more difficult.

She checked her watch. Only eight. Still early. She decided to go down to the café on the corner. As she entered the elevator she realize she'd forgotten to ping Sasha. The café was only two doors from the main entrance. It seemed silly to bother Sasha for a quick cup of java. When she exited the building she noticed a woman on a bench across the street. She looked familiar, but Zoe couldn't quite place her. Then it hit her. It was the woman in the town car from the train station. She began to get anxious. So she was, in fact, being followed. *By two people.* She wanted to kick herself for not alerting Sasha. She thought about hitting the panic button, but she didn't feel as if she was in immediate danger.

Zoe tried not to stare and hightailed it into the café as the woman crossed the street. Now the sweat was pouring down the back of her neck. Before Zoe knew it, the woman following her was bumped by someone on a bicycle. The cyclist stopped and made profuse apologies while Zoe rushed into the coffee shop.

"You people!" the woman who'd been bumped growled. "Watch where you're going! You should be on the street, not the sidewalk!"

"Sorry. Sorry." This gave Sasha an opportunity to get a good look at the other woman and take a quick snapshot of her face with her watch, which doubled as a camera. Sasha moved her bike to the street and sent the photo to Avery. She pedaled a few feet to a spot where she could keep an eye on the café door.

Inside the café, when Zoe got to the counter she could barely speak. "Hi. I . . . I . . ."

"I think you need some decaf, Zoe," the barista said.

Zoe regained her composure. "You're right, Diane. Thanks." She looked over her shoulder. The woman following her was now pretending to be window shopping, and Zoe could see Sasha was not far away. "I'll have a chocolate croissant, too."

"Going wild today, eh?" The barista smiled.

"Maybe just a little crazy." Zoe laughed nervously. She pulled out her wallet, paid the tab, and then stepped to the side as they got her order ready. She was visibly shaken. She took some slow, deep breaths. She'd thought after her meeting with Fielder the day before, they would no longer suspect her of being suspicious. It occurred to her that Fielder might not be the one having her followed. Maybe it was Walsh. He seemed to be much more squirrely about things. She bit her lower lip in contemplation. Then she jumped when she heard her name being called.

"Zoe? Decaf cappuccino?"

"That's me." She grabbed the cup and moved quickly through the crowd, all getting coffee on their way to work. She thought she was going to hyperventilate. When she got outside, the woman was back at the bench across the street. Sasha had repositioned herself as well, and Zoe was still in her sights. Sasha would remain outside the office building from the minute Zoe entered until the minute she left to go back to her apartment. If Zoe had any plans after work, Sasha would be biking along.

Zoe stood by the elevator bank, anxiously watching the

numbers on the light above the doors indicating what floor the elevator was on. *Why are they always so slow?* It was a thought every New Yorker had at least once a week. The elevator finally reached the lobby level. She wiggled inside as a throng of people tried to smush themselves into the tiny car. Zoe found herself looking at the notice about the weight limit. She started counting heads and noticed how much bigger people seemed, especially after COVID. She'd read that a weight gain of ten percent was average. Then she tried to calculate the weight gain times the number of people in the elevator. *Did the engineers consider the possibility of a pandemic and people getting fat?* She was starting to get goofy. *Get a grip,* she admonished herself. Then she gave it more thought. Her engineering brain kicked in. It would take ten three-hundred-pound people to max out the elevator's weight limit. Or twenty-one hundred-fifty-pound people. That wasn't too farfetched if you thought about it. Zoe's mathematical musings were interrupted by someone saying "Yoo-hoo!" It was Kyle in one of his ever-so-fabulous moods. He was wearing his thematic bow tie of the day.

They squeezed through the swarm of people as they exited onto their floor. Would Kyle know this was not Zoe's first trip in the elevator today? She decided to say nothing. She knew she'd left the light on in her office and her beautiful D & G bag behind. *Big mistake.* She'd left it sitting on the chair in her office under her jacket. She'd been so anxious to get to Kyle's computer, she hadn't hung up her jacket or stowed away her tote. At least she'd had the smarts to lock the burner phone in her desk drawer after she'd removed it from her pocket.

When they passed the reception area, Zoe saw there were a handful of other employees scattered about and that all of the overhead lights were now on. Kyle probably wouldn't notice. Then she froze. The Dolce & Gabbana bag. Kyle would certainly notice that! She walked swiftly ahead of him to move the bag before he saw it. It wasn't that she hadn't planned on showing it to him; it was that she didn't want him to know she had already been at work. He would wonder why. Then she thought if he asked she would say she'd had a zoom call with someone in England. This lying and storytelling was coming a little too easily to the normally straightforward, upstanding Zoe Danfield. She comforted herself with the notion that she was part of a grand play and she was one of the players. Produced and directed by Annie de Silva and Myra Rutledge. She could imagine the credits rolling in her head.

Kyle couldn't resist stopping by one of his coworkers to gossip. Zoe took the opportunity to dash into her office, and pretended she'd just arrived there for the first time that day. She sat back in her chair and gave a huge sigh of relief. The past fifteen minutes had produced more adrenaline than she'd experience since . . . since she couldn't remember when. *When Izzie said I'd get used to it, I should have asked her to clarify how long it would take.* She made a mental note to inquire the next time they spoke. She also wondered how often they would have their private conferences, and if she would be kept in the loop with everyone else's activities. Zoe knew her only job was to keep doing her job, nose to the grindstone and to keep Charles and Fergus informed of anything unusual. The challenging part was to pretend as if nothing was happening behind the scenes. But Zoe was becoming a good liar. She simply had to remind herself of the production she was part of and play her role accordingly. If she needed any moral support she could count on Izzie, and Sasha was also within reach.

She removed her glasses and gave them a good wipe with a special cloth. There was nothing else for her to do that day except her normal job. She checked the timeline log to see when the shipment would release for the school in Italy. It was within the week. She had to let Charles know as soon as she could. Kyle was approaching his cubicle and waved to her. Zoe waved back, then gestured for him to come in.

"Look what I got!" Zoe said with amusement, holding up the bag.

"Oh. My. God. That is gorgeous! Give it here." Kyle reached out his hand.

"You have croissant fingers. Not until you wash your hands!" Zoe smirked.

"Party pooper," Kyle said sulkily and turned away.

"Kyle, please close the door behind you. I have a personal call to make." Zoe raised her eyebrows.

"Oh my. You *have* been busy!" Kyle was an inch away from giggling as he shut the door behind him.

Zoe unlocked her desk drawer and grabbed the burner phone. She typed Charles's number and sent off a quick, all-caps text:

SENT JOB POSTING.

Several seconds later, she got a reply: **RECEIVED.**

What a rollercoaster ride this has been, Zoe thought. And it was just starting.

Charles perused his monitor, scouring the dark web for information. He and Fergus had spent hours trying to follow the money. It was one shell company after another. It could take days to unravel the transfers and find out who or what El Cemento really was.

After Charles had received the job description from Zoe, he configured a résumé that would be a perfect fit for the position. He also created false identities for Alexis and Maggie. Alexis would be Estelle Johnson and Maggie would be Eve Marlowe. Fergus ordered up the fake IDs, passports, driver's licenses, and credit cards. All would be delivered by the end of the day.

Avery would provide the necessary credentials for Eileen. Myra and Annie could travel under their own names.

As the computer program kept churning under Fergus's supervision, Charles checked out REBAR's home page. It was a typical corporate page with the usual information: ABOUT. CONTACT. OUR TEAM. PRESS. Under OUR TEAM Charles easily found Donald Walsh's company photo and his title: Director of Quality Control. Then came the mug of Malcolm Fielder, Vice President of Manufacturing in the Caribbean. He downloaded Walsh's and Fielder's photos and printed five copies for the women to bring with them.

Annie would use her charm to wheedle information from Mac, the bank's general manager. Annie had met Mackenzie Stoddard in London in the late 1980s when Mac was a teller at her bank. Over the years he'd been promoted to general manager of Cayman National. She knew he would never divulge the name of an account holder. Nor could he. But what he *could* do was indicate with a facial expression whether he recognized either of the men in the photos. Annie was confident she'd get a hint of information out of him, whether he realized he was divulging it or not. She and Myra were adept at reading body language.

Charles and Fergus were continuing to dive deep into REBAR's business dealings when Fergus got a message from Avery about the mystery woman tailing Zoe. The text read:

ID says name is Louise Phillips. Works for a small P.I. firm. Will find out who hired her. Stand by.

"Avery is on the mystery woman," Fergus said and then he read the message to Charles.

"That information will be extremely helpful," Charles said with a nod.

"Indeed."

While Fergus and Charles were engrossed in the technological aspect of the mission, Annie phoned the pilot and informed him to have her Gulfstream ready. There would be five of them. First stop, Cayman Islands, and then on to Santo Domingo. It was a good thing they were taking Annie's private jet. Commercial flights took no less than six hours to their first destination with a two-hour layover, and then another six from island to island. Their flight would be direct and take just under four to Grand Cayman, and then another five when they reached the Caribbean. It was going to be a long day.

Annie also made hotel arrangements at the Ritz-Carlton, about an eight-minute ride to George Town and the bank. Then she made reservations for lunch at the Lobster Pot, where they would meet up with Mac. The plan was for Annie and Myra to spend two full days on Grand Cayman. She sent Mac a text with the reservation information. He immediately replied:

Looking forward to seeing you, Countess!
Annie laughed and replied: **Should I wear my crown?**
Only if you wear your rhinestone cowboy boots! LOL.

Annie continued making arrangements for everyone. The nature of their work was very sensitive; having an assistant make the bookings would be out of the question. Besides, Annie enjoyed chatting with her contacts. She dialed a number in Santo Domingo. Unfortunately for Maggie, Alexis, and Eileen, they wouldn't be beachside, but Monaco Residences in Santo Domingo would provide a very comfortable stay in one of their luxury apartments. For the most part none of them would be spending a lot of time there, but it was a convenient "base camp," as Maggie would say. They decided to plan for a full workweek to get an idea of the factory's routine. The comings and goings. Deliveries and shipments. It was an intricate plan but not outside the realm of the Sisterhood. Annie ordered two rental cars to be ready for the others when they arrived at the Santo Domingo airport. Alexis would have one, and Maggie and Eileen would take the other.

Later that afternoon Alexis and Maggie met at Alexis's apartment. Alexis had an entire room dedicated to her disguises. It was like an international fashion festival. Dozens upon dozens of traditional cultural outfits lined one wall. Another wall held everything from casual wear to grunge. Boots, shoes, sandals, and slippers were in cubbyholes, along with hats and handbags. Over fifty scarves and pashminas hung from a ballet bar. Wigs of every color and style were on a pegboard. Down the center of the room ran a long vanity table with drawers. Two five-foot Broadway-style mirrors with marquee lights sat back-to-back on top. The vanity drawers were lined with over forty shades of foundation, lipstick, eyeshadow, and false eyelashes. A full-length three-way mirror was in the corner. It could all be mistaken for a dressing room on a film set or musical production.

Alexis sat in the swivel chair in front of the vanity while Maggie stood in front of the three-way mirrors. "Geez, I hate looking at myself." The petite, curly-haired, freckle-faced imp scowled.

"So don't look. It's more important that I look at you." Alexis folded her arms and tapped her finger on her cheek. "Turn left." Maggie obliged. "Now right." Again, Maggie obeyed.

"You are very pale." Alexis kept staring at Maggie's light Irish complexion. "We should give you a slight spray tan."

"Ew. Do we have to? I hate that stuff," Maggie protested.

"There isn't enough SPF to keep you from frying in the sun. Just a shade or two darker. I'll bring a touch-up kit."

"But I'll mostly be in a vehicle or inside."

"Not twenty-four-seven. You need to try to blend in somewhat. I think you'd look more conspicuous with your porcelain skin, sitting in a car. You might as well hold up a sign that says, 'Hello! I don't belong here.'"

"Yeah, yeah," Maggie huffed.

"Now, what can we do about your hair?" Alexis stood and picked through Maggie's curls. "Wig or color rinse?"

"It's gonna be hot, so let's ditch the wig and do some color," Maggie said. "I'll wear a hat, too."

"Good idea." Alexis went to a cabinet that contained a variety of hair products. "Medium brown should do it."

Maggie rolled her eyes. "Whatever you say."

"What kind of hat? Baseball cap?"

"Sure. Got something Caribbean?" Maggie was half joking. She knew if anyone had it, Alexis would.

"How about the Jamaican Reggae Boyz soccer team?"

"Will it match my hair?" Maggie joked.

Alexis tossed the black, green, and yellow cap at her. Maggie plopped it on her head and gave it a thumbs-up of approval.

"Next, probably a few pairs of khaki cargo pants, T-shirts, and a pair of overalls."

"You mean like my regular outfits?" Maggie snorted. She was not known as a fashionista, so Alexis's ideas were good ones.

"Do you know what kind of vehicle you'll be in?" Alexis began to collect the hair-coloring items.

"Probably an SUV. Something nondescript, obviously."

"Right." Alexis began to mix the concoction that was about to transform Maggie into a less conspicuous Orphan Annie. "Come. Sit here." Alexis wrapped a plastic cape around Maggie's neck. "Comfy?"

"Indubitably." Maggie laughed. "And who are you going to be?"

"Since it's an office job, I'll wear a simple pantsuit and an ombre brown, chin-length wig. I'm used to wearing them." She glanced at her collection.

"Oh yes. I like that one on you. Reminds me of Rihanna's latest. As in today's latest. It will probably be different tomorrow."

Alexis chuckled. "That's what wigs are for, baby cakes."

While Maggie sat with her hair color developing, Alexis grabbed several pantsuits. She held up a bright blue one under her chin. "Hillary Clinton?"

Maggie burst out laughing. "You? Hardly. I think you should tone it down though."

Alexis went through one of the racks. "How about these?" One was a mustard-colored suit, another was olive green, the third burgundy. "Muted enough?"

Maggie scrunched her nose. "Boring. But good!"

"All I need are some flat shoes." Alexis had legs that went on forever. Heels would be out of place in an office in the Caribbean. A club? For sure. Alexis went through the cubbyholes and plucked out a simple leather attaché case. She hung the pieces on a rack and studied the outfits. "That should do it."

The timer went off, indicating that it was time to unveil Maggie's new hair color: medium brown. Alexis pulled out the blow-dryer and went to work on Maggie's hair, making it as straight as possible. "I think we should use a flat iron on it," Alexis suggested. "That should last for a few days, and I have a serum that will keep your hair from frizzing."

"You're the master of disguise. So whatever you say." Maggie finally looked into the mirror. She hardly recognized herself. Her new brown hair fell against her collar boncs. "I kinda like it."

"That's a relief. I wouldn't be able to stand your whining if you didn't," Alexis joked. Sorta.

Maggie stuck out her tongue.

Alexis heard her computer chime, alerting her to an incoming email addressed to Eve.Marlow@gmail.com. Alexis knew she would get the proper documents before they boarded the plane. Now she hoped she would get the interview at REBAR. She read the new email:

> *Dear Ms. Marlow,*
> *Your résumé is impressive, and we would like to discuss employment opportunities with you. If you are still at Monaco Residences, would you be available for an interview?*
> *Kindly,*
> *Alberto Segundo*

"Yes!" Alexis exclaimed. She quickly responded, pretending she was already in Santo Domingo. She wrote that she could meet the day after next. Segundo replied with the time and address. She sent off a text to Charles and Zoe informing them of her interview. She also knew not to mention Zoe Danfield during the interview. No one knew who all the players were in this fraud.

For Zoe the rest of the day was uneventful, and she was relieved. At the end of the day when she stepped outside her office, Kyle was shuffling papers and tidying up his desk.

"Got plans for this evening?" Zoe asked casually.

"Yes, and I would invite you, but you have to let me see your precious new thing." He snapped his fingers at her tote.

"Let me see your hands," Zoe joked.

"Oh goodness. I've washed them at least a dozen times today." Kyle rolled his eyes. "Hand it over."

Zoe had anticipated being stalked by Kyle until she

showed him her new purchase, and had already locked the tablet in her desk drawer along with the burner phone. "Tsk. If you insist." She handed the soft calf-leather bag over to him.

Kyle rubbed his hand over the embossed logo and sniffed the bag. "Delicious. I can't wait until I have a job like yours and can buy something this fabulous."

"If you must know, it was a gift." Zoe made a good salary, but a twenty-five-hundred-dollar purse was not in her budget.

"Oh, do tell." Kyle rolled his chair closer to Zoe.

Some bosses would not approve of Kyle's overly friendly demeanor, but he was good at his job, and he was a decent human being. Besides, there was very little in Zoe's life that would be of interest to anyone else. Except for Donald Walsh. And probably Malcolm Fielder.

"My friend Izzie. The one I visited this past weekend. She said it was an accumulation of birthday presents she owed me."

"Who knew that was a thing?" Kyle kept stroking the bag.

"I'm not sure it is, but I'll pretend it is." Zoe chuckled. More lies. "Okay. Hand it over."

"Are you coming for cocktails?" Kyle asked. "At Parker and Quinn." Kyle was referring to the retro-style bar with a prohibition vibe, complete with a speakeasy entrance.

"Sure." Zoe had nowhere else to go. "Give me a minute." She went back to her desk, unlocked the drawer and sent Sasha a quick text:

Going to Parker and Quinn.

Sasha promptly sent her response: **Roger that.**

Zoe slipped the tablet in its case and placed it and the burner phone in the D & G bag. She draped her folded scarf over them. She hooked the bag onto her arm and confidently strolled out of her office. As long as she was back home by nine, she might as well enjoy a cocktail with her assistant and his friends.

As they exited the building, Zoe spotted Sasha at the corner near the crosswalk. Zoe was still waiting for Charles to figure out who the mystery woman was.

Once at the bar, Zoe was happy to have the time to relax and enjoy a cocktail with upbeat people. The entire REBAR situation had been weighing heavily on her. Now, with the Sisters' involvement, Zoe was reassured that the perpetrators would be stopped. But how? She had no idea, but after what she'd experienced over the past few days, she had no doubt the Sisters would accomplish something. Zoe sat back and enjoyed the banter and jokes traded among Kyle and his friends. She promised herself she would be more social once this nightmare was over.

Back at Pinewood, Charles received another message from Avery:

Louise Phillips niece of Mason Chapman in London. Works for small P.I. firm in NYC.

Charles stared at the text. "Didn't Zoe mention someone named Mason Chapman in London?"

"Ay. What about 'im?" Fergus asked.

Charles showed him the message.

"Sounds a bit dodgy, doesn't it?" Fergus scowled.

"Indeed. I'm going to check with Izzie." Charles hit the speed dial button. "Iz, what do you know about that bloke Mason Chapman?"

"He was a romantic interest for Zoe when she was in London."

"That's a problem," Charles said with dismay.

"Why? What's the problem?" Izzie's tone held concern.

"It seems he is related to the mystery woman who's following Zoe. It's his niece and she works for a small private investigator firm."

Izzie was crestfallen. And here she had encouraged Zoe to pursue the relationship. "I don't understand."

"It's a conundrum, certainly. I'll try to get more info."

"Thanks, Charles." Izzie ended the call with an ache in the pit of her stomach.

How? And why?

After a few cosmos, Kyle was loosey-goosey. "Oh, I forgot to mention, a friend of yours stopped by the office on Friday, but you had already left."

"What friend?" Zoe knew the list was rather short.

"Huh. Come to think of it, she didn't leave her name. I told her you were going to D.C. and would be back in the office on Monday. She smiled and said, 'Taking the Acela?' " Kyle patted his lips with a cocktail napkin. "I said, 'For sure, is there any other way to travel?' I asked if she wanted to leave a message but she said she was going to text you."

Zoe's blood went cold. "She didn't leave her name?"

"No. Sorry. She seemed really friendly. She had a slight accent. British, I think. Didn't she text you?"

Zoe struggled to maintain her cool. "No. No, she didn't. I wonder who it was."

"She was average looking. About your height and maybe early twenties in age."

"By any chance did you tell her what train I would be on?"

"Uh, maybe." Kyle was straining to remember. "Sorry, Zoe."

"No problem," Zoe lied. Again. She needed to message Charles as quickly as possible. She waited a few more minutes and then checked her watch. "I better get going before the cats wreck the apartment." She pulled out a fifty-dollar bill and set it on the table. "See you tomorrow." She tried to move normally, but the urge to rush took over and she dashed out of the bar. She strained her neck to find Sasha, then heard the ding of a bicycle bell. Zoe gave a big sigh, thankful she was being watched over—while she was also being watched by someone else.

Once the cab pulled in front of her building, she hurried out and blew through the front door. "Hey, Carlton," she said as she whizzed by.

"Good evening, Ms. Danfield. Have a good night," he called out as she bounded into the elevator.

Upstairs, she disengaged the alarm, entered her apartment, shut the door behind her, and then reset the alarm.

What was happening? Who was that woman who came to her office asking questions? She threw her belongings on the sofa and sat down on the floor to hug her cats. Then she pulled the burner phone from her bag and dialed Izzie's number.

"Zoe. Are you okay?" Izzie asked.

"I'm not sure. Why do you ask?"

"Mason Chapman. What do you know about him?" Izzie had to get straight to the point.

"Honestly, not a whole lot. He went to school in Oxford. Worked for the royal family's estates since. Why?" Zoe was beginning to sense something was afoot.

"I don't know any easy way to say this . . ."

Zoe's skin began to crawl. "Say what?" She tried to keep her breathing normal.

"That woman who's been shadowing you? She's related to Mason Chapman. It's his niece."

Zoe thought she was going to puke. "What do you mean?"

"Exactly what I just said. Charles confirmed it. Her name is Louise Phillips."

Zoe squinted, thinking hard. *Where had she heard that name before?* "Louise Phillips. What is she doing here?"

"She works for a private investigator." Izzie paused. "Zoe, I am sure there is a reasonable explanation for this. Don't get all worked up. At least not until we can find some answers. Okay?"

"I'll try." Tears began to run down Zoe's face. She wiped at them and then looked at her hands. She couldn't remember the last time she'd cried.

Chapter Ten

Wednesday

England

Mason Chapman limped over to the gurney with the help of an emergency responder. "I'm quite alright," Mason protested as the ER tried to talk him into getting in the ambulance.

"You really should have a doc take a look at ya," the ER cautioned. "You could have broken somethin'."

Mason tried to put pressure on his right leg, but the pain shot up to his hip. "Right." He sat on the ledge of the NHS ambulance. "Just give me a minute, eh?"

He felt his cell phone vibrate in his pants pocket. It was his niece, Louise. He rolled his eyes and ignored the text message. He looked at the ER and agreed to be taken to the hospital. They took down his information on a medical clipboard and placed it at the foot of the gurney.

"Yer lucky you didn't break yer neck." The ER looked at the crumpled platform. "Or worse!"

Mason Chapman looked at the mangled pile of pipe and wood. He had been standing at the edge of the building when the scaffold collapsed directly in front of him. As he ducked, he'd twisted his leg and a piece of the wooden platform fell on top of it. All he could think about were the questions he would be asked by the safety inspector. Questions for which he had no answers.

The ER helped him inside the ambulance, closed the doors and got into the passenger side of the cab. Mason lay back on the stretcher while another ER took his blood pressure.

"A bit high, sir, but considering what you've been through, it's not too bad," she said.

Mason stared out the small windows as the tops of buildings passed by. He was stunned, but not in shock. Stunned because something like this should not have happened. Thankfully no one was standing on the scaffold when it collapsed. *So how did it happen?* He shut his eyes, trying to imagine the scenario. Were the bolts not properly tightened? It didn't occur to him that the accident was not an oversight, but something deliberate. His phone vibrated again. *Louise. What on earth could she possibly want?* Whatever it was, it was going to have to wait.

About twenty minutes later the ambulance pulled into the emergency entrance of the hospital. They wheeled him into the large triage center, where a half dozen other patients were waiting for medical attention. One man had a knife stuck in his arm, wrapped in makeshift bandages soaked in blood. Another was a woman about to give birth. Mason knew he would be waiting a long time before he was tended to. Another hour had passed before a nurse came by to take his temperature. He was unsettled, but still maintained a polite façade and cool demeanor.

"I'm not feeling ill," he said to the nurse.

"Then why are you in hospital?" the sourpuss nurse asked.

He pointed to his leg. "I may have broken it."

She again checked the clipboard that held his information. "Oh, sorry, sir. I thought you were someone else. The doctor should be with you shortly."

Her indifference did not give Mason a sense of confidence,

but there was little he could do except wait. Another hour passed and his cell buzzed yet again. This time it was Louise phoning him instead of texting. "Louise? What on earth is going on?" He tried to keep his voice down, but his impatience with the entire situation was getting the better of him.

"Mason! You know I've been working for a private detective agency in New York."

"Yes, of course, Miss Marple." Mason held his hand over the phone and mouthed apologies to his fellow patients-in-waiting.

"Well, don't poke fun at me just yet."

"And give me a reason why I shouldn't."

"That woman you met. The one from the States. Zoe?"

"Yes. What about her?" Mason's concern was obvious. "Is everything alright?"

"Yes. Why?" Louise asked.

"Because you are phoning me from the States about someone I know who I haven't spoken to in weeks." Mason revised his response. "We've emailed but . . . but what is this all about?" He started to raise his voice again.

"My boss gave me an assignment, kind of learning on the job. I was to pick a mark, follow them, and deliver information."

"Louise, you need to be more concise. What kind of information?"

"Now don't get angry, but I wanted to check on your lady friend, Zoe Danfield."

"You what?" This time his voice boomed across the entire room, rousing chastising remarks and scolding sounds.

"Okay, okay. Remember you said that you two had been in touch via email?"

"Isn't that what I just said a few seconds ago?"

"Yes, yes. Anyway, you told me she was going to visit someone in Washington, D.C. I know you're keen on her, so I wanted to see if she was involved with anyone."

Mason was grateful they had already taken his blood pressure because now it would have been through the roof and they would be admitting him for a stroke. "Louise, you need to explain everything to me."

"Just so you know, my boss was happy with my work."

"He may be the only one. Please continue."

"I remembered you said she was leaving Friday afternoon, so I went to her office."

Mason was shaking his head and taking deep breaths. "And how did you get into the building?"

"You're gonna love this."

I doubt it, he thought to himself.

"I made an appointment for a job interview so I could get past the security guards. But instead of going to the interview, I went to her floor."

"And then what happened?"

"I chatted up her assistant and got him to tell me she was visiting a girlfriend in D.C. and would be returning Sunday on the Acela. So I wasn't worried about a romantic involvement anymore, but I still needed to complete my assignment. I glanced at the assistant's desk diary and it had her arrival time in New York." Louise was very chipper. "And then I checked the Acela schedule to see what time the train got in."

Mason was afraid to ask but he did. "Did you meet her at the train station?"

"No, I did not."

"That's a relief." He let out a heavy sigh.

"I followed her to her apartment."

"You did what?" His voice boomed again. More complaints and admonishment. A nurse walked over to him.

"Mr. Chapman, if you do not lower your voice, I am going to have to take away your phone. Now please show some respect for the rest of the patients. And the staff!" She stood with her arms akimbo.

"Sorry." He placed his hand over the phone again. "It's a relative calling from the States."

The nurse waved him off and stomped back to her station.

"As I was saying, I followed her to her apartment," Louise continued.

"Did you speak to her?" Mason asked in a much quieter voice.

"Don't be ridiculous. That would have blown my cover. Anyhow, I surveilled her Monday when she went to work early and then went out for a coffee. Some idiot almost ran me off the sidewalk."

If only, Mason thought to himself.

"My boss was very impressed that I was able to infiltrate her office, get information, and follow her."

Mason sighed. "Is there anything else you would like to share with me?"

"She went out for drinks with her assistant and a few of his mates." She paused. "Not to worry. They play for their own team."

Mason knew what she meant. "Anything else?"

"I don't think she is seeing anyone in New York either."

"And what makes you say that?" Mason was finally interested.

"Just a feelin'."

"I know you, Louise. What else have you done?"

"I had a little chat with the doorman of her apartment building."

"Oh, for the love of Pete." Mason was exasperated.

"I asked him if there were any vacancies or single people in the building. Stuff like that."

"What did he tell you?"

"That there were several single women. A few my age."

"So you assumed he was referring to Zoe?"

"Well, I couldn't come right out and ask him now, could I?"

"No, of course not," he said sarcastically.

"But it's been two days and I haven't seen her with anyone."

"I suppose that's the good news."

"Where are you, by the way?" Louise asked. "What's all that dinging in the background?"

"I had a slight accident. Nothing serious, but I need an X-ray."

"Why didn't you say so? You let me prattle on and on!"

"As if anyone could stop you?" Mason chuckled for the first time that day.

"Is there anything I can do for you?"

"How about finding another 'mark,' as you put it, and leaving Zoe alone?" Mason looked up at the heavens for help.

"Well, fine. I was just looking after ya."

"I know and I appreciate your concern, but please stop."

"Oh, alright. Besides, my boss is putting me on a real case."

"I can't wait to hear about it." Mason was only half serious. He only cared that Louise didn't meddle with his personal life any longer. A doctor was now walking toward Mason. "I must go. Good luck with your new job." He ended the call before Louise could say another word. He wondered if he should tell Zoe. Tell her what? That he had an overly enthusiastic niece with a penchant for mysteries? Stalking? He thought better of it for now. At the moment he needed his leg tended to, and then he needed to find answers to the questions that would follow. His biggest concern was potential violations of the Building Safety Act. He would be blamed, and he would most likely lose his job.

Maggie began packing the clothes Alexis had put together for her. They really weren't much different from what she usually wore, but these were a bit more climate friendly. She went through her pantry and stuffed packages of cookies, chips, protein bars, and bottled water in another bag. The food on the plane would be excellent, but these were supplies for their stakeout. She took one last look before she heaved the strap of the goodie bag onto her shoulder and almost toppled over. *That ought to do it.* She'd never been to the Dominican Republic and didn't know what kind of snacks would be available. She didn't want to take any chances. The bag must have weighed fifteen pounds. She lifted her suitcase, which weighed about the same. She was confident she had enough supplies for a few days. Then she drove to Pinewood, where they had agreed to meet.

Alexis had a much bigger suitcase, but she also had to dress according to her role. When she arrived at the farm, they went through the logistics again.

"Alexis, what is your story as to why you're in the Dominican Republic and why you want a job there?" Myra asked.

"I just went through a very difficult time. My fiancé and I broke up and I went to Punta Cana to get away. While I was there I fell in love with the beautiful turquoise water, the soft breezes, and the relaxed atmosphere. One afternoon while I was having lunch, I overheard a couple talking about moving there and that many companies were trying to fill positions that were vacated after the last two hurricanes. I asked around about companies with ties to the U.S. and began a job search. I have no family to speak of and I was tired of the Detroit weather."

"Brilliant!" Charles said.

"Always blame a man." Myra chuckled.

"Oh, love, you don't mean that." Charles gave her a peck.

Myra rolled her eyes at Annie. Almost every one of their missions involved men behaving badly. Myra patted Charles on the cheek. "Not you, dear."

Eileen, one of Avery's operatives who had worked with the Sisters on other past missions, was the next to arrive. She, too, had a small suitcase filled with casual, comfortable clothes and one decent outfit should they get the occasion to be around other people.

It was eight A.M. Right on time, the five-passenger SUV pulled up and Charles and Fergus loaded the luggage and Maggie's stash into the back. Hugs, kisses, and good wishes swirled about, along with a few woofs from Lady and her pups.

The women soon arrived at the small airport where Annie kept her private jet. The pilot was going through the final checklist as the caterer rolled a cart onto the plane. The interior of the jet was like a comfortable living room, decked out with a large-screen television, deep leather seats, a fold-down table, and plenty of outlets for their computers and devices.

As they were settling in, the flight attendant asked what they would like for breakfast. The choice was French toast or quiche, with fruit and yogurt on the side. Maggie asked if she could have both. No one flinched or said a word. Not even the flight attendant. She'd met Maggie several times before.

The pilot got on the speaker. "Wheels up in fifteen minutes. We should arrive in Grand Cayman at approximately one P.M. We'll have a half hour layover and then continue to the Dominican Republic. Our flight time from Grand Cayman to Santo Domingo will be four hours. ETA approximately five thirty P.M. Sit back, relax, and enjoy the ride. And, of course, should you need anything, Carol and Raul are at your service. Breakfast will be served when we reach our cruising altitude." Carol and Raul strapped themselves into the jump seats while the others buckled their seat belts.

The women busied themselves checking their tablets. Myra turned to Annie and asked, "What do you make of this niece of Mason Chapman's?"

"According to what Fergus just sent, she went to school

here in the States. Her parents, Margaret and Cecil, worked for Lloyd's of London, the insurance company, and were stationed in Boston, which is where Louise grew up. They eventually moved back to the U.K. but Louise decided to stay in the States and attended the University of Connecticut. She graduated a little over a year ago and is now employed by a small private investigation firm in New York."

"Rather an odd choice for a young woman, wouldn't you say?"

Annie peered over her reading glasses. "You make me laugh. Look at us! We're not exactly conventional."

Myra chuckled. "True."

"Believe it or not, a lot of women are getting into the field," Eileen said. "Take me, for instance. I always had an insatiable curiosity and loved murder mysteries. *Murder, She Wrote* was one of my favorite TV shows growing up. At first my parents thought there might be something wrong with me. They actually met with my guidance counselor!" She chortled. "But much to their surprise and relief, the counselor decided I was normal."

"Hardly," Maggie blurted.

"Excuse me?" Eileen raised her eyebrow. "You're not exactly Nancy Normal."

Myra and Annie burst out laughing. "Oh, we are *so* not normal!"

Annie continued. "Anyway, the company Louise works for does mostly cheater surveillance."

"So why on earth would Louise be tailing Zoe?" Myra looked befuddled.

"I have no idea."

"How old is she?"

"According to Fergus, she's twenty-two. This is her first job out of college."

"Do you think her uncle hired her to follow Zoe? And could he be involved in this scam?" Myra asked.

"Both are very good questions. I'm going to get in touch with Izzie and see if she knows anything else. I know she was going to speak to Zoe last night." Annie typed a message to Izzie asking how Zoe was doing.

Dejected was the reply. **I might go to NYC to see her,** Izzie added.

Good idea. Her head must be spinning, Annie typed back. Then she said aloud, "Izzie may go to New York over the weekend. She thinks Zoe is a bit depressed, but won't show it or admit it."

"Poor girl. First she discovers something unsavory is happening with her employer, then she finds out the person who has been following her is related to a romantic interest. And let's not forget the big part," Myra said.

"What big part?" Alexis asked.

"The part where she came to Pinewood," Myra said. "I can only imagine what is going through her head."

"Makes me nauseous just thinking about it," Maggie said.

"You mean you're not going to eat anything?" Myra asked dubiously.

"Don't be ridiculous," Maggie chirped.

"We'll have to leave the Louise situation to Fergus and Charles and hope they can come up with a reasonable explanation," Alexis said.

Carol unhooked the straps that were holding her in the jump seat. "The pilot has informed me we have now reached cruising altitude. Shall I get you breakfast?"

"Yes, please!" Of course Maggie was the first to answer.

Back in London the doctors were finally tending to Mason's leg. He had been waiting for hours. The X-ray showed no signs of a fracture, but he had a very bad sprain. They released him with a pair of crutches and instructions. He checked his watch and saw that it was now ten P.M. He thought of Zoe. He knew he must phone her and explain what his niece had been up to. He hobbled to the sidewalk, hailed a cab, and headed to his flat. He sent a text to Zoe saying he needed to speak to her and would call shortly.

In her office in New York, Zoe looked at her phone and deleted the text. "Well, I don't need or want to speak to you," she said out loud.

"Did you say something?" Kyle's voice floated across the threshold.

"Oh no. Just talking to myself." Zoe was past being hurt. After a restless sleep the night before, she was now angry. *How dare he play me like that?* But something was nagging at her besides Louise. In spite of trying to maintain her indignation, it just didn't feel right. Time would tell.

A half hour later her cell phone rang. It was Mason. Zoe promptly hit the END button. She didn't want to speak to him. Not yet anyway. She needed more ammunition before she blew his head off. Figuratively speaking. Several minutes later her phone rang again. This time it was Izzie and she answered.

"Hello, my friend."

"Hey there. Wondering if you want some company this weekend? Abner has more work to do on his project and won't be back for another week. I haven't been in the city for ages. What do you think?"

"I think that would be great. We can go to a museum and eat ourselves senseless."

"Love it!" Izzie exclaimed. "What's your schedule like?"

"I can be outta here late in the afternoon on Friday."

"Perfect. I'll take the noon train. Gets me in at three-ish. Shall I meet you at your office?"

"Sounds good," Zoe said. "Izzie? I really appreciate your friendship, ya know."

"I do. And likewise. See you soon."

Zoe felt much more content knowing she would have some good company over the weekend. She called out to Kyle, "Hey, can you get me two tickets to an opera? Anything but *Don Giovanni*. One scoundrel at a time," she said softly to herself.

"Sorry, I didn't hear that last part," Kyle called back.

"I said, see if *La Traviata* is playing. It's impossible to be in a bad mood when they sing 'The Drinking Song.' "

"Verdi must have hated sopranos," Kyle responded.

"Why do you say that?"

"They say it's the most challenging part ever written."

"I disagree. *Lucia di Lammermoor* is by far the hardest." Zoe marked down *Izzie* in her desk diary.

"Whatever. Opera's not my jam." Kyle spun around on his chair and called American Express concierge service. "Matinee or evening?" he asked over his shoulder.

"Whatever. Make a dinner reservation depending on which show you can get."

"Saturday matinee?" Kyle asked while he was still on the phone.

"Perfect. Then dinner at seven at the Union Square Cafe."

Kyle finished his call and bounced into Zoe's office. "Okay, chief. You are all set. The opera at two at Lincoln Center, then seven for dinner. What are you going to do in between?"

"Shop? Cocktails? We are going to play it by ear."

"Was that supposed to be a pun?"

"What?"

"Play. It. By. Ear."

Zoe rolled her eyes and made another note in her desk diary. Another text from Mason arrived. Again, she deleted it.

* * *

The flight from the Manassas Regional Airport, not far from McLean, Virginia, to the Cayman Islands was smooth sailing. The Sisters watched a movie between chatting and checking emails. "Izzie confirmed she is going to New York to visit Zoe," Alexis announced.

"Do you think they should find out more about Louise Phillips?" Maggie asked.

"If I know Izzie, she'll sniff it out," Alexis said.

"Do you think Zoe will go along?" Maggie asked.

"It depends on how angry she is," Annie replied.

"Let's not forget, we don't know why Mason had his niece follow her. He could be involved in the REBAR corruption, and it could be dangerous," Myra suggested.

"I'm just not getting that vibe," Annie said.

"I know. Me neither, but until we know more, I would advise Izzie to simply enjoy spending time with her friend," said Myra.

"Well, if Izzie thinks she can scope it out, you know she will," Maggie stated.

"True." Annie opened her tablet and sent a message to Izzie:

Under no circumstance should you pursue Louise. Not until we get more intel.

A minute or so later Izzie responded with:

Understood.

Annie shut off her tablet and placed it in its case. "Maggie, Eileen, when you get to the airport you'll have an SUV rental waiting for you. Alexis will take a taxi."

"Right," said Eileen.

"But when you get to the Monaco, there will be a 1970 turquoise and white pickup truck in the rear of the parking lot. You are to use that to come and go. You'll blend in better."

"Turquoise?" Maggie wrinkled her brow.

"Matches the water. It's a very popular color there," Annie said.

"Cool. I always wanted one of those," Maggie said with glee.

"If you're a good girl, I'll get you one for your birthday." Myra chuckled.

"Really? Seriously?" Maggie was almost begging.

"If this mission goes well, everyone will have a new toy," Myra said and gave each of the other women a high five.

The pilot came on the speaker, announcing their descent into Grand Cayman. "We should be touching down in approximately ten minutes. We'll refuel and then on to Santo Domingo."

Santo Domingo was a busy city with skyscrapers and all the other trappings of a metropolis. Punta Cana, a popular vacation resort, was on the far eastern end of the island. The two cities were as different as night and day. Grand Cayman was a total resort island. With lots of banks. Beaches and banks.

Maggie was the first to chime in after they landed in Grand Cayman. "I wonder what's for lunch," she said, knowing everyone was anticipating her question.

"An assortment of sandwiches and salad," Annie replied. "And, yes, there's enough for you."

The plane taxied to the small terminal, where they were met by a driver who would take Myra and Annie on to their hotel. The women kissed and hugged and wished one another good luck, punctuated by shouts of, "Whatever it takes!"

Myra and Annie's ride to the Ritz Carlton and Seven Mile Beach was postcard perfect. Several hundred yards offshore, the ocean appeared a deep cerulean blue, lightening to various shades of turquoise at the shoreline. The silver thatch palms, blossoming lantana plants, and soft white beaches embodied the word *paradise*.

"It's absolutely gorgeous here. The smell of the salt air

mixed with fragrant tropical notes. Divine." Myra sighed. "It's too bad we can't stay a bit longer."

Annie eyed her. "Anything is possible." She patted Myra on her knee.

When they arrived at the hotel, they were welcomed by not one, but two bellmen.

"Nice to see you again, Countess, Ms. Rutledge," said the first of the two bellmen. He then circled to the back of the vehicle and saw there were only two small suitcases. "A short stay?" he asked.

"Afraid so," Annie answered. "But you never know."

"Right this way," the other bellman announced. He placed their bags on a cart and rolled it in the direction of the elevator.

The women were met by the concierge in the usual fashion, with smiles and joyful greetings. He handed them the keys to the suite and bid them a good afternoon.

Their top floor suite had a spectacular view of Seven Mile Beach from the outdoor terrace. "This is absolutely the bomb!" Myra said, trying to use a more youthful vernacular.

Annie laughed out loud. "Listen to you! But you are absolutely correct."

"Too bad Fergus and Charles can't join us," Myra said as she unpacked her bag.

"Let's see how the next few days go," Annie replied with a twinkle in her eye. "If not now, then we'll come back for a long-overdue vacation."

"I like the sound of that," said Myra. "What's on our agenda for today?"

"Check in with the others and then some relaxation."

"I like that plan."

The Gulfstream jet continued east with Cuba to the north and Jamaica to the south, the blue Caribbean below. "I don't

know why I don't take any vacations down here," Maggie
said.

"I don't know why we don't take any vacations at all."
Alexis was almost grumbling.

"Me either." Eileen held up her hand. "But a girl's gotta do
what a girl's gotta do."

"And we do it well," Alexis remarked.

Lunch was served and they watched another movie. After,
Maggie's tablet pinged.

"This just in—Izzie said Mason has been trying to get in
touch with Zoe. Zoe is ignoring him," Maggie relayed.

"Good move if you ask me," Alexis said dryly.

"Izzie told Zoe to keep ignoring him until we can get more
information."

"Splendid idea," Eileen added. "Ignoring men seems to be
the one thing that gets their attention."

"Yeah, but do we want her getting *more* of his attention?"
Alexis asked.

"Good point," Maggie said. "Although I try not to judge
until I have all the information."

"Spoken like a true journalist," said Alexis. "And I, too,
try not to jump to conclusions about my clients. But as the
saying goes, 'If it looks like a duck and walks like a duck—' "

"It must be a duck!" the other women chorused. Then they
busied themselves with various entertainment selections until
the pilot got back on the speaker.

"The flight time was a bit shorter than expected because of
a tailwind so we will be starting our descent shortly."

Alexis excused herself to change into one of her pantsuits
and a wig while Maggie and Eileen stayed in their capri
pants, tank tops, and flowered shirts. No one would question
whether or not they were tourists. At least for now.

After the plane landed, Maggie and Eileen got into their
rental and Alexis hailed a taxi. They all headed to the Mon-

aco Residences where a two-bedroom apartment was re-
served for Maggie and Eileen and a one-bedroom for Alexis.
Maggie and Eileen checked in first under their aliases, Eve
Marlow and Marie Chrysler. A few minutes later Alexis, aka
Estelle Johnson, signed in. It was important for Alexis to
maintain her singularity in case anyone inquired.

After they settled in, Maggie pulled up a map to see how
far REBAR was from the hotel. "It's on Calle Nicolás de
Ovando, about a half hour away," she said to Eileen. "What
time should we head over there?"

"Probably after dinner."

"Good idea. Food, I mean." Maggie giggled.

"Ha!" Eileen snickered. "I feel bad we can't eat with
Alexis."

"Yeah, me too. But as you said, 'A girl's gotta do what a
girl's gotta do.'" They finished the last bit of the sentence in
unison.

They changed into even less conspicuous clothes and Maggie slung her bag of snacks over her shoulder. There was a
bistro a few blocks away and Maggie suggested they check
the parking lot first.

"Ah, there's our beauty," Maggie said as she gestured to
the pickup truck. "Annie said the keys would be under the
passenger seat." They checked the parking lot for security
cameras. There was only one above the rear door, which was
easily avoided. They meandered around the other cars and
approached the truck. The keys were exactly where Annie
had promised. Maggie plucked the keys from underneath the
seat, shoved her goodie bag into the small space behind the
driver's seat, and then locked the truck doors.

After a quick dinner, they made their way back to the
parking lot and drove to the REBAR complex. They passed
by it slowly. There was a small, two-story office building behind the first gate with a few parking spaces nearby. A sec-

ond gate led to the batch plant in the back that housed the equipment needed to mix concrete. The machinery they could glimpse was massive.

Eileen got out of the truck about a block away from the complex to check for security cameras and motion detection lights. She pulled out a device that could detect high frequency cameras. There was a motion detector on every corner of the building. It was going to be more difficult to breach than they'd thought. They would have to make their way through the dense vegetation that surrounded the fence. It was a good thing that they had packed bug spray, though they had no idea just what creatures inhabited the plant life. "I guess we'll find out," Eileen said under her breath. She took several photos of the area and met up with Maggie down the road where she had parked the truck.

"You're not going to like this . . ." Eileen said.

"Now what?" Maggie was almost whining.

Eileen broke the news to Maggie. "We need to be on foot. You're going to have to trim down your snack bag. And we'll be in the woods, more or less."

"Bugs? Please, not bugs."

"I have that part covered. It's the other creatures we'll have to deal with."

"Say it isn't so."

"I would, but I would be lying."

"Dang!" Maggie shuffled through her bag. "I have pepper spray!"

"That might come in handy. As far as I know the snakes are only in the jungle areas so we should be okay."

"That's a relief. On to the important decision—popcorn, protein bars, or cookies? Take your pick."

"Protein bar, please."

Maggie had a small, nylon backpack folded inside one of the pockets of her snack bag. She filled it with a few essen-

tials and some small electronic devices. "Ready?" she asked
Eileen.

"Ready!"

They looked both ways as they crossed the street. The road
was dark and deserted now except for the lights on the building several yards away. Eileen told Maggie about the cameras
and the security guard in the small shack at the front of the
gate. They began picking their way through the trees and
vines until they were at the back of the gated property. They
positioned themselves so they would have a good sight line to
the loading docks. But there was no activity. Not a soul was
about. They cleared a few branches so they could sit. And
wait. And wait. And wait.

Chapter Eleven

Thursday

Outside REBAR

The sun was creeping over the horizon when Maggie and Eileen decided that they should hightail it out of there before the morning crew arrived. The night had proven fruitless and they decided to go back to the apartment, shower, and get some rest. If anything unseemly was going to happen, it was going to be at night. Unfortunately, it hadn't been that particular night. When they got back to their rooms, Maggie phoned Alexis and reported, "Nothing. Nada."

"Sorry to hear that."

"Me too," Maggie said. "The place is like Fort Knox. We had to sit in the bushes."

"Interesting. Why would they have such high security for a cement manufacturer?"

"Exactly."

"The security is top of the line and very recent," Eileen called out from across the room. "The cameras they're using have only been made available within the past year."

"Interesting. That's about as long as Malcolm's been there," Alexis noted.

"I repeat—exactly," said Maggie.

"My interview is this morning. I'll check out as much as I can and let you know when I get back."

"Sounds like a plan," Maggie said. "Good luck with your interview."

"Thanks. Talk later."

London

Mason Chapman hobbled to the door of his flat. It was late morning and he was nervously anticipating a grilling. When he opened his door, a nondescript man in a suit was standing on the other side.

"Mr. Chapman? Inspector Crenshaw of the building authority. May I come in?"

Mason hopped to one side and let him in. "Tea? Coffee?"

"No, thank you."

"Please sit down." Mason gestured to his dining table and chairs. "What can I do for you, Inspector?"

"It's about the accident yesterday."

"Yes. How can I help you?"

"Can you tell me if the scaffolding was properly secured?"

"To my knowledge, everything was up to snuff. I walk around the premises myself every morning."

"Indeed." The inspector jotted down a few notes. "About how long was the scaffolding there?"

"Several weeks."

"Were there workers on it every day?"

"Actually, no. We were supposed to start a renewal project, but the job was canceled."

"And who was responsible for the scaffolding?"

"The contractor erected it."

"Why hasn't it been dismantled?"

"I've been waiting for the contractor to come and retrieve it."

"I see." He jotted down a few more things before asking, "What is the name of the contractor?"

"Cotswell Contracting."

"I've heard they declared bankruptcy."

"Yes, which is why it's been a problem having the scaffolding removed. Something about the bank and all that."

"I see." More notes. "Anything else you can tell me?"

"Aside from spraining my ankle? No. Sorry."

"Fine. You will be hearing from us again." The inspector stood and unceremoniously left the flat.

Mason stared down at his lukewarm tea. Why was life becoming a nightmare? He tried again to contact Zoe. This time he phoned. But once again, there was no answer; the call went straight to voice mail. Then he realized it was still only five A.M. in the States.

New York

Zoe jumped up from a deep sleep, awakened by her phone ringing. Who would be calling at this hour? *Mason.* She slid her finger to the red button, sending the call to voice mail. Betty and Buster lifted their heads in annoyance, repositioned themselves on the bed and went back to sleep. "Easy for you," Zoe said to her fur family.

She was now wide-awake. She wondered how long she could go without taking Mason's calls or answering his messages. She thought about the Sisters' motto: *Whatever it takes.* But it was hard. On the one hand, she wanted to blast him with expletives. On the other, she wanted to hear him out. Maybe Izzie was right. Maybe he had a good explanation for why his niece had been following her. Zoe was glad her friend would be arriving the next day.

She got up and made a pot of French press coffee and toasted an English muffin. She scowled at the word *English* on the package, a reminder of Mason. "Ugh." She was curious as to what was happening in the islands, but didn't want to disturb anyone. Then she remembered there was an option to have a message delivered at a future time. Zoe began to type a message to all concerned letting them know Mason was still calling, texting, and emailing her. Then she asked how the rest of the mission was going. She set the message to be delivered at eight A.M. That left only three hours to pace the floors. Instead, she opened her work laptop and checked the latest timelines. The shipment for the school in Italy had been moved ahead. It was to leave the port in Santo Domingo in two days. She quickly typed a second message to the Sisters. But this time she sent it immediately.

Maggie was just stepping out of the shower and about to get some rest when she saw Zoe's message. "Oh no! Eileen! The shipment is leaving the port the day after tomorrow."

"I guess that means they'll be loading the truck tonight." Eileen grabbed her tablet and sent a message to Avery. "Between Charles, Fergus, and Avery, I am sure they'll come up with a plan."

Fergus was staying at the farm while the women were away. Charles teased that he needed Fergus around to clean up the kitchen. They were still in their pajamas when they saw Zoe's message. They quickly contacted the harbormaster in Santo Domingo. They spoofed REBAR's email signature and sent a message:

> *Shipment from REBAR to Abruzzi must be delayed.*
> *Need two to three days. Saturday at the earliest.*
> *Donald Walsh*
> *Director of Quality Control*

Several minutes later they got a confirmation of a new slip and time. Fergus and Charles were quite pleased with themselves.

"Brilliant, old boy!" Charles slapped Fergus on the back. "While the driver is cooling his heels in the overflow parking area, the International Maritime Organization will inspect REBAR's shipment."

Fergus gave Charles a sly look. "Do you want to tip them off or should I?"

"I'll flip you for it!" Charles chuckled. "I'll fetch more coffee and grab a few scones. We need to be fortified!"

Charles was fleet-footed as he sailed past Lady Liberty and gave her the customary salute. A few minutes later he returned, settled down in his chair and sent messages to everyone letting them know the shipment would be delayed, but they still had to finish by Saturday. He and Fergus had only been able to buy them two extra days. Otherwise someone from REBAR might grow suspicious waiting for a copy of the bill of lading to be sent to the office. Charles also sent Zoe an email letting her know, so she wouldn't fret or feel compelled to do something rash. Besides, she already had plenty to stew about. The situation with Mason and his niece was unsettling. He'd look into that once they got everything else handled.

Santo Domingo

Clad in her ombre wig and olive-green pantsuit, Alexis carried a leather portfolio under her arm. She spoke with the guard at the entrance to the REBAR complex, notifying him that she had a job interview. He phoned the main office and then buzzed her through the gate. Alexis secretly took photos with her phone and sent them to Eileen. This way they would have an inside view.

The short walk from her vehicle to the main entrance was sweltering. The air conditioning inside the building felt good on Alexis's skin. "Good morning. I'm Estelle Johnson. I am here to see Mr. Segundo."

The pretty receptionist had a singsong Caribbean accent. "Take the elevator to the second floor. Someone there will direct you."

"Thank you." Alexis kept her phone in her hand, surreptitiously snapping photos along the way, ever mindful of any security cameras. There was only one at the front desk and one in the elevator. When she reached the second floor, she noticed it had a wall of windows overlooking the plant outside. Again she took several pictures and sent them to Eileen.

A short, round, middle-aged man with an accent greeted her. "Good morning, Miss Johnson. I am Alberto Segundo. Thank you for coming in."

"Thank you for seeing me on such short notice."

"My pleasure. Please follow me."

Not wanting to draw any further attention to herself, Alexis took mental notes of the layout. Segundo didn't have an office. Instead he brought her to an area in the middle of the floor, where his desk faced the view of the plant and production line. There was little or no privacy.

"Please sit." He gestured to the chair opposite his desk. "You have a very impressive résumé. Tell me, why do you want to work here?"

As rehearsed, Alexis gave him her tale of woe, her epiphany, and her desire to change her life.

Segundo nodded sympathetically. "I am glad you found our island to your liking. You have many years to look forward to and I believe you will enjoy spending them here." He began to review her résumé again. "I see you have a broad experience in contracts."

"Yes. Some people find it boring, but I look at it from a forensic point of view. They say the devil is in the details."

"You are correct, Miss Johnson."

"Please call me Estelle."

"Of course. I tell you, Estelle, this is a stroke of luck for us. We have been in need of a contracts manager for almost a year. It is not my specialty, but currently it is my responsibility. It would take a big burden off me if I could fill the position."

"I can start as soon as tomorrow, if you want me."

Segundo's face lit up. "Splendid!"

Alexis looked around. "Would you mind taking me on a tour?"

"It would be my pleasure." Segundo got up from his chair. "Please, follow me." As they meandered among the desks, the various employees busied themselves while also acknowledging their boss.

"Here is where you will be working." Segundo gestured at a wall of filing cabinets where a desk was positioned. Alexis noticed it was as private as a football field. Looking through the documents would be challenging, although Segundo seemed anxious to get that off his plate. He introduced Alexis/Estelle to several of the other employees and then walked her back to his desk.

"Could I get a peek at the production line?" Alexis hoped she wasn't overstepping. "I'm always fascinated by how things are made."

With great pride, Segundo replied, "We have limited access due to safety concerns, but I would be happy to point out the important features. I must warn you, though—you may get dust on your lovely suit."

Alexis placed her hand on his arm. "I think my suit can handle it."

He grabbed two N95 masks and waited to hand one to her while she secured her phone in a pouch on her belt. "This is for your lungs," Segundo said. He sounded almost giddy at the prospect of the tour.

They took the elevator to the first floor and walked toward the plant. The noise of trucks, forklifts, mixers, and conveyor belts was deafening. Segundo handed Alexis a set of plugs, which she gladly stuffed into her ears. He took her by the elbow and began to point out the various machines, but she couldn't hear a word he said. She hoped the microphone on her cell phone could pick up his monologue as it was being sent to Charles and Fergus.

Segundo was thrilled to have an audience. Rarely did he see anyone from outside, with the exception of Mr. Fielder coming once a month, and Mr. Walsh periodically. Therefore having Estelle to speak to was a refreshing change. He rambled on about the raw materials: Portland cement, water, gravel, sand. The concrete was formed when the raw materials were mixed together. Depending on the ratios, the finished blocks could range from lightweight to high density. Once the batching was complete the cement went through the molding process, then curing and packaging. After the show-and-tell, Segundo and Alexis moved back inside. Segundo offered her an espresso, which she accepted.

Alexis was well aware they were now on an accelerated timeline. "Since I'm already here, why don't I familiarize myself with the filing system?"

"That would be wonderful!" Segundo exclaimed. "Come. I'll explain." They moved to the back wall and he told her that they kept a paper copy of every job file. There was a lot of computer hacking going on and a paper copy was good insurance.

Alexis bit her lip to stifle a smile. *Computer hacking, in-*

deed. When Segundo finished giving her an introduction to their filing system, he excused himself and went to his area of the floor. Confident she was out of his sight line, Alexis went to the appropriate drawer and began to look for a file with the name *El Cemento.*

Grand Cayman

Myra and Annie were up before the crack of dawn. They wanted to watch the sunrise. The hotel packed a basket with pastries and a thermos of coffee, and one of the porters set two lounge chairs at the water's edge. The sky began to shed the darkness, illuminating the horizon. They sat in silence as the waves gently lapped at the sand. Soon a bright orange ball of fire crested in the distance, signaling the dawn of a new day.

Annie checked her cell phone. It wasn't quite five A.M. There was a message waiting from Zoe about the shipment. Shortly after came a message from Charles. "Things are moving fast," she said and then read the messages to Myra.

"Good thing we're meeting Mac today."

"Alexis has her interview this morning, and Maggie and Eileen will go back to the plant tonight." Annie ticked off her list. "Charles and Fergus are looking into Fielder's and Walsh's financials. If everything goes well, we should be able to wrap this up by Saturday."

"We haven't come up with a plan for Walsh and Fielder yet." Myra was referring to the justice they would impart.

Annie raised her eyebrows. "Oh, I have an idea, my sister!" She put her arm around Myra as they headed back to their hotel suite.

Later that morning, as they were about to leave for the Lobster Pot, they got a message from Alexis:

Secured job. Starting today. Sent recording and photos to Charles, Fergus, Maggie and Eileen.

"Maybe Charles and Fergus will get some background on Fielder and Walsh today, too," Myra said as she crossed her fingers on both hands.

When the two women arrived, Mac was already at the restaurant, leaning on a railing and enjoying the ocean view.

"Mac! Darlin'," Annie called out.

They all kissed on both cheeks, and then Mac also kissed the backs of each of the women's hands. "Lovely to see you, Countess." He was grinning from ear to ear. "And you, too, Mrs. Rutledge. What a pleasure to be able to spend a little time with you."

The restaurant hostess approached them and asked that they follow her. After she showed them to their table, Mac pulled out chairs for both Annie and Myra. He had the finest of manners.

Annie ordered a bottle of sparkling rosé, Billecart-Salmon Brut, for the table. She wanted to loosen Mac up a bit. She knew he wouldn't get plastered, but one glass of wine was often enough to cause a person to shed their outer layer. The atmosphere and conversation were delightful. Mac had the perfect personality for dealing with the public. He was charming, yet exacting; confident and polite at the same time.

Annie was contemplating her timing before she started to interrogate him. The opportunity came when he said, "Countess, I know we have a long history, but there must be another reason you wanted to meet. You are a busy woman and rarely do you take lunch. Am I right?"

"You are very intuitive." Annie took his hand. "I am going to show you photos of two men. I just need to know if you have ever seen them."

Mac smiled. "Is that all? I wouldn't be violating any customer's trust or anonymity. And who said they even were customers?"

"I certainly didn't say it, did I?" Annie was playing along. She held her purse on her lap and pulled out the photos so only Mac could see them.

"The one on the left," Mac said, indicating Fielder. "He comes in about once a month." Mac looked at the second photo again. "I've never seen the other one."

Annie and Myra were about to burst. "Mac, you are a love." Annie gave him a kiss on the cheek and Myra planted one on the other side.

Lunch had lasted for two hours when Mac began to say his goodbyes. "I do hope to see you again soon. You two always brighten my day. My most sincere gratitude for a divine afternoon." He tipped his Panama hat and left.

Myra and Annie were beside themselves. Fielder was behind the scheme. Walsh was probably his lackey.

They scurried to the restaurant entrance and took a taxi back to their hotel. As soon as they arrived at their rooms they powered up their tablets and had a video call with Charles and Fergus. Annie and Myra explained what they had discovered; then the men shared their information.

"We know Fielder has been with the company for about a year," Charles said. "According to Eileen, the security equipment is very up-to-date and must have been installed within the past year. Maybe it was a necessity, but given the cost of the system, they must have a lot more to protect than just the factory. Perhaps a secret.

"Alexis is at the office now. They keep paper copies of all their files. It's really not a bad idea. Much harder to hack. People forget that's how the Allies planned the Normandy invasion—on paper. But don't ask me to give up all my devices." He chuckled.

"Or vices," Myra teased.

"What else do we know?" Annie asked.

"We know that the woman who was following Zoe is Mason Chapman's niece. She works for a private investigator in New York," Fergus added.

"We also know Mason has been trying to reach Zoe, but she is ignoring him," Myra mused.

"And Izzie is going to New York tomorrow to spend the weekend with her," Annie said.

"But we still don't know the connection, if there is one, between Mason and Walsh. Or Fielder," said Charles.

"The only seeming connection is that the company where Mason works was supposed to purchase materials from REBAR, but the job got canceled. In fact, all of REBAR's jobs in the U.K. were canceled," Fergus explained.

"Do we know why?" Myra asked.

"We do not," Fergus replied.

"I've asked Avery to check up on this Mason chap. Avery said he'd get back to me by EOD today," Charles informed them.

"Good idea," said Annie.

Myra spoke next. "Maggie and Eileen are going back to the plant tonight. If the shipment is supposed to go out in the next two days, they will most likely prepare it tonight, don't you think?"

"According to the recording we got from Alexis, the plant only does custom work, so, yes, it would make sense for them to do it tonight or tomorrow," Charles agreed.

"What have you gotten on Fielder so far?" Annie asked. "He seems to spend a lot of time here."

"We're still trying to get his bank records, but what we *do* know is that he purchased a sixty-foot yacht for one-point-five million, via a promissory note. One third upon delivery and then two more subsequent payments." Charles snickered. "I wonder if he went the cheap route. A new Hatteras is around three million."

"How does one go cheap with a yacht?" Myra squinted at him.

"Brass bathroom fixtures instead of fourteen karat gold."

"I see." Myra fidgeted with her pearls. It occurred to her she hadn't fiddled with them as much since she had been breathing sea air. She made a mental note.

Charles continued. "In addition to his seafaring interests, his condominium in South Beach, Miami, is a one-point-three-million-dollar investment."

"He can't be making *that* big a salary," Annie said.

"He isn't," Fergus said. "That is one thing we were able to find out. His annual salary is a half million, including a bonus. That wouldn't cover his lifestyle."

"Doesn't he come from money?" Annie said. "Didn't his family own a liquor distribution business?"

"They did. He worked there for a bit, but then he left to work for FREDO and then REBAR."

"Strange change in professions, no?" Myra asked.

"According to one of our sources, he blew through his trust fund when he purchased the condominium. His mother wasn't too keen on it and she was the one who arranged for his transfer into concrete."

"Interesting," Annie said. "Why would his mother banish him from the family business, if that's what she actually did?"

"We need to do a little more digging. He left FREDO under a cloud. Maybe it followed him," Charles suggested.

"Looks like we still have work to do. There must be several more jobs he has planned going forward. Shall we reconvene this evening?" Annie asked.

"Nine our time?" Myra asked.

"Roger that. You girls behave." With that, Charles and Fergus signed off.

REBAR *manufacturing plant*
Santo Domingo

Alexis busied herself opening filing cabinet drawers, getting accustomed to the company system. It was easy. Old-school. Everything was in alphabetical order. She was making her way through when Segundo popped up behind her. He nearly scared her wig off. "Oh my, you startled me!" she exclaimed, then quickly batted her eyes at him.

"My apologies." Segundo seemed quite sincere. Alexis wondered just how involved he was with this charade. "I wanted to check and see if you needed anything."

"Thank you. I see your files are very well organized." She looked over at her desk, where a wire basket held a ream of contracts and papers. "I'll start work on those in a few minutes."

"We normally take a lunch break. Could I interest you in some of our local cuisine?"

"Thank you, but I really feel as if I should go through that stack on my desk. Would you mind bringing something back for me?"

"It would be my pleasure. But I don't want you to think we do not treat our people well." He was almost blushing.

"Not at all. I've found everyone most kind. Thank you." Alexis tried to end the conversation and get back to her snooping. She shut the file drawer and moved toward her desk.

He clasped his hands in front of him. "I am very grateful to have someone with your level of commitment." Then he turned and walked away.

Alexis was beginning to feel guilty. Not about what she was doing, but how disappointed Segundo would be when she left. He seemed like a nice man.

As it turned out, everyone took their lunch break at the same time. The phones could ring off the hook, but there was no one to answer them. Alexis knew it was not unusual for Latin and South American companies to operate that way. She remembered a trip she once took to Brazil to check on a shoe manufacturing facility. At one o'clock a whistle blew, the machines stopped, and people went to the cafeteria. It was almost like school. When the last person left the floor, she went back to the cabinets and flipped through the files. There it was: *El Cemento*. She pulled out her phone and began to snap photos of the invoices. The one thing that was not included on the paperwork was the company's address.

What *was* there was the routing number to a bank in the Cayman Islands. She also found information for an order that had completed its curing process and was awaiting shipping. It was destined for a school in Italy. She flipped through the rest of the invoices and was stopped in her tracks. A folder containing invoices for processed goods indicated that another shipment had already reached the U.S. and was enroute to a school in Ohio. Alexis quickly sent a pic of the paperwork to Charles, Avery, Myra, and Annie. Now she had to do what she'd actually been hired to do—go through the pile of contracts.

New York
REBAR corporate office

Malcolm Fielder booked a flight to Miami. Previously he'd had his hand slapped by the CEO for using the company jet one too many times. So first class on a commercial jet would have to do. His plan was to spend a few days carousing about, and then it would be a quick hour and a half hop to Grand Cayman. He had his eye on a new car. This time it was an Aston Martin DBS with a price tag of three-hundred-fifteen thousand, almost two hundred grand more than the Maserati. It was time for a step-up. He phoned Walsh. "I need to see you before I leave. Be in my office by two. I have a flight at six."

Walsh showed up on time. He was nervous. It seemed he was always nervous. Perhaps it was because he was always on the brink of being found out, and he really wasn't the brightest bulb in the chandelier. Walsh knew in the world of criminal offenders he would be considered a two-bit crook. Unlike his father, he had no expectations of being a mob boss. "Getting over and getting a taste" was enough for him. He was a miserable, sour, pathetic man who resented anyone who he perceived had a better life. One could almost feel sorry for him, but he had no redeeming qualities.

"Walsh. Come in. Close the door." Fielder had his feet up on his desk, displaying his fancy red-soled leather shoes. "I take it we have that Danfield situation tidied up?"

"Yeah. I don't think she'll be a problem anymore."

"And what of that chap she knows in the U.K.?"

"I don't think he has anything to do with any of our business. Besides, we pulled out of there." Walsh tried to suppress a grin.

"What's so amusing?" Fielder asked.

"Let's just say he had a bit of an accident."

Fielder pulled his legs off his desk and sat upright. "What?" he roared. "Listen, I told you that little stunt at the subway station was unnecessary. Now you're telling me her friend had 'an accident'?" He was standing at this point. "We're not thugs, Donald. I want no more of that sort of thing. We do not need any more attention. Do you understand?"

"Completely." Walsh hung his head. "I was just trying to scare her."

"What about him?"

"Yeah, him too."

"Your only job is to hire the trucks, fill them with coal ash and deliver them to the plant. It's not rocket science." Malcolm was beginning to think he needed to find a replacement for Walsh. He was becoming careless and taking matters into his own hands. "Don't ever do anything without consulting with me. Am I making myself clear?"

Walsh was still staring at the carpet. He had to conceal the smirk on his face. It was lucky Fielder didn't know about his recent visit to Zoe's apartment building. If he'd gotten in, he could have shut her up for good. *We're not thugs?* He supposed even criminals have their class system. "Crystal."

"Fine. Now I have to get ready to leave. Phone me when the shipment leaves Santo Domingo and you have a copy of the bill of lading. I want to be sure it's out of the port by tomorrow."

Walsh didn't move. "Anything else?"

"No. Just shut the door behind you."

REBAR manufacturing plant
Santo Domingo

In spite of her real purpose for being at REBAR, Alexis felt compelled to do some of the work she'd been hired for. But before she settled at her desk, she took one more walk around the office space, taking a few more pics. When she passed Segundo's desk she noticed a framed photo of a woman and two children at a beach. They all looked very happy. Normal. She was convinced Segundo had no idea about all of the corruption he was fostering. She knew what it was like to be accused of something you were not guilty of. Just to be sure her soft side wasn't taking over, Alexis double-checked with Charles, sending him a text:

Any connection between Segundo and the others?

A few minutes passed before Charles answered:

Not that we can find. His bank accounts match his salary.

Alexis pinged back:

Got it. Thanks. Someone should alert Zoe about Ohio shipment.

Another response from Charles:

Roger. Will see what she knows.

The contracts Alexis worked on were all standard. She zipped through them like the pro she was. By the time Segundo and the others returned from lunch, her wire basket was empty. Segundo stopped by her desk to drop off a sandwich. "Miss Johnson. What have you done with all the files?" He looked genuinely befuddled.

"All done, sir." She looked up at him and smiled.

"But that cannot be possible!" Segundo scratched his head.

"They were all quite standard. All the *t*'s were crossed and the *i*'s dotted, and the signatures were in place."

"You are a miracle worker." He stood with his arms folded and gazed at the paperless desk.

"Not really." Alexis stood. "As I said, all routine."

"It seems you are finished for the day." Segundo could not have been more pleased.

"What time shall I come in tomorrow?" Alexis asked, knowing she would probably never see him again.

"Any time before ten." Segundo smiled.

She shook his hand. "Thank you again for the opportunity."

"The pleasure is mine. Have a good evening."

Alexis made sure she had all of her belongings before she said her final farewell.

*   *   *

By three P.M. Maggie and Eileen had gotten several hours' sleep and were getting ready for their next night in the woods. Alexis pinged Maggie to see if she could stop by their apartment, which was two floors above hers. First Alexis went to her apartment and changed out of her pantsuit. She removed the wig and stuffed her real hair under a straw pork-pie hat. Even if she was caught on camera, no one would recognize her. When they'd first arrived at the hotel, Eileen had done a sweep of the floors and elevators to locate the security cameras. They were in the usual places: above the door of the stairs and one in the corner of each of the elevators. Alexis checked the hallway. Empty. She sprinted the two flights up the vacant stairwell and slowly opened the door to check the hallway. Empty, as well. She scooted to Maggie and Eileen's suite, where Maggie had left the door unlocked so Alexis wouldn't have to knock.

Alexis zipped into their room with a huge smile on her face. "I got the routing number for the account in the Caymans. In the file, it was labeled El Cemento, but we know it actually belongs to Fielder."

"Holy smoke!" Maggie gasped. "Now that is real sleuthing!" She gave her a high five. "Do Annie and Myra know?"

"Yes."

"So what's the game plan?" Maggie asked.

"We're going to have a Zoom meeting tonight at nine."

"Eileen and I will have to do it from the truck," Maggie said.

"Since there was no activity last night and we have the photos Alexis took, we probably don't need to wait in the woods," Eileen said. "There is only one entry and exit on the property. It's at the gate. The trucks have to be cleared by security before they can get in."

"From what Zoe explained, it's the ratio of the combination of materials they use that determines the density," Alexis added.

"Which means a truck has already delivered raw materials that could have been something else." Maggie tapped her pen against her notebook. "It takes twenty-four hours for the blocks to cure, so the ash had to have been delivered before we arrived."

"If our assumption is correct, and the load destined for Italy is being loaded tomorrow, the truck with the bad blocks will be leaving the plant tonight," said Alexis.

"That sounds about right. So tonight we watch all the traffic in and out of the plant and send photos of the trucks and their plates to Charles and Fergus. They'll alert the International Maritime Organization, who will inspect the cargo at the port and have it tested," Eileen said.

"Can we be sure they'll inspect the right trucks?" Maggie asked.

"Not entirely, but we could always follow the trucks and tag them with my trusty, laser-sharp paintball gun." Eileen pulled it out of its holster.

"Oh . . . wee! Let me see that thing!" Maggie was like a little kid.

Eileen made sure the safety catch was on it. "It's not available to the general public. But some DEA agents carry them when they're trying to track a drug haul and can't get close enough to plant a GPS device."

Maggie turned the gun over in her hand. "This is way cool."

"Okay, Annie Oakley, hand it over." Eileen put her hand out and Maggie obliged.

"That sounds like a safer plan than trying to climb over a fence without becoming part of someone's cinderblock foundation." Alexis snickered.

"For sure." Maggie was intrigued and excited. "A low-speed chase?"

"Kinda," Eileen said. "We just need to be careful they don't realize we're following them."

"What if there's more than one truck?" Maggie asked.

"If there's more than one, chances are they'll be carrying similar loads. According to the papers I looked through, each job is custom ordered. That way they're not sitting on inventory. They do one job and while it's curing, they start the next."

"Got it. So they've already made the subpar concrete?" Maggie asked.

"Let's hope we're on the right track. We are making a lot of assumptions, but based on shipping manifests and timing, I think it's a good bet the trucks will pick up the load tonight and bring it to the port," Eileen said.

The room fell silent for a moment and then Maggie asked, "Alexis, do you think our disguises are good enough?"

Alexis replied with a completely straight face. "I think you should both have mustaches." After the snickering, Alexis continued. "Two guys in a pickup truck would look less suspicious than two women."

"Very true," Eileen agreed.

Alexis thought for a moment. "I think I can fake it with one of my extra wigs, eyebrow pencil and some eyelash glue. We should also get another baseball cap and make it look worn out."

Maggie folded her arms. "So we leave the apartment looking like Cheech and Chong?"

"Since I'm not planning on going back to the REBAR office, I'll go with you. I can plant the lip foliage on your faces when we get in the truck."

"Sounds like a good plan. We can grab another cap at a store on the way," said Eileen.

"Remember we have that Zoom meeting with everyone at nine. What time should we get over to the plant?" Maggie asked.

"To be safe, I suggest right after it shuts down. According to Segundo, the office staff leaves at five and the factory workers leave around seven," Alexis said.

"And we only saw one guard on duty last night," Maggie added.

"Okay then. Let's plan on leaving at six. That will give us enough time to find a good spot to park where we can also make a quick exit as soon as the trucks leave the lot," Eileen said as she double-checked for extra cartridges for the paint-ball gun.

"I can't wait to see how it all works out!" Maggie said with a little too much glee.

New York

Zoe was wrapping up her workday when she checked the burner phone for any messages. Much to her horror she saw the text from Charles about the Ohio shipment. *How did that get away from me?* She went back to her computer and typed in the name of the school: *Riverwood Elementary.* Sure enough, it wasn't in her account file. *So where was it?* She looked in every file where she thought it might be, but to no avail. She wondered if this was a Donald Walsh deal and he had fudged the records. Zoe immediately looked up the school and found the main phone number.

"Good afternoon. This is . . ." She had to think quickly. "Louise Phillips. I'm calling regarding some building materials that are enroute to your school."

A pleasant voice responded. "Oh yes. That's for the new gymnasium they're building. How can I help you?"

"We seem to have conflicting addresses. Can you please tell me where the shipment should be delivered?"

"Certainly. Just one moment."

Zoe heard some papers rustling in the background. "The truck needs to enter on River Road. It's to the north of the building. They'll be able to see the entrance from the street."

"Can you give me the exact address? My boss is a stickler for that sort of thing."

"Of course. It's 115 River Road. Is there anything else I can help you with?" the pleasant voice asked.

"No. Thank you very much. You have been very helpful. Enjoy the rest of your day." Zoe realized she had been holding her breath for what seemed like an hour. She immediately contacted the team with the address.

Charles then sent off a quick text to Myra asking what direction Kathryn was coming from or going to.

Myra answered Charles, saying she thought Kathryn was picking up a load in California and was heading to Nebraska. Charles quickly sent a message to Kathryn that she needed to intercept a truck going to Florence, Ohio.

Kathryn decided this required a phone call and hit Charles's speed dial number.

"Hey, Charles. What's happening?" Kathryn asked calmly.

"There's a truck delivering subpar materials to an elementary school in Florence. We need to intercept it."

"I'll reach out to some of my road warriors and see who is in that area. I'll get back to you ASAP."

Kathryn picked up her CB radio and sent out an APB. "Anyone heading to Florence, Ohio?" No response. She tried her VHF radio instead and sent the same message. Still nothing. She knew she had no other alternative but to scramble and head to Ohio herself. Her cargo of bok choy would be taking a detour. If she hustled she could be within the vicinity of Florence within the next twelve hours. She phoned Charles again. "I can't get anyone on the wire right now so I'll head off in that direction. I should be able to make contact with the truck the closer I get."

"Right-o. Mind as you go!" Charles exclaimed.

"Will do!" Kathryn took the next exit to I-80 East and put the pedal to the metal. If there weren't any detours she would be near Florence around two A.M. But she still had to find that driver or her trip would be for naught.

Santo Domingo

Alexis left her room first and strolled to the parking lot. Five minutes later Maggie and Eileen headed toward the pickup truck. Maggie rolled her baseball cap in the dirt and Eileen scuffed hers on the asphalt. Alexis's porkpie hat was already a little frayed around the edges.

The three piled into the truck and began changing into their disguises, arms and legs flailing and knocking into one another. It could have been a scene from an episode of *I Love Lucy.* When they finally accomplished the bizarre quick-change routine, they burst out laughing.

"I don't think we could do that again if someone paid us!" Maggie roared.

They gave each other the once-over. No one would mistake them for tourists now. They looked like they were on their way home from a long day at a farm. Once they drove to the complex, Eileen spotted an area on the side of the road where they could park and be hidden by a few shrubs. Now all they had to do was wait. Again.

Cayman Islands

Annie checked her watch. Not quite six P.M. She thought Mac might still be at the bank. She dialed his number.

"Countess! First lunch and now a phone call? I don't know if I should be flattered or concerned," Mac joked. "To what do I owe this unexpected pleasure?"

"I have an account that I'd like to close out tomorrow."

"Close?" Mac sounded very confused and truly concerned.

"I want to make a donation."

"I see." Mac sounded defeated.

"Not to worry, Mac. I will open another account with the same amount of money."

Mac was perplexed, but it was Countess de Silva. You didn't ask questions. "If I am understanding you correctly, you want to close out one account and open another?"

"Correct," Annie said. "I know it sounds odd, but that's how the money rolls." Annie could certainly afford to make any amount of donation herself, but on principle, she wanted to use Fielder's own ill-gotten gains for a more humanitarian cause. She could let her own money sit in the Cayman account forever if necessary. And she didn't want Mac to take any heat for losing such a large sum. A sum over two million dollars. Annie could hear the relief in Mac's voice.

"Very well, Countess. Whatever your heart desires."

"Perfect. What time should we come in?"

"Is ten agreeable?"

"Absolutely. Myra and I have decided we like to get up early to watch the sunrise."

"Brilliant, Countess! See you in the morning." Mac ended the call and patted his forehead with his handkerchief. He hated losing an account, but this situation was certainly agreeable.

Annie looked at Myra. "So who shall we endow with Fielder's ill-gotten gains?"

"Since it seems as if he's been targeting schools, let's send it to a few schools in need of computers."

"I like that plan." Annie smiled. "I only wish I could see the look on Fielder's face when he tries to withdraw funds."

Myra sighed. "Me too, but we'll have to console ourselves with our imaginations!" Then she hooted, "Whatever it takes!"

"The girls should be on their stakeout soon, and Kathryn is slamming her way toward Ohio," Annie said.

"I have no doubt our girls will be triumphant. So, what did you have in mind for Mr. Fielder and Mr. Walsh?" Myra raised her eyebrows.

"Something that includes concrete." Annie gave her a wink.

"I cannot wait to hear the details. Should we alert Pearl?" Myra was referring to Pearl Barnes, the woman who facilitated in the disposal of the perpetrators. Nobody was ever killed—but most probably wished they had been.

"Yes. We'll need two large empty oil drums, Portland cement, and two hand trucks." Annie ticked off the items on her fingers.

"Sounds like a scene from *The Godfather*."

"Funny you should say that. It's actually a mafia legend. Rumors were if anyone crossed them, they would put their feet in cement and toss them in the river so the body wouldn't float. I suppose it could be true; however, there is only one known case where a body was found on a Brooklyn beach and the feet were encased in cement."

"Interesting." Myra stroked her pearls for the first time since their sunrise inspiration.

"There is also another euphemism. 'A Chicago overcoat.' It means death."

"Well, I certainly don't like that wardrobe collection!" Myra chuckled.

Annie followed with a guffaw. "Touché!"

Myra decided to phone Charles. She hadn't had a private conversation with him since she and Annie had arrived in Grand Cayman.

"Hello, love." Charles's smile could be felt over the airwaves. "Are you girls enjoying yourselves?"

"Very much so, but it would be much nicer if my favorite companions were here." Myra sighed. "And, of course, you, my dear." She laughed.

"Aren't you being the funny one now?" Charles teased. "What is the latest, love?"

"Annie and I are going to the bank to close out Fielder's account. Annie is going to open a separate account with the same amount of funds so as not to upset Mac's applecart. The plan is to send Fielder's funds to several schools who are in need of supplies."

"Splendid idea," Charles said. "That should fix the pants on that tosser. Do you want Fergus and me to send you a list? This way you can make all the transactions at the same time."

"That would be very helpful," Myra replied. "We also need you to get in touch with Pearl. Annie will send details. Sounds like she's fitting Fielder and Walsh for concrete shoes."

Charles laughed. "I haven't heard that expression in a dog's age. And I know better than to ask questions. What's on your agenda for this evening?"

"Annie and I are going to have dinner on our beautiful terrace tonight before our call. Then we wait."

"Right," Charles said. "Enjoy your dinner. We shall see you in a bit."

After Myra had ended her call, Annie pulled out the room

service menus. "I think we should order a bottle of champagne."

"But the mission isn't over yet."

"We have the routing number and there is no way Fielder can get to his account before we do."

"You always put a positive spin on everything." Myra chuckled.

"That's my job." Annie gave Myra a hug.

Santo Domingo

Alexis, Maggie, and Eileen made themselves as comfortable as possible within the close confines of the truck cab. Luckily Maggie was petite, but Alexis's long legs were battling the dashboard. "I have to get out. I'll stand on the other side of the truck," Alexis said. The turquoise-and-white pickup was parked about a hundred yards away from the main entrance to the REBAR complex. They didn't know which way the truck would turn when it exited, so Alexis had moved a little bit of brush out of the way in case they had to make a quick U-turn.

Just before nine o'clock a tractor trailer's headlights almost blinded them as it made a sweeping turn into the driveway to the plant. They all ducked down. Maggie stretched her neck, Alexis peered over the truck bed, and Eileen snapped photos with a telephoto lens. The guard pressed a button inside the small hut and the gate swung open.

"This could be it," Maggie said in a loud whisper. The truck was unmarked, but it bore a commercial rental license plate and sticker. "Figures it's a rental."

Eileen read the numbers off the license plate and Maggie scribbled them down. She tore off the page of her notebook and handed it out the window to Alexis, who sent the information to Charles and Fergus.

The women had waited for over an hour when they saw the gate swing open again. Eileen and Maggie switched places to give Eileen free hands to tag the truck. The big rig took another sweeping turn from the lot and Maggie inched their way onto the road. Lying flat in the back on the truck bed, Alexis sent another message to Charles and Fergus:

ON THE MOVE.

It looked like they might be late for their nine P.M. virtual meeting. They had to be sure to tag the truck before it got to the port. Otherwise, it could get lost among the dozens of carriers waiting to be hoisted onto one of the cargo ships.

Izzie, Yoko, Annie, Myra, Zoe, Charles, and Fergus called in and gave their updates.

Annie went first. "Alexis got the routing number for the bank. Myra and I are going to the bank tomorrow to transfer funds to schools. Charles, do you have that list for us yet?"

"Still working on it, but should have something by the time you get to the bank."

It was Fergus's turn next. "Alexis sent the plates from the truck we believe is carrying the merchandise heading to Italy. I contacted someone who contacted someone at the International Maritime Organization. They are going to do a 'random' check." He raised his eyebrows, almost as if to salute. As the retired head of Scotland Yard, Fergus made every attempt to remain invisible and, if possible, anonymous. Using his complicated web of contacts in dozens of departments and organizations was a much better tactic then anything coming directly from "the gov," which could be considered interfering with matters that should not concern him. It was good to know people who knew people.

Izzie told everyone she was going to New York the next day to visit Zoe, who was also on the call. "I need to talk to a few of you offline later," Izzie said. She did not want to discuss Mason in front of Zoe.

Charles continued the conversation, bringing up Kathryn. "She was supposed to stop in Lincoln and deliver a trailer of bok choy to a grocery store chain, but she's making a detour and is heading toward Florence."

"How are the plans coming for the café and square?" Annie asked. "Did my contact Danny Lodge get in touch with either of you?" She directed her question to Izzie and Yoko.

"Yes, he phoned this afternoon. Yoko is going to meet with him tomorrow," Izzie said.

"Excellent. Anything else we need to cover?" Myra asked.

Everyone murmured about what was on their list. "Alright. Let's check in tomorrow. Charles, we'll be leaving for the bank around ten A.M."

"Right. Will have something for you in the morning." Charles was culling a list of schools that could benefit from Fielder's money.

Everyone signed off except Charles, Izzie, Myra, and Annie.

"Charles, you haven't found any connection between Mason and Walsh, have you?" Izzie asked.

"Nothing. The only thing they have in common is Zoe."

Izzie pursed her lips. "So strange. Maybe I should pay Ms. Phillips a visit while I am in the city."

"Are you sure that's a good idea?" Myra asked.

"Zoe really likes this guy. The first man who has garnered her attention since she broke up with Brian. I know she's heartsick about this. If anything, I'd like to give her some closure, even if it means verifying the guy is a creep. But it would be nice if he isn't. She's not taking any of his calls, and, if I know Zoe, she may never respond to him. When she closes a door, it's slammed shut, bolted, and sealed."

"I'll get you the info about the company Louise Phillips works for," Charles said.

"Are you going to tell Zoe?" Myra asked.

"I'm going to have to play it by ear. See what kind of mood she's in. If he's called again. That sort of thing," Izzie explained.

"Sounds like a good approach," Myra said. "Keep us posted. I'd like it if Mason was a stand-up guy, too."

Maggie was able to keep up with the semi and still maintain a safe distance. When they finally came upon an intersection, Eileen looked in both directions; leaning out the passenger window, she had a clear shot at the right rear. She pulled the trigger. It made the popping sound of a can of soda being opened. And then there it was, a luminous orange spot the size of a quarter, with an embedded GPS tracking device placed right above the rear taillight.

"Nice shot!" Maggie whispered in awe.

"I do my best." Eileen put the safety lock on the paint gun and put it back in the case. She pressed a button on the side of her watch. A very small light blinked back at her. "We got 'em." She transferred the data to Avery, who would continue to track the truck once it reached the port area. In turn, Avery would send the information to the inspectors at the port who had been alerted to "possible fraudulent documents and misinformation of content of goods." With this tip-off, the inspectors had license to check out a few other suspicious shipments while they were at it.

Maggie continued to follow the truck until they were approaching the security gates of the port. They had no documents, so they would not be granted access. "Is this where we say goodbye?" Maggie asked.

Eileen nodded toward the tractor trailer with the little orange button.

Maggie shrugged and sighed. "Better check in." She pulled

the pickup around to the side of a service road where they could remain relatively out of sight, but still see who came and went into the loading stations. It was a very long parade of trucks. Charles had told Maggie it would be several hours before the agents went into action.

There was a tremendous amount of maneuvering taking place, with containers, trailers, cabs and cranes, all orchestrated by the central planners. They had to be sure any toxic chemicals were stored away from other cargo and organized by destination. The trailers would be assigned to containers where they were lifted by large cranes. Sail guides held the trailers as they were stacked like Legos into the containers. A hatch cover would be placed on the first layer of trailers, and the process began again until the containers were full.

Keeping the facility safe was top priority. The Caribbean was a playground for unscrupulous activity. Uniformed security personnel were on high alert for terrorists, human trafficking, drugs, or weapons smuggling. Dozens of cameras demanded vigilance and observation of any possible hacking into the entire system, which could cripple an already battered supply chain still recovering from a pandemic and war. The port was still short on staff and tensions were high. Everyone was on their one last nerve.

Alexis remarked on how different the ships in the industrial port were from cruise liners.

"When you are a passenger on a luxury liner you have no idea what goes on behind the scenes," Maggie responded. "It's like the expression, 'You don't want to know how the sausage is made.' "

"Ew." Alexis's nostril twitched.

Maggie dug into her snack bag. She handed Alexis a protein bar and Eileen accepted a bag of trail mix. "I think we're going to be here all night."

Somewhere in the Midwest

Kathryn was racing against the clock to get to a popular truck stop that she knew some of her fellow travelers frequented, just outside of Toledo. It was almost midnight. Two more hours to go. Someone in the vicinity should be able to check if anyone was headed to Florence. She pulled into the big lot and parked her truck close to the back. She heard a voice calling out.

"Yo, Kathryn! What brings you to these here parts?"

Kathryn squinted and recognized Benny and Drew, partners in a big rig. Kathryn approached the two men. "Hey, guys. How's it going?"

"Ya know. Same. Traffic. Detours. Tourists," Benny replied. "And you?"

"I was headed to Lincoln, but I need some help."

"Fire away!" Benny said.

"It's a long story. Care for some breakfast?" Kathryn asked.

"Only if you're buyin'. But I'd rather have a burger," Drew answered.

"Whatever. It's on me!" She grinned and slapped the two men on the back.

As they entered the truck stop diner, Reba, the owner's wife, waddled over, with her permanent big grin flashing her two gold teeth, and a pot of coffee in her hand. "Howdy! Ain't you boys done eatin'?" She chortled.

Benny looked at Kathryn. "Truth up. We just had somethin'."

"Well, you can have more somethin'," Kathryn encouraged him. The place was relatively empty. Most drivers were back on the road, but to be safe she picked a booth in the far corner of the diner.

Reba followed them to the table. "Getting cozy?" she joked.

"You betcha!" Kathryn responded. "I know what I'm having. Two eggs, over easy, bacon, nice and crisp, grits and biscuits."

Benny was next. "Give me a double cheeseburger, bacon, and fries."

"I don't know where you put all that food," Reba remarked.

"Since Kathryn's buyin', I figure I'll find a place!" Benny said.

Drew chimed in. "Make it two burgers, bacon and fries."

Reba clicked her tongue. "Whatever you boys say."

"So, what can we do ye fer?" Benny asked.

Kathryn leaned in closer. "I heard there is someone who is messing around with construction materials."

"Heck, that happens all the time," Drew said.

"I know, but we have an opportunity to stop a potentially hazardous situation."

"Do tell." Benny leaned in closer. Kathryn's eyes almost started to water from the smell of his chewing tobacco.

"I need you to find the guy who is driving a load to Florence, Ohio. It's going to Riverwood Elementary School."

"Kids?" Benny looked horrified.

"Yes. A shipment of bad blocks is supposed to be delivered tomorrow morning, and I have got to stop it."

"What ya got in mind?" Drew asked conspiratorially.

Kathryn looked around the diner to be certain no one could hear her. "I want someone to meet up with me and swap trailers."

"Huh. In-ter-est-ing," Drew commented.

"We swap trailers and he delivers my load to the construction site."

Benny began to rub the stubble on his chin. "I dunno, Kathryn. That's a big ask."

"I'll make it worth his while. Or hers if there are any women out there."

Benny looked at Drew.

"You say all he's gotta do is deliver your trailer?" Drew asked.

"Yep. He's got the bill of lading from the manufacturer. He turns the load and the paperwork over to the foreman and moves on."

"What kind of trouble can he get in?" Drew asked.

"None, really. He can't help it if the dispatcher hitched the wrong trailer to his rig."

Benny nodded. "True."

"And he'll have all the correct documents," Kathryn reminded him.

"And you say you'll make it worth his while?" asked Benny.

"I will for sure." Kathryn winked as Reba brought over their food, balancing two plates on her left wrist. She set a plate down in front of Benny, then Drew, and Kathryn.

"Be back with those biscuits in a snap."

They waited for Reba to leave before they continued their conversation.

"If I hustle, I can meet up with him in two hours," Kathryn said.

Benny wiped the ketchup off his chin. "You're really gonna have to hustle."

"Yeah, but he won't be able to deliver the load until the morning when someone is on the lot."

"True, true," Drew agreed. The threesome then focused on their food, gobbled their meals and Kathryn placed a hundred-dollar bill on the table.

"Ooo-wee, lady. Got any more of that?" Benny exclaimed.

"Only if you're carrying bad concrete." She slapped him on the back again.

They walked over to Benny and Drew's rig. Drew pulled out his cell phone and opened the Trucker Path app. He did a search for anyone going to Florence, Ohio. Several seconds later he got a response from Willie Walnuts. He had gotten that handle hauling walnuts from California.

Willie called Drew in response to his message on the app. Kathryn leaned in to listen. "Got a load to deliver first thing. Getting some shut-eye. What's up?" Willie asked.

Drew looked at Kathryn for a cue.

"Tell him the truth. That you need to swap bad goods," Kathryn urged.

Drew obeyed and Willie replied, "What bad goods?"

"You're carrying a load of subpar blocks," Drew answered.

"What are you talkin' about?" Willie asked.

"Trust me," Drew said. "You gotta meet up with my . . ." He was searching for the right word.

"Colleague," Kathryn coached him.

"My colleague."

There seemed to be an interminable pause on Willie's end. Then he answered: "Okay. What time?"

"Tell him I can be there in two hours. Just name a place," Kathryn said.

Drew sent the info and Willie replied, asking them to meet at another truck stop just outside of Florence. Drew thought it was also a good idea to let Willie know he was meeting up with a woman.

"Lady's name is Kathryn," Drew explained.

"Lady?" They could hear the shock in Willie's voice. Even to this day there weren't a whole lot of female truckers. Maybe seven percent of the entire business.

"Yep. A good one." Drew smiled at Kathryn and then ended the call with Willie.

"I can't thank you guys enough," Kathryn said. "Just

think—you probably saved a bunch of kids a lot of injury."
She reached into her shirt pocket and pulled out two more
hundred-dollar bills and handed one to each of them. "Take
your ladies out for a nice dinner when you get home."

The men looked shocked. "Aw, Kathryn. You don't need
to do this," Benny protested.

"Put it in your pockets before I change my mind."

She gave them a quick salute and hopped back into her rig.
She gave two toots as she pulled out of the lot and pulled on
to the ramp for I-280, following it to I-90.

Chapter Twelve

Friday

Ohio

Somewhere around two thirty A.M., Kathryn spied the lights of the Buckeye Truck Stop and Diner. She wondered how many other similar spots in Ohio shared the same name. Kathryn spotted a guy who fit Willie's description: skinny with a scruffy beard, wearing a Grateful Dead T-shirt, tattoos on both arms, and a Super Mario cap. *Interesting wardrobe choice*, Kathryn thought. He was leaning against the passenger door smoking a cigarette. She walked in his direction. "Willie Walnuts?" she asked with a smile.

"You found 'im." He tipped his finger to the brim of his cap.

Kathryn held out her hand. "Kathryn Lucas. Nice to meet you. I really appreciate your helping out."

"Yeah. About that. I'd like to know more about this little scheme you have goin' on."

"Oh, it's not a scheme. But I don't blame you for being skeptical. Shall we go inside and have something to eat? Some coffee?"

"I could use somethin'." Willie pushed off from the truck and started walking toward the diner.

"I was wondering, how many Buckeye truck stops do you suppose there are in Ohio?"

Willie snorted. "Never thought about it. Maybe a dozen." He opened the door for Kathryn. "After you."

Once again, Kathryn surveyed the room, looking for some privacy. A young woman wearing a pink uniform appeared. Kathryn tried not to stare at her over-plumped lips. *Talk about a bee sting.* Kathryn had nothing against women doing whatever they wanted to look good, but some women took it way too far. She thought about something Annie had once said: "When it looks like you've had something done, then you've done too much."

Kathryn was still digesting the bacon from earlier, so once they were ensconced in a booth, she only ordered a cup of coffee. Willie ordered the "Three-fer Trucker Special," which consisted of a three-egg omelet stuffed with cheese, peppers, and onions, three pancakes and three sausage links. A side of grits and toast came with it.

While they waited for their order, Willie checked out the other customers in the diner. Two guys, who looked like they'd been on a bender and were taking some time to sober up, sat a few yards away. Even if they did hear anything, it probably wouldn't register. He leaned across the table. "Okay, Miss Kathryn. What's the deal?"

Kathryn conveyed the same story to Willie that she had to Benny and Drew. As he listened, Willie had an expression that made him appear be in a far-off land. Then he snapped back. "So, if I'm hearin' you correctly, there is a scam to use junk for building materials?"

"Basically, yes." Kathryn waited until he had a mouthful of food before she told him what he would be delivering instead.

He almost choked. "Cabbage?"

Kathryn's eyes went wide. "Shh."

He lowered his voice. "For real?"

"It's technically called bok choy, but yes."

Instead of putting up a fuss, Willie tried to stifle a laugh. "That's one way to get your greens!" He was truly amused at his own joke.

Kathryn had to agree. She checked the room again. The few people who were there weren't paying any attention. Kathryn pulled an envelope from her back pocket. She always kept a stash of cash in one of the door panels of her rig in case she needed it for an emergency. This qualified as an emergency. She slid the envelope across the table. "Two grand good with you?"

Again, Willie almost choked. That was more than he would make in ten days if he hustled. He swallowed and cleared his throat. "Yes . . . yes, ma'am. Happy to oblige."

Willie finished his breakfast without saying another word. He was still trying to digest the amount of cash in the envelope. Now his stomach held a Three-fer on top of it all. Kathryn signaled for the check. She also left this waitress one hundred dollars. People worked hard and a nice little show of appreciation could make someone's day.

Willie got behind his rig and disconnected the trailer hitch. Kathryn did the same. They jockeyed their cabs around so they would be in position for the switch. The entire process took less than ten minutes. They were both pros. Willie snapped a photo of the bill of lading for the inferior building materials and sent it to Kathryn's phone. He would ping her when his load was delivered.

Willie slowly pulled out of the lot and could immediately tell his new load was much more odiferous than the one before. He gave Kathryn a wave and a thumbs-up as he pulled away. Kathryn gave a big sigh of relief. She pinged Charles to let him know the bok choy was on its way with a copy of the BOL. He sent her instructions to stop at the next inspection station and gave her the name of one of the officers there. She wasn't sure what they would do with her cargo—but the important thing was that it was no longer a threat to elementary schoolkids.

Around seven A.M., Willie pulled into the construction site and parked the trailer as far away as he could from anyone's nasal passages. By now the smell of the rotting bok choy filled his cab. It might take days for him to get the smell out of his nostrils. He walked over to the foreman and handed him his clipboard and his tablet.

"You can leave the trailer where it is," the foreman instructed. "We won't be unloading it until Monday morning."

Willie suppressed a snort. Two more days in the sun would make for a very rancid stew. The foreman signed off on the documents and Willie hightailed it out of there, laughing all the way. He texted Kathryn:

Signed, Sealed, Delivered.

After Kathryn relayed the good news to Charles, he sent a message to everyone:

Phase One Complete.

Brooklyn

Donald Walsh was finishing his regular breakfast of cereal, orange juice, and instant coffee. He gazed around his small one-bedroom apartment. Sure, it was a step up from the railroad apartment he first lived in when he started at REBAR, but it was still drab and dank. He never spent any money on furnishings, depending on the local Goodwill to provide the basics. For a fifty-five-year-old man, he had very little to show for his life. A few bowling trophies and a stuffed bass he hung on the wall. He'd won it at a fishing tournament. It had been sheer luck. He knew little about fishing, but thought it would be good for him to develop another hobby, one that required fresh air. He kept stashing the extra funds from Fielder in a savings account, promising himself he'd move to a warmer climate and buy a boat. He heard there were some decent places in Alabama where he could live cheaply, something he was well accustomed to.

He cleared the old maple table with the mismatched chairs and placed his dirty dishes in the old enamel sink. Part two of his morning ritual was to buy the newspaper on his way to the subway station. The daily grind was wearing on him. He resented people like Malcolm Fielder, who had everything handed to them. But it was never enough for Malcolm. And now Donald was complicit in Fielder's scheme. There was something about that Zoe Danfield woman that bugged him. Even though she claimed she was satisfied with his answers, his gut was telling him something different. She had been too nice to him lately. Walsh knew if anything went sideways, he would be the one to take the fall. Fielder had more money for better lawyers. He decided to start checking out retirement communities and get a head start before anything hit the fan.

The creaking, noisy subway train rocked back and forth, jostling everyone from side to side. The straphangers continued to check their phones with one hand and steady themselves with the other. *Some life*, Donald thought to himself as the other passengers seemed to remain oblivious to the crush, smell, and noise.

For several months Donald had enjoyed periodic trips to the Dominican Republic, but Fielder had put a stop to it. Malcolm had said, "We don't want anyone recognizing your face."

"Then how will I be able to carry out your plans? The people and factories of Santo Domingo are not as hooked up with technology as we are," Donald whined, his resentment growing.

"I have every faith you'll figure it out," Malcolm had said dismissively.

Yes, it was time for a change. When Donald arrived at his office he searched the internet for "active retirement communities." Several popped up and he sent email queries using his personal email account. He knew Fielder had people in the I.T. department that could trace almost every search from the company's system. He gave himself a short window. His exit strategy would start over the weekend, and he would go to the bank first thing Monday morning and withdraw his funds. He'd give his landlord thirty days' notice, but planned to be out as soon as he could, even if it meant heading south with no forwarding address. Which wasn't really a bad idea.

Santo Domingo

The sun had been up for over an hour. Alexis, Maggie, and Eileen had taken turns catching a few z's in the truck parked outside the port entry. Now Maggie began to squirm. "I have to pee."

Alexis and Eileen groaned in unison. They looked around for vegetation, but there were only a few straggly trees along the side of the road. Maggie remembered spotting a gas station about a quarter mile down the road. They decided Maggie and Alexis would dash over while Eileen kept vigil. Once they returned, Eileen would take her turn. She was much better at holding her bladder from all her time doing surveillance, but she still hoped they would hurry. As the two women rounded the bend, Eileen received a group message from Charles:

Trailer confiscated. Well done. Phase Two complete.

Eileen sent back a "woo-hoo" emoji and started the truck. The girls would be happy they didn't have to walk back, and Eileen was elated she wouldn't have to wait much longer to use the restroom. She caught up with the women as they were walking out of the dismal restroom. Maggie and Alexis ran up to the truck, where they did a couple of high-fives and fist bumps for good measure as Eileen bolted past them into the dingy bathroom.

All three of them felt a sense of relief—in more ways than one. A feeling of jubilation filled the pickup on the ride back. "I'm going to miss this thing," Maggie said as they were pulling up to the Monaco Residences.

"Yeah, I was growing rather fond of it myself." Eileen laughed and elbowed Maggie.

The three dispersed to their apartments and took long, well deserved hot showers. Maggie ordered a breakfast tray of muffins and scones and Alexis ordered massages for all of them. Eileen made a dinner reservation at Nacan, a beautifully restored former bank turned restaurant. The three would spend the remainder of the day recouping from their midnight-to-dawn adventure.

Grand Cayman

Annie and Myra were once again up with the birds. It didn't matter how many missions they had been on—they were always giddy when things were coming to a head. They had their coffee on the terrace and took a walk on the beach. Mac had promised a continental breakfast for them when they arrived at the bank.

When they got back to their suite a list of twenty deserving schools was waiting for them from Charles. They changed

into more appropriate outfits, gathered their things, and proceeded to the bank.

Mac greeted them in the lobby with a big smile. "Good
morning! How is everyone today?"

"We are just ducky," Annie replied.

"Sensational," Myra added. *At least we will be in a short
bit*, she thought to herself as Annie gave her a little tap with
her elbow. At this point in their lives they could almost read
each other's minds.

Mac ushered them into his private office, where a sideboard of breakfast pastries, quiche, fruit, smoked fish, and
an assortment of beverages was displayed on the credenza.

"Mac, you are going to make me fat!" Annie exclaimed.

"Nonsense." He smiled and gestured to the sideboard.
"Please. Enjoy."

They spent about twenty minutes enjoying light conversation and the delicious offerings. Both Annie and Myra were
trying to contain their excitement and anxiety. Until the confirmation of the account status came through, anything could
go horribly wrong.

Mac sat behind his desk and put on his reading glasses.
Annie handed him the paper with the account information.
His computer was situated where only he could see what was
on the screen. He typed a few keys, and then another set of
numbers, and then a third password. "There are two million
dollars in the account," Mac reported.

"That sounds about right." Annie nodded as if it was her
own account.

Annie pulled out the list of schools along with the name of
their respective banks. "I would like the money to be divvied
up and sent to each of these." She turned the list over to
Mac. "One hundred thousand per school."

"I can have someone get the routing numbers. Just give me

a few minutes." He switched off his computer, got up from his desk and walked out to the lobby, where he spoke to a colleague.

Annie couldn't hear what Mac was saying but she could see from their body language that nothing was amiss. She tapped Myra on the knee and gave her the "okay" sign with her thumb and forefinger. After what seemed like an eternity, Mac returned to his desk. "Very well. We'll close out this account and put the money in escrow until we get all the routing numbers for the schools. If there are any issues, I will certainly let you know." He returned to his computer and went through the same process of security passwords. He typed a few more numbers, and then a few more. He looked up from the monitor. "The account is officially closed." Then he waited.

Annie was so distracted by the word *closed,* she almost forgot to hand over the check for two million! Myra tapped Annie's knee with her own. "Oh, Mac, before I forget . . ." Annie opened her purse and presented him with the check, but this time the account would be in her name, with her own private account number. The relief in Mac's face was obvious. Not that he didn't trust Annie, but moving large sums of money required much finesse.

"Thank you, dear Countess," Mac said with great appreciation.

"Always a pleasure doing business with you, my dear friend." She stood, followed by Myra.

Mac walked from behind his desk and approached the two women. "It would be nice if you could stay on our patch of paradise a little longer, no?"

"Yes. Yes, it would," Myra answered.

Mac gave the women a kiss on both their cheeks and walked them through the lobby to the large glass doors. They bid each other farewell and then Annie and Myra linked arms and skipped down the sidewalk.

As soon as she was able, Myra sent Charles a text: **Phase Three Complete.**

Charles answered with: **Bravo!**

"I think we should reward ourselves," Annie said.

"What do you have in mind?"

"Parasailing?"

"Have you gone mad?" Myra squealed.

"Kidding. But a stroll through Chanel might be nice. We can pick up a few presents for the girls."

"I like that idea." Then Myra stopped short. "What about Fielder and Walsh?"

Annie raised her eyebrows. "I shall fill you in as we browse the shop."

"I like that idea, too!" Myra said with glee.

South Beach, Miami

Malcolm Fielder was doing his morning workout on his Peloton bike as his mind sailed across the Miami Beach skyline. He was lucky he'd gotten into the condominium complex when it was first opened. It had almost tripled in value. He thought about his mother's chastening him for his extravagant lifestyle. In this particular case it had paid off. Now, with plans in place to continue that lifestyle, he was rather proud of himself. Or at least his ability to make money. Shady money. But wasn't that how most people made their millions now? If it wasn't hiding it from the government, it was crazy tax shelters, or hostile takeovers. Even inflating one's worth was a way to get people to invest in projects. It was one scheme after another. Less than a handful were ever caught and even fewer prosecuted. With his elaborate plan it could be years, even decades before any of the foundations gave way. He would be long gone before paramedics arrived at the scene. It gave him a bit of a thrill thinking about a family sharing a holiday meal and having no clue they could be sitting on potential quicksand. His greed was only matched by his evil nature.

After his workout he strolled into the lavish master bathroom with the six-foot ultramodern shower stall. One wall was made of natural stone and the others were clear glass. He turned on the tower of shower heads, each with variable pressure. The pulsating water hit all the right spots on his back. It was relaxing and invigorating at the same time. When he was done, he placed a lush Turkish wrap around his waist and phoned his assistant.

"How are the plans coming for tomorrow night?" he asked.

"All set, sir. Hors d'oeuvres, champagne, and a playlist of cool jazz for your sound system. The caterers will arrive at four, as will the servers."

"Perfect!" Malcolm almost had an erection thinking about the lavish party he was going to throw for his posh friends on his new yacht.

His assistant continued. "The yacht has arrived and is docked as per your instructions. And the Aston Martin dealership is expecting you around two o'clock this afternoon for your test drive."

"Perfect!" Again a tingle. He would ask the dealership if he could keep the car over the weekend. And why wouldn't they allow it? He was dangling the fine sum of three hundred thousand dollars in front of them. Well, not exactly all of it. He would make a down payment and finance the rest.

"Will there be anything else, sir?" his assistant asked.

Malcolm could barely manage his delight. He would be

fashionably late for his own party, arriving in the Frosted-Glass-Blue Aston with Glacier Blue interior. It was a beauty. He'd paid the marina director extra money to get a berth close to the parking lot and a parking space close to the pier. "Just be sure you're on time to greet the guests. And when you see the Aston pull up, make sure you announce my arrival."

New York

Zoe checked her watch. It was already past noon. She made a list of things she needed to do before the weekend. Kyle sauntered in and plopped down her tickets to *La Traviata* as he whistled the melody of "Brindisi." He pirouetted and left. Zoe called out, "Bravo!" He turned and took a bow. Zoe could always count on Kyle to keep the mood light.

A few hours later Kyle made the announcement, "Company!" as he ushered Izzie into Zoe's office. Zoe was genuinely happy to see her friend. It was the one thing she was looking forward to. Working at REBAR had taken its toll since she'd discovered what had been going on. And then there were all those calls and texts from Mason. A good friend would be the distraction she needed.

"Hey!" Zoe shouted and gave Izzie a big hug. "So, so happy to see you!"

"Ditto!" Izzie said. "How are you doing?"

"Meh." Zoe shrugged.

"We're going to fix that."

"I sure hope so." She lowered her voice. "I don't know how long I can keep up this front of pretending I love my job."

Izzie winked. "I hear ya." She cleared her throat. "There's something you and I need to do."

"What is it?" Zoe looked concerned.

"I'll tell you while we are on the way. I'll leave my stuff here," Izzie said.

"Where are we going?" Zoe asked.

"You'll find out. Keep your shirt on."

As they walked out, Zoe placed her hand on Kyle's shoulder. "Why don't you wrap it up? It's the weekend."

Kyle spun around in his chair. "You're aces, boss!"

Izzie looked at Kyle. He reminded her of the actor who played Jamie in the Progressive Insurance commercials. "Did anyone ever say you looked like an actor?"

He propped his hand on his fist. "You mean like Chris Hemsworth?"

Zoe tried not to laugh. "I can't see you throwing lightning and thunderbolts!"

"You've never seen me dance!" He batted his eyes.

"I still think you're handsome even if you aren't a Norse god." Izzie chuckled.

"You girls have fun! Don't do anything I wouldn't do!" He gave them a finger-flutter wave.

Zoe rolled her eyes at Izzie. "That leaves a *lot* open."

When they reached the sidewalk they saw Sasha sitting on her bike. Izzie nodded and made a gesture indicating Sasha could call it a day. They hailed a taxi and Izzie gave the driver the address. It was in the fashion district on Twenty-Ninth between Seventh and Eighth Avenues.

"Okay—where in the world are we going?" Zoe asked.

"To visit a Miss Louise Phillips."

"We're going where?" Zoe was shocked. "But why?" She was close to livid. "How could you do this?"

"Trust me on this. Please." Izzie placed her hand on Zoe's arm. "Really. You want to get to the bottom of this, right? So trust me."

Zoe was almost hyperventilating. "I can't believe you . . . we are doing this."

"Relax."

Zoe sat back and sulked. "How do you know she'll be here?"

"I made an appointment."

"You did what?"

"Please, Zoe. Take a few deep breaths. It's going to be alright."

"Yeah. Says you."

"Exactly."

The taxi made a turn off Seventh Avenue. The neighborhood looked much the same as it had almost a century ago, with old stone buildings, crowded streets, and racks of clothes being pushed by vendors down the sidewalk. The taxi stopped in front of one of the more tired-looking structures. The two climbed out of the cab and pushed a broken button over a worn nameplate that read EMPIRE STATE INVESTIGATION SERVICES. A garbled voice asked who it was and Izzie announced herself. A moment later the buzzer let them in the old wooden door.

They climbed an equally old set of steps to the second floor, where they found another old door with frosted glass and the name EMPIRE INVESTIGATIONS inscribed on it. Izzie rapped on the door.

"Come in!" a male voice called out.

Izzie cautiously opened the squeaky door. She blinked. It was as if she'd stepped into a time capsule circa 1930, in a Dashiell Hammett novel starring Sam Spade. She was expecting to see a man in a zoot suit wearing spats and a woman with a short, wavy bob, seamed stockings and a fox stole. And both would be smoking cigarettes. But the man was wearing a long-sleeve polo shirt, jeans, and Nike sneakers. The woman looked more the part in a shirt-waist polka dot dress.

"Hi. We're here to see Louise Phillips," Izzie announced with Zoe standing behind her.

"Sure. Come on in." The man jerked his head toward the woman sitting in the corner. As Zoe passed his desk he asked, "Have we met before?"

"Met? No," she replied dryly.

The woman at the desk stood, gasped, and began to stutter. "I . . . I . . ."

"Yes, *you*." Izzie pointed to the woman's chair. "*You* have some explaining to do."

Zoe and Izzie sat down in the vintage wooden chairs across from the very nervous woman's desk. They both folded their arms and glared at Ms. Phillips. "Explain yourself," Izzie ordered.

Louise took a huge breath. "It's not what you think. Thought."

"How would you know what I am thinking?" Zoe snarled. "Or is it because you've been stalking me that you presume to know what I am thinking?"

"No! No. That's not it. Really." The young woman's English accent was bleeding through her reinvented American accent.

"Then what. Is. It?" Izzie punctuated each word.

"It was for my Uncle Mason."

"So he hired you to follow me?" Zoe fought valiantly to keep her cool.

"No! Not at all." Louise's eyes went wide. "He's quite cross with me now." She nervously shuffled some papers on her desk.

Izzie leaned forward. "And why is that?"

Louise regained some composure and began to explain. "Uncle Mason was always talking about this Zoe woman. Zoe Danfield. How smart Zoe was. How interesting Zoe was. How cool and fashionable she was."

Zoe bit her lip to keep herself from smiling.

"Anyhoo, I could tell Uncle Mason was rather smitten with her and was gutted when she left England."

"*She* is sitting right here." Zoe scowled at her.

"Yes. Of course. Sorry. My apologies. I wasn't expecting this."

"I am sure you were not. Please continue," Izzie directed her.

"Uncle Mason had a bad go of it with his previous girlfriend. I knew he was quite besotted with you, Zoe." She looked directly at her. "My boss asked me to pick someone and follow them for a week. It was part of my training. To file a report, that is." She took another deep breath. "Uncle Mason said he might take a holiday and visit New York, but I wanted to be sure he wasn't going to walk into a situation where he would be horribly crushed."

"Therefore, you chose me as your assignment," Zoe concluded.

"Yes. Exactly." Louise lowered her head. "I meant no harm. Honestly. In fact, you can thank me for keeping you from bouncing onto the subway tracks."

"That was you?" Zoe exclaimed.

"I saw someone nudge you and I was worried you might lose your footing, so I grabbed your sleeve."

Zoe was mystified.

"I don't think you would have fallen, but crowds on subway platforms can be dangerous. I knew if anything happened to you, Uncle Mason would be devastated."

Zoe stared blankly. She was speechless, as was Izzie.

"I promise you Uncle Mason had nothing to do with my actions. I take full responsibility. When I told him, he was in the hospital and was thoroughly cheesed off. If you don't believe me, you can ask him."

"Hospital?" Zoe sprang forward.

Louise looked surprised. "Yes. Didn't you know?"

Zoe felt a huge pang of guilt. "No. I did not. Is he alright?"

"He's getting on. A sprained ankle. He's back at his flat now."

"But what happened?" Zoe asked with alarm.

"Something about a scaffold falling. A few feet of difference and he would have been a goner. Lucky, he is."

Izzie and Zoe remained silent for a moment and then Zoe pulled out her cell phone and dialed Mason's number.

"Zoe?" Mason answered immediately. "Is everything alright?" He was truly concerned. "I've been trying to reach you for days."

"Yes. I know. I'm very sorry about that." She pushed the speaker button so everyone could hear their conversation. "I'm sitting in an office in the Garment District with a woman named Louise Phillips."

Mason's voice boomed through the speaker. "You're where? What? Louise?"

"Yes, Uncle Mason. Zoe and her friend Izzie are here."

"But why? How?" Mason was totally befuddled.

"Honestly, Uncle Mason, I don't know how they found me. I suppose they are better detectives than I am." Louise frowned.

"I should think so." Mason was filled with mixed emotions. Zoe had finally called him back. That was good. She and Izzie were with his niece. He wasn't sure how to feel about that.

Zoe spoke next. "Mason, I'm so glad we were able to unravel this situation."

"But how did you find Louise? Did she explain I had nothing to do with it all?"

"Never mind the first question. As to the second, yes, she explained it was an assignment. For both your and her own benefit."

"Yes, that's what she told me." Mason, too, was feeling relieved. "Zoe? May we speak privately?"

"Of course." She pushed the speaker button to the off position and moved to a more private corner of the room. "How are you feeling? Is your leg alright? How did it happen? Too many questions?"

"You can ask as many as you want. I'm much better now that you've called. Leg is better. Lots of bruises. Not exactly sure what happened, but an Inspector Crenshaw of the building authority was here to speak to me. There is going to be an investigation." He didn't want to tell her he would likely lose his job. That was a conversation for another time. If there *was* another time.

"What do you suppose happened?" Zoe asked.

"I really have no idea. Thankfully no one was on the platform at the time or it could have been deadly."

Zoe furrowed her brow. *Both of them had recently avoided deadly accidents. Coincidence?* She made a mental note to discuss this with Izzie. Perhaps Fergus could have someone check into it. "I'm so glad you're alright."

"All in one piece." Mason smiled into the phone. "They put me on leave." He paused. "I was thinking of taking the time to go down to Cornwall."

"Sounds lovely. I so enjoyed our weekend there." Zoe smiled back.

"Do you have any holiday time?" he asked.

"Holiday?" Zoe thought, running through a mental list: *Thanksgiving, Christmas, Fourth of July . . .*

"Vacation," he clarified.

"I do, actually." *Vacation* and *likely unemployment,* she thought to herself.

"Do you think you could find the time to cross the pond and join me?"

"I would be delighted," Zoe cooed. "When did you have in mind?"

"Week after next?" he asked.

"Perfect." It would give her time to plan and get kitty-sitters. Then it dawned on her that he hadn't said for how long. "Oh, and how long will we be there?"

"How much time do you have?" he asked.

"Let's say ten days?" Zoe didn't want to overstay her welcome, and the cats would have hissy fits if she stayed away for too long. For real.

"Splendid." Mason's voice was jubilant. "Just send me your flight details and I'll do the rest."

"Mason?" Zoe's voice grew softer. "I am so happy you called."

"I'm chuffed."

"Chuffed?"

"Over the moon," he replied.

"I need to learn more of your idioms."

"I teach a master class."

"I promise to be a good student."

"I have no doubt."

"I better go. Louise and Izzie are dying to know what we've discussed."

"No doubt."

"Talk later." Zoe ended the call. She practically floated across the room.

"Spill!" Izzie demanded.

"Yes! Do!" Louise echoed the request.

"I'm going to take a holiday in Cornwall with Mason." Zoe was blushing.

"Blinding!" Louise shouted.

"Excellent!" Izzie concurred. "Our work here is done." She got up from her chair. "Louise, I could say it was a pleasure meeting you."

"You mean it wasn't?"

"It's lucky for you that things turned out the way they have." Izzie was an inch away from scolding her.

Louise looked sheepish. "Glad I wasn't a blighter."

"There is an entire vocabulary I have to learn." Zoe laughed.

Louise scrambled out from behind her desk and threw her arms around Zoe. "I am so happy you're not a trollop."

Izzie and Zoe howled, said their goodbyes and left the office, but not without Izzie snagging one of Louise's business cards. You never knew when you were going to need an extra gumshoe.

By the time they left the building, it was rush hour. People were moving in all directions. They stood on the corner for several minutes before they could catch a cab. "You must be relieved," Izzie said as they waited.

"I'm flabbergasted. I don't know how to thank you, Izzie. I would have written him off. Period. End of story."

"I'm glad that it's the beginning of a new one." Zoe finally flagged down a taxi and gave him the address of her office.

On their way up Sixth Avenue, Zoe explained the scaffolding accident to Izzie. "It sounds like it could have been deliberate," Izzie observed.

"Yes. There is going to be an investigation." Zoe sighed.

"We will have one of our own." Izzie patted her friend's knee and pulled out her cell phone. "What's the name of the building again? And when did this happen?" Zoe gave her the details and Izzie immediately sent them to Fergus with a brief explanation. If anyone could investigate something, it was the former head of Scotland Yard.

They pulled up in front of the office building and went inside. The place had pretty much emptied out. When they got to Zoe's floor, it was empty, which was not a big surprise for a Friday night. Just to be sure, Zoe did a quick walk around her corner of the floor. It was deserted. The two women went into Zoe's office and closed the door. "Lock it," Izzie instructed. "We don't want anyone interrupting us."

Izzie pulled out a small electronic device and checked for any hidden audio or visual surveillance. Nothing turned. Fielder and Walsh were probably depending on tracking Zoe's movements via her computer. But they were not expecting the magic touch of Izzie Flanders.

Zoe gave her a quizzical look and Izzie responded, "That shipment to Ohio was not in your files, correct?"

"Correct," Zoe answered.

"Which means there are probably a whole lot more you don't know about."

"True. But I didn't want to risk searching for anything else."

"That's why you have me." Izzie winked and sat in Zoe's chair. Izzie was able to access the mainframe without using any passwords. Zoe was quite impressed.

"Wow. I knew you were good, but this is exceptional."

Izzie searched for anything that contained the words *El Cemento*. Over a hundred jobs came up on the screen. Izzie plugged in a thumb drive and copied them. "I'll send this on to Charles."

Zoe was dumbfounded. "How did I miss all this?"

"Because there was no way for you to find out. Fielder and Walsh had them password protected once they suspected you were on to them."

"But you . . ." Zoe trailed off.

"Abner is an excellent teacher." When the download was complete, Izzie erased all traces of her intrusion. She pushed her chair away from the desk. "Shall we go?"

Zoe looked around her office. She knew she wasn't coming back. She couldn't. Wouldn't. She took the one personal item off the wall. It was a chalk sketch she'd drawn when she was in high school. It was of a bridge. She tucked it under her arm and then thought about Kyle. "Izzie, I feel badly about Kyle. He's an excellent administrative assistant. Fielder will toss him out when he discovers I'm not coming back."

"We can fix that." Izzie handed her a business card. "Just give him this."

Zoe quickly wrote a note:

> Dear Kyle,
> Apologies for the short notice, but I am taking an in-determinate leave of absence. Please call Jack Emery as soon as you read this note. Tell him Izzie sent you. I wish you all the best. You're aces.
> Warmly,
> Zoe

She placed the note and Jack's card in an envelope and left it under a paperweight on top of Kyle's desk diary, already opened for the coming week.

Izzie placed her hand on Zoe's arm. "He's going to be alright. I promise. But he has to get in touch with Jack."

"Wasn't he a prosecutor?"

"Yes, he was. Now he has a private law firm."

"With Nikki?"

"No, but they often work together on cases. Especially the ones where people don't have the money for good legal counsel."

"You have a marvelous group of friends." Zoe sighed.

"Yep. Them's my peeps! Come on, before you change your mind."

"No chance of that happening." Zoe let out a big burst of air. "I feel as if I've been holding my breath for days."

"I know the feeling," Izzie said. "But you are starting a new adventure. You should be excited."

"I don't think all of this has sunk in yet. It's been quite a whirlwind. So much has happened in just a week."

"That's how we do things. We don't like to waste time. Important information can get lost. People disappear." She chuckled. "I mean, those who disappear on their own."

Zoe gave her an odd look. "Dare I ask?"

"Nope." The elevator doors opened. Zoe stepped in and didn't look back.

Chapter Thirteen

Saturday

Cayman Islands

Myra was sitting on the terrace of their suite, enjoying the view and her morning tea. She picked up her phone and called Charles.

"Good morning, love. How is my girl today?" Charles sounded very chipper. "I'm looking forward to seeing you tonight."

Silence.

"Love? Everything alright?"

"Yes, Charles. Everything is fine."

"You sound a bit distant, aside from the miles."

"Charles, when was the last time you and I had a holiday?"

He paused for a moment.

"Exactly," Myra broke in. "I can't remember when either. We've talked about it, but we never do it. There always seems to be something urgent we have to tend to."

"I can't disagree. What do you have in mind?"

"What if you came down here for a few days after we finish this mission? Nikki can look after the pups."

"That sounds like a marvelous idea."

"How much longer do we need to wrap things up?" Myra asked.

"Fielder's Cayman account is empty. The IRS will be freezing whatever assets he may have. That should come down on Monday."

"What about Walsh?"

"Seems like he's planning on skipping town on Monday. Heading south from what we could glean from his internet searches. A stopover in Nashville and then he booked a motel just outside of Mobile. Of course, if things go according to plan, he'll be canceling that reservation. Or should I say someone from our group shall?"

"But not until Kathryn has him," Myra said.

"Correct," Charles concurred.

"What about his bank accounts?" Myra asked.

"We're not going to touch him until he's several hundred miles away. If he thinks we're on to him, he might alert Fielder and we could lose them both."

"And then what?"

"Now that we know why Louise Phillips was following Zoe and she's no longer on her tail, we'll send Sasha to Walsh's and place a GPS on his car. Kathryn is going to have to make a hairpin turn from Ohio. After she releases the trailer to the authorities, she'll head to Nashville and catch up with him there. I already booked her a room at the same motel where he made his reservation."

"What about Pearl?" Myra stroked her own pearls at the same time.

"Pearl is awaiting instructions. She has the oil barrels and cement. What else does she need?"

"Annie hasn't shared the final details. Every time I ask she just giggles."

"It's not like her to keep anything from you," Charles said.

"I know, but I think she's saving it as a surprise. I'm fine with that. I know whatever she has up her sleeve will be perfect justice." Myra chuckled. "But back to my original question."

"Holiday?"

"Yes, Charles, a holiday. Just you and I." Myra was quite serious. "I'll keep the suite while Annie and I finish up in Florida and then meet you back here."

"What about Annie?"

"I'm sure she will understand. Plus, she has to get back for a board meeting."

"My next question—if Walsh is in Tennessee and Fielder is in Miami, how will Pearl be able to do her job?"

"Annie has her private jet. I am sure we can use that to transport Fielder to a shared destination with Walsh."

"Brilliant."

"Speaking of brilliant, Annie just came out to the terrace." Myra turned to Annie and said, "Speaking to Charles."

Annie leaned in and called out, "Mornin', Charles!"

Myra put her cell on speaker phone.

"All right, Annie!" Charles called back.

Myra gave Annie a quick rundown of what Charles had already shared. "And I have some intel from Fergus," Annie replied.

"Charles asked about getting Fielder and Walsh in the same place so Pearl can relocate them together."

Annie's eyes brightened. "This is what I'm thinking. The dealership has allowed Fielder the use of the car he's buying over the weekend. An extended test drive, if you will. Just to be sure he wants to keep it. But when he gets to the dealership on Monday, he'll discover he *can't* keep it. He will be informed the account from which the deposit was drawn was closed late Friday. Of course he'll start making phone calls, but Mac will not be available for Mr. Fielder. That in turn will cause Fielder to have a major conniption. Account closed? No car? He will be mortified. I'll happen to be at the dealership at the same time to overhear the conversation. Next he'll get a phone call from his bank in New York telling him the IRS has frozen his funds. He will have to get back to the city, but can't use his credit card, which has also been frozen. He'll be on the verge of hysteria at that point. I'll introduce myself at that point and tell him I'm on my way to New York. I'll offer him a seat on my private jet. Again, an offer he couldn't possibly refuse. While we are in flight, I'll slip him something to help him relax." She winked at Myra and snickered. "While he's unconscious, the pilot will fly us to Nashville, where we will meet up with Kathryn, Walsh, and Pearl."

"Sounds like you women have it all in hand," Charles said proudly.

"There are a few loose ends. We have to get Mr. Segundo a new job. I'm going to ask Mac to take care of that. Izzie gave Zoe Jack's card, to help her assistant Kyle get other work. He'll also be mincemeat when the hammer comes down on REBAR. Speaking of which, when do you think that will happen?"

"First, I'm putting a call in to the FTC, SEC, and every other alphabet in government agencies. Even with the best lawyers, Fielder will never dig his way out of this. I am certain his family isn't going to help bail him out of this mess, and he won't have the money. Secondly, we won't know what dark place he'll be spending the rest of his days."

"And Walsh?" Myra asked for clarification. "What about his cash reserve?"

"What's that expression? He's a dumpster fire in a trainwreck?" Charles laughed.

Annie began. "According to Fergus, Walsh's cell records show he phoned the bank late Friday morning. Most banks don't have that much cash on hand and need twenty-four hours' notice.

"Chances are he will have cash on him, especially if he thinks he is putting a down payment on a place to live. We'll take what we find on his person and forward it to one of our charities." Annie paused. "Then he and his cohort will be sent to Pearl's parts unknown." She couldn't help but chuckle. "But not without a little suffering first."

"Are you finally going to tell me what you have in mind?" Myra pressed. Annie whispered in her ear. Myra roared. "That is hilarious!"

"Care to share?" Charles asked.

"Later, darling," Myra said. "I need to talk to Annie now. Bye."

"Talk to me about what?" Annie gave her a sideways look.

"I'm going to stay down here for a bit longer. A week. Charles is going to meet me once everything is sorted."

"Oh, Myra, I think that's wonderful!" Annie gave her a big hug. "You both deserve some R and R."

Myra placed her hand on Annie's arm. "Sure you don't mind?"

"Mind what? Mind that my best friend wants some alone time in a beautiful tropical setting with her husband? Don't be silly." Annie kissed Myra on the top of her head. "I couldn't be more pleased."

"Thanks, Annie. I'll let the concierge know I'll be staying on."

"No, you won't. I'll take care of that." Annie was going to surprise Myra and Charles with a romantic dinner on the terrace as soon as Charles arrived. And, of course, a lovely bottle of bubbly.

"Let's go over the rest of the plans," Myra said.

"I'll stay on another day and keep you company. I'll fly to Miami tomorrow so I can accidently bump into Mr. Fielder on Monday. By Monday evening we should be winging our way to Nashville." Annie picked up her phone. "I also need to speak to Mac about Mr. Segundo." She dialed his private line.

"Countess! Again, I have the delight of hearing your voice. Is everything alright?" Mac asked nervously.

"Yes. Everything is quite fine. I decided to stay another day and Myra is going to stay on through next week. Her husband, Charles, is going to meet up with her."

"That's wonderful. I know it is very difficult to leave this island. So to what do I owe the pleasure?"

"I need a favor."

"From me? What could I possibly do for someone of your stature and wealth?" His tone held sincerity rather than flattery.

"There is a very nice gentleman in Santo Domingo who will be in need of a job."

"And how can I be of service?"

"He has meticulous management skills. Not necessarily in banking, but general office management. I was wondering if, by any chance, there might be an opening for an office manager in any of your branches in Santo Domingo. And if not, surely you must know someone at another bank?" Annie was businesslike but also kind.

"As you know there has been a mass exodus from Santo Domingo over the past two years. There must be some openings. How soon do you need this to happen?"

"Monday would be ideal."

"As in . . . the day after next?"

"Yes, Mac, as in the day after next."

"We close early on Saturday. That will give me about three hours to see who I can reach."

"Please make it sooner. The man cannot go to his current place of employment on Monday."

"Is he in some kind of trouble?" There was growing concern in Mac's voice.

"No. Not him personally. I really can't get into the details, but I want to protect him."

Mac was envisioning guns. Annie could sense his trepidation. "Nothing violent, Mac. Let's just say he's been working for some very bad people who are about to get into a lot of hot water, and not from a tub. He's an innocent bystander, but chances are they will close down the company he works for and he won't have a job. He has a wife and family."

Mac was relieved. "And you say he's on the up-and-up?"

"You have my word," Annie said. Even though she had never met the man, Alexis's word was as good as her own.

"Alright then. I am going to need some information."

"Yes, of course. Give me a few minutes and I will get right back to you. Mac, I truly appreciate what you are doing."

"Countess, if this is important to you, then it's important to me as well."

"Thank you. Will be back in a flash." Annie quickly phoned Fergus. "Hello, cookie." She loved teasing him. "Can you send me the dossier you have on Alberto Segundo from the REBAR plant? I've asked Mac to get him a new job and he needs a bit more information than the man's name and my word."

"Right. Will send now. Talk later, my sugar plum." Fergus gave it right back to her.

Annie snorted. "I just love that guy," she said as she hung up the phone.

About a minute later a Word document appeared on her tablet's screen. It was all there: Alberto Segundo's full résumé and background information. He was an upstanding member of a small community outside of Santo Domingo. No criminal record. Married for twenty-three years, with two teenage boys. He volunteered at his church's soup kitchen and coached his kids' rugby team. Before REBAR he was a clerk at a big hardware supply store and became the section manager. Several years later he was offered a job at REBAR as the assistant to the plant manager. When the plant manager retired everyone moved up the ladder, including Segundo, who took on the responsibility of Plant Manager. According to the chain of command, he eventually became the person who made sure everything ran on time. Plant Manager. He was the boss. As much of a boss as he could be. He had no control of the size of the jobs, nor did he control where they were being shipped. But keeping the office operating efficiently was something he did control, and he did it well without bullying. He was respected and liked by his staff.

Annie finished reading. "I think he will be a valuable employee wherever he goes." She forwarded the information to Mac.

Brooklyn

Donald Walsh hadn't felt this level of excitement since his bowling team won first place in the Borough Bouncers League. He eyed his trophy. It was one of the few things he could call his own. Every stick of furniture came from a thrift shop. The mismatched dishes were from his mother and two grandmothers. He could barely make a place setting with all of them combined. But he didn't care. He never had dinner guests, nor did he want any. There was nothing he cared to bring with him except his clothes and his television set. It was his one splurge: a seventy-five-inch Samsung Neo QLED 8K.

It took up most of the wall. One could argue it was a tad too big. At first it was unnerving to see people on the screen with heads much bigger than your own. But he would just pretend he was in the front row at the movie theatre. Not ideal, but so what.

He knelt down next to the Early American–style maple bed, also from Goodwill. Two black nylon duffel bags were covered with dust. He remembered when he took his first trip to Santo Domingo. Fielder called him into his office and advised him to make sure he had respectable luggage. Right then and there Walsh wanted to punch Fielder in the mouth, but he didn't want to smash the face of the man who was about to feed him. Walsh once again made a quick trip to a big-box store and purchased two inexpensive matching nylon duffel bags. They were presentable enough. At least they didn't have holes in them.

It dawned on him he would need to wrap his television. He smiled at how clever he'd been to keep the original box just in case something went wrong with it. That, too, was under his bed.

He tossed the two duffel bags on the bed and began to pack. He decided to take only one of his blazers. Just in case. In case of what, he had no idea. Maybe he'd make a lady-friend down there. They said Southern women were the most charming and friendly. Maybe someone like Susan Sarandon in *Bull Durham*. It hadn't occurred to Walsh that Durham was in North Carolina. Not Alabama. But like many people born in New York, anything south of the Mason-Dixon Line was the South to him.

He shook himself out of his daydream of meeting a beautiful woman, although the thought of meeting *any* woman hadn't crossed his mind in years. He smiled to himself. Things were about to change. Little did he know exactly how much.

New York

After their meeting with Louise Phillips and then hacking the REBAR central data base, Zoe and Izzie dropped off Izzie's overnight bag, said hello to the kitties, and went to a local café a block away from Zoe's apartment. When they finished dinner they decided to bring some New York–style cheesecake back to Zoe's and completely unwind. Before they went to bed they promised they would sleep in and hang out in their pajamas the following morning.

Zoe was the first one up, thanks to Betty and Buster. They didn't care how tired their mommy was. They wanted breakfast. And if Zoe didn't feed them, they would find the remote to the television and turn it on. She reminded herself every night to put it in a drawer. If they couldn't access the remote, they would find something to knock off her desk or the counter. As long as it made a loud noise, they didn't care. Betty was the blabbermouth of the two, meowing orders for Zoe to move faster.

"Shush . . . we have company," Zoe said as she tiptoed past the second bedroom, which doubled as Zoe's home office. Or vice versa.

"I'm awake," Izzie called out.

"Sorry. Did we wake you?" Zoe asked.

"Nope. First it was the garbage trucks. Do they always come by at three in the morning?"

Zoe pursed her lips. "I haven't noticed."

"And ambulances? Do they come around often?"

"I also haven't noticed." Zoe made a curious face. "I seem to be immune to the noise."

"I guess that's a good thing if you're going to live here."

Zoe entered the room where Izzie was lounging on the bed. "You know, that's kind of scary. I remember one time when I was at a convention in Las Vegas. We were in a huge, relatively new hotel. One morning when I went down for breakfast, one of my colleagues asked me where I was during the fire alarm. 'What fire alarm?' I asked. And then they told me. An alarm went off around four A.M. and I slept right through it. I was horrified. But then when I got back home, it occurred to me how lucky I was that the hotel hadn't gone up in a blaze."

"That *is* scary. Was there a fire?"

"No, just some smoke from the kitchen, but it got through a few vents and set off the alarms." Zoe shook her head. "There is so much you become immune to when you live in a city like New York."

Izzie clutched one of the pillows in front of her. "I suppose you have to."

"True. But that doesn't mean it's a good thing." Zoe frowned. "You have to wonder how oblivious you've become."

"Speak for yourself, girlie," Izzie joked. "I'm only oblivious when Abner is discussing things I know nothing about."

"But hasn't he taught you lots of stuff?"

"Oh, sure. But so much of it is data drivel." She rolled her eyes. "So how about some coffee?"

Betty and Buster were complaining about being ignored. "Them first," Zoe said and exited to the kitchen, where she pulled out two small cans of cat food. Each of her pets had their preferences. Betty liked chicken; Buster preferred salmon. Zoe chuckled to herself about how similar cats were to people.

Izzie padded into the kitchen and pulled out a bar stool. "I never understood why kitchens in New York were so small."

"I think landlords have a deal going with the local restaurants and takeout joints."

"I mean, it's not like people don't cook. I cannot imagine raising a family with a toy-size oven and stove."

"I remember those when I was a kid. When I first moved in here I had something that looked like it was from the 1950s."

"Speaking of kids' toy kitchens, I saw one that was going for almost two thousand dollars!" Izzie remarked. "You can buy a regular-size range for that kind of money."

"That kid better end up on the Food Network." Zoe laughed. She pushed the plunger down on the French press. "Cream?"

"Oh yes, please. I never understood putting skim milk in coffee. Why bother? I get it if you're going to drink a glass and are concerned about the fat content, but please. A tablespoon of cream isn't going to kill you."

"But drinking lousy coffee can!" Zoe chuckled. "I'm a coffee snob."

"What time is the opera?" Izzie asked.

"Matinee is at two. Then dinner reservations at the Union Square Cafe."

"Fabulous! So what are you wearing?" Izzie asked.

"A long black skirt, tank top, and a jacket."

"Fancy?" Izzie cocked one eye.

"I'll show you." Zoe scurried into her room and returned with a black, white, and gray patchwork leather jacket with big black buttons.

"That's gorgeous," Izzie remarked. "I'm going to look like a plain Jane next to you."

"I seriously doubt that," Zoe said.

"It's the opera. I am sure I'll look like a hillbilly."

"Then you can borrow something of mine." Zoe eyed her up and down. "How about that turquoise pantsuit I wore when I went down to visit you? I had it dry cleaned the other day."

"Really? I'll feel so chic!" Izzie said with excitement. One

wouldn't call Izzie plain. Not by any stretch of the imagina-
tion. It just so happened she wore simple clothes. Business
casual clothes that were appropriate for her work.

"Done!" Zoe said with a grin. "I always wanted to dress
you."

Izzie snorted and her coffee shot out of her nose. When she
regained her composure and wiped her face she replied, "Better than *un*dressing me."

"Not that there's anything wrong with it," Zoe and Izzie
said in unison.

Later, when they were both dressed and ready, Izzie looked
at their reflection in the mirror. "We look fabulous!" she proclaimed.

They took a taxi to Lincoln Center and were escorted to
their seats. Fifth row, center—probably the best in the house,
both visually and acoustically. The production was masterful
and the entire audience could not help but sway back and
forth during the first act as the cast sang "Brindisi (The
Drinking Song)," one of the most famous arias of all time.
But years before the opera had been written, Alexandre
Dumas wrote *La Dame aux Camélias*, the story of Marie
Duplessis, a twenty-three-year-old woman who was considered the most fashionable courtesan in Paris. The story,
thought to be true, became the inspiration for Verdi's opera.
The themes were love and class discrimination, as the viva-
cious heroine, Violetta, succumbs to consumption. But before she dies, she asks her closest friend to donate her money
to the poor.

The performance brought the audience to their feet, with
tears and applause that went on for almost fifteen minutes.
Izzie and Zoe kept swapping tissues during the curtain calls.

As they were leaving, Izzie turned to Zoe and said, "That
was one of the most remarkable experiences I have ever had.
The energy in the room. Incredible. At the risk of using an

overused word, that was totally awesome." She dabbed her eyes with another crumpled tissue.

It was now late afternoon and they decided to walk several blocks down Broadway, their arms linked as they hummed the familiar strains of the opera. They passed several people along the way who were also humming and singing the same refrain. It was a glorious experience, especially when shared with total strangers. Several streets later, when the energy of the opera-goers had waned, they hailed a taxi and started downtown to the Union Square Cafe, Danny Meyer's flagship restaurant. "I love eating at his restaurants," Zoe said during the cab ride. "They support many of the local food banks and educational programs for underprivileged kids. Plus the food is so, so good."

"Zoe, you are spoiling me." Izzie smiled as she watched the interesting architecture—old and new—of New York pass by.

"It's the least I can do. I believe you saved my life."

"Me and the Sisters."

"For sure." With that, Zoe gave Izzie a high five.

Santo Domingo
Earlier that same day

Maggie and Eileen had a leisurely morning and were waiting for Alexis to join them for breakfast. They no longer needed their disguises, but Maggie was beginning to like the sleek look of her hair. "Maybe Alexis can show me how to do this," she said as she ran her fingers through her smooth mop.

"You may need to get one of those Brazilian straighteners," Eileen commented.

"I've heard of Brazilian waxes, but not straighteners. What are those?"

"For someone who is in the news industry, your lack of fashion know-how is mind-boggling," Eileen teased.

"I work in news. Fashion isn't news, even when they pretend it is. The Met Gala has become a circus sideshow. I don't get it."

"I think they consider it art."

"That reminds me of a story I did about how the worth of art is calculated."

"And?"

"It's as much as anyone is willing to pay. Take that non-fungible-token stuff. You pay for something you can't touch, or hang on your wall, or place on a shelf. It's a unique digital identifier that can't be copied or substituted through what they call a blockchain."

"You're losing me," Eileen said.

"Precisely. It's all digital and has come under a lot of scrutiny. Some say it's the equivalent of a Ponzi scheme and others defend it by comparing it to cryptocurrency. I dunno—I still like to feel those green bills in my wallet."

"I'm with you on that part. I have to admit that technology is what pays my bills. Without it, I wouldn't be as good at what I do."

"Eileen, you are one smart woman. I think you'd be great regardless of what tools were at your disposal."

"Thanks. Yes, I've had to count on my wits on many an occasion."

"That's what I'm talking about."

There was a knock at the door. Maggie thought it might be Alexis. Instead, it was a messenger. "Maggie Spritzer?" he asked.

She was almost afraid to answer him. "Yes. I'm Maggie."

"This is for you." He handed her an envelope. "Please sign here."

Maggie wasn't sure what to do. She held the pen in the air. "Can you tell me who it's from?"

He checked his paperwork and said, "It says, 'The Countess.' "

Maggie breathed a sigh of relief, although Annie rarely sent her anything via messenger. "Just a moment." She pulled a ten-dollar bill from her wallet and handed it to the gentleman.

"Thank you. Enjoy your day." He turned on his heel and walked down the hallway as Maggie watched with a confused look on her face.

As the elevator opened to let the messenger in, Alexis walked out. Maggie gave her a vigorous wave to hurry her up.

"What is it? Everything okay?" Alexis asked.

Maggie closed the door behind them and showed her the large white envelope. "It's from Annie. Or so he said. All three of our names are on it."

"Well, don't just stand there—open it!" Alexis insisted.

The three women huddled together as Maggie gingerly peeled opened the envelope. Inside was a note:

> *Maggie, Alexis, Eileen,*
> *You've done the Sisters proud. Excellent work deserves excellent praise and a little fun. Please spend the next three days as my guest at the Excellence Club in Punta Cana.*
> *Big hugs,*
> *Annie.*
> *P.S. A car will be picking you up at eleven, so get busy. Maggie, don't forget sunscreen!*

"Wow. That boss of mine is the bomb!" Maggie exclaimed.

Alexis and Eileen were equally ecstatic. "I don't remember the last time I had a real vacation," Eileen said.

"You mean sleeping in a pickup truck isn't your idea of rest and relaxation?" Maggie joked.

"Not one bit."

"But I brought snacks!" Maggie pouted.

"You need to get a handle on your dietary needs," Alexis kidded.

"How long have you known me?" Maggie asked innocently.

"I could say 'way too long,' but I don't want to hurt your feelings." Alexis gave her a grin.

"Gee, thanks. You're such a pal."

"Like the note says, get busy. We need to pull our stuff together pronto!" This time it was Eileen who was bossing them around.

"Aye-aye, captain!" Maggie saluted, scooted to her room and then stopped abruptly. "We don't have any resort clothes with us."

Alexis was still holding the envelope in her hand. "Wait, there is another envelope in here. Inside is a thousand-dollar gift card with another note." She read the note aloud. " 'Buy some appropriate clothing. I don't want you to look like you just fell off a turnip truck.' "

"Who me?" Maggie said defensively. The two other women laughed.

"As we were discussing earlier, you're not known for your fashion sense." Eileen laughed.

Maggie stuck out her tongue. "Well, all we really need are bathing suits and a couple of sundresses. I think I can figure that out."

Alexis sent a thank-you message to Annie, as did Maggie and Eileen. Then the women hustled, as instructed. They gathered up their things and skipped down the hallway to the waiting elevator. As promised, a car was waiting to take them for a much-deserved weekend of pampering, sun, and sand.

Miami

Fielder had filled out all the required paperwork before he was able to drive his new car off the lot. At the moment, it was technically still a test drive until the final approvals came through. After he left the dealership, he drove the car through Coral Gables to see how many other people had a similar vehicle. He only spotted one and it was a few years older than his model. He was tempted to try to talk his way into one of the gated communities like Star Island or Hibiscus Island, but thought better of it. It would take only one phone call from security to have the Miami-Dade police asking him questions. Not a good way to end the day. Instead, he pulled up to Bagatelle on Collins Avenue, making a big fuss with the valet about being careful with his car. Unfortunately most of the valets were accustomed to obnoxious patrons and Fielder was no exception. He sauntered into the exclusive eatery and slipped a fifty-dollar bill into the hostess's hand. It was the only way he was going to get a table without a reservation. He ordered an expensive bottle of wine and flirted with several women who were sitting at a nearby table. Before he paid the check he asked the waiter to deliver his business card to the table of nubile females. On the back he wrote: *Party. Tomorrow. Six. Venetian Marina. Yacht named "Superlative."*

It would have been more gallant if he had bought them a drink, but chivalry was not in his wheelhouse. There was no room. His overblown ego took up all the space.

Now it was a new day. His yacht was secured at the marina and he was on his way to give it a good look. As he crossed the Venetian Causeway he was riding an enormous high. Everything was falling into place for him. His only complaint was his office in Santo Domingo, which he rarely visited. If he kept bringing in new work he might suggest moving the office to a much more luxurious island. He'd promise larger contracts and a wider reach. It was entirely possible, but he knew he would have to actually do some real work. But it would be worth it. In five years he could retire to the South of France or Barbados or wherever he wanted to be. With all the jobs he had lined up and with Walsh doing his bidding, the world would be his oyster.

As he approached the marina his excitement was off the charts. Sexual ecstasy couldn't match what he was feeling at that particular moment. Two crew members dressed in official regalia were positioned at the top of the gangway to his yacht.

"Welcome aboard, sir. I'm Captain Reggie Tucker. A pleasure to meet you in person, sir."

Malcolm shook the captain's hand. "Indeed."

Captain Tucker proceeded to introduce Fielder to First Mate Douglass Walters. "A pleasure, sir. Shall I give you the tour, sir?" Tucker asked.

"Certainly," Malcolm replied. He had seen the boat weeks earlier, but now that it was going to be his, he wanted to familiarize himself with all the amenities.

They started in the grand salon and made their way to the master suite, fully appointed with a king-size bed. The VIP suite was on the forward deck and there were also two guest suites, one on the port and the other on the starboard side. The lounge featured a bar with six stools, a circular sofa and a large LED television and a Bose sound system. It would be a vacation home on the seas. Enough space for a half dozen people to be completely comfortable. Malcolm met the rest of the crew, including the engineer, who made his home in the underbelly of the boat. The engine room was even more pristine than the galley. No one was allowed to wear their shoes in the room in order to keep all dirt particles from the intricate electronics. Booties were issued to anyone going below deck.

Malcolm made his way to the bow, where he stood looking out at all the other vessels. He felt like Leonardo DiCaprio in *Titanic*. He was the king of the world. For now.

Crew members began to assist the caterer who was setting up glassware and the bar. Satisfied things were going as planned, Malcolm bid everyone adieu, saying he was looking forward to the soiree that evening. As he walked along the pier he eyed the other yachters to see what they were wearing. It was nothing like he expected. Most had on chino pants, with the women in capris. It wasn't as glamourous as he'd imagined. He wondered if perhaps they dressed more formally in the evening. He pondered what his attire should be. He didn't want to be over-the-top—but then again it was *his* party.

Just as he was about to climb into his shiny sports car, one of the people from the catering company came jogging toward him. "Excuse me. Mr. Fielder?"

He stopped and turned. "Yes. What is it?"

"My boss just called and said your credit card was denied."

"That's impossible," he said with a hint of arrogance.

"Would you like to speak with her?"

"Certainly." He took the cell phone from the young woman's hand. "This is Fielder. What seems to be the problem?" He listened, but didn't quite understand what the woman on the other end of the line was telling him. "That's not possible." He listened again. "I see. Unfortunately, I don't have another one on me." Suddenly he had to back off his arrogance. "If you don't mind, I can bring another card later this afternoon or pay you by check." Again, he listened. He thought throwing his family name into the conversation would alleviate the caterer's concern. "Surely you know my family, the Fielders. The liquor store Fielders." The color began to return to his face. "Yes. That was my grandfather." The person on the other end said a few more words and Malcolm responded with, "I am terribly sorry for this issue. A total misunderstanding, I can assure you, and I will get it resolved by this evening. Thank you for your consideration. Yes, here she is." He handed the young woman her phone. "It's all been arranged." Then he got into his car in a slightly less jovial mood.

When he got back on the causeway, he resisted the temptation to floor the accelerator. A speeding ticket would send him over the edge. He hurriedly parked, taking up two spaces in the lot of his condo building. He didn't want some guileless idiot putting a ding into that beautiful metallic paint, especially since he wasn't yet the official owner. He would have to pay for the damages in full.

Once he'd stepped inside his condo, the first thing he did was call the credit card company. It was a Saturday and for whatever reason, credit card companies didn't have enough staffing over the weekend. *Isn't that when most people shop?* he mused. *As long as they had your money, they were able to charge double digits on unpaid balances. So why would they care when you shopped?* It was a scam, and he was able to justify his own misdeeds by comparing them to even bigger ones. As far as he was concerned, the system was rigged. Therefore, why shouldn't he rig it for his own benefit?

Malcolm spent what felt like an interminable amount of time on hold, listening to insipid music on a loop. Finally, a woman who could barely speak English got on the line. By then, steam was coming out of his ears and he laid into her like a punching bag. It was no surprise that she disconnected the call. He dialed again, this time screaming into dead air as the same tune played on and on. He was infuriated, but resisted the temptation to throw his phone across the room. He didn't have time to buy a new phone on this particular day, a day that was moving much too fast. His guests were arriving in four hours. He poured a shot of tequila and sat staring out at the Miami skyline, trying to calm his nerves. He told himself it would all be okay. He'd bring a check for the caterer and deal with the customer service nitwits on Monday.

As the Casamigos Reposado began to flow through his veins, his mood improved. No wonder it was a very popular tequila. It proved that its founder George Clooney was not just a pretty face. Fielder made up his mind to focus on the present and prepare for the party. But as hard as he tried, he couldn't escape the feeling of trepidation that was beginning to deflate his earlier exhilaration.

To Nashville

The government freight and cargo inspectors were efficient, polite, and expedient in processing Kathryn's paperwork. *If only the rest of the government performed the same way*, she thought to herself. Drug trafficking was a huge problem, so the inspectors had to be on top of things. But in her case, it was claims for subpar concrete and not fentanyl. Easy-peasy for the authorities. It was also helpful that they had already been informed by some people at the top.

After Kathryn finished up she got a little shut-eye in the sleeper compartment of her semi. By noon she was ready for the seven-hour drive to Music City. Annie had made a reservation for Kathryn at the Vanderbilt Hotel, where she would stay until Monday. Then she would be relegated to the no-tell-motel where Walsh also had a reservation. Even though she was accustomed to sleeping in her truck, a real bed with clean sheets was always a luxury. The Vanderbilt was an indulgence. Annie and Myra always looked out for the Sisters, especially when they were putting their own safety at risk. Whenever possible, they were remunerated with some niceties, and for Kathryn this was bliss.

She took a long, hot shower and climbed between the sheets to finish the sleep she desperately needed. She had asked for a wake-up call at five P.M. Her plan was to go to Martin's Bar-B-Que Joint and then on to the famous Bluebird Café. Garth Brooks and his wife, Trisha Yearwood, had been known to show up there unannounced and sing a few duets. Kathryn was looking forward to an evening of anything but diner food with a diverse group of people, some good music, and then winding down in a soft, comfortable bed.

Chapter Fourteen

Sunday

Brooklyn

Donald Walsh checked all the drawers in his dresser. Empty. The two duffel bags were stuffed. Whatever he wasn't going to bring with him, he was dropping off at Goodwill. After all, they'd provided most of his amenities, if you could call them that. He planned on leaving a note for the landlord that read: *You can rent this as a furnished apartment.* He then checked around to be sure there was no paperwork or anything that could reveal his trail. He didn't know who might come looking for him, but he wanted to take no chances. He even planned on bringing his garbage with him and tossing it in some strip mall dumpster along the way.

He realized he was being a bit paranoid, but he had good reason. It was just a matter of time before the hammer fell on REBAR. Someone somewhere would figure out they'd been shorted on the quality of their goods. Heaven forbid it became an incident where lives were at risk. But wasn't that the case all along? He hadn't given it much thought before that Danfield woman started sniffing around. He knew the blocks were solid enough. Enough to last maybe twenty years. It would take an earthquake, or a flood, or a hurricane, or a lot of stress for anything to come tumbling down. But that was the problem. There were too many earthquakes, floods, and hurricanes of late. Fielder had assured him that no one would be put in harm's way, but Donald had grown skeptical, especially after Fielder halted Donald's trips to Santo Domingo. He was sure Fielder had even more to hide than he let on. Donald couldn't wait until he crossed the Delaware Memorial Bridge on Monday afternoon. He would be on his way to a new location. A new life. He wondered what had taken him so long.

Cayman Islands

Annie and Myra were packed and rip-roaring-ready to get to Miami and finish off this nasty business of Malcolm Fielder. They sat on the terrace and enjoyed a last cup of tea before they boarded Annie's jet to Florida. Before they checked out, Myra phoned the front desk and made another reservation for the end of the week. "I'll be back on Wednesday," she said to the desk agent.

"I am so very happy you and Charles are going to spend some quality time together. It's not like you don't spend quality time together, but here, in such a tranquil, peaceful place . . . it will refresh your souls," said Annie.

"You're right about that. All of us have been in high gear with one mission after another. It's time Charles and I pampered ourselves." Myra giggled. "And each other."

Annie cackled. "Glad I won't be around for all the moaning and groaning."

"Don't be fresh." Myra giggled again. "Young lovers on the beach. Well, young in heart and in spirit."

"If I had a glass of champagne, I'd drink to that!" Annie smiled. The phone in the suite rang. It was the concierge telling them the car was waiting and he would send up a bellman to get Annie's bags. Myra was leaving hers with the bell captain. No sense in lugging luggage. She wondered if that was where the word came from.

"Okay, my friend. Off to spank Mr. Fielder and slap Mr. Walsh," said Annie.

"From what you told me, your plan is to do much worse."

"Of course. I was downplaying."

The flight to Miami took an hour and a half. While aboard the jet, Annie checked in with Fergus via phone.

"How are things coming along?" she asked.

"Splendid. Sasha planted the GPS on Walsh's car so we'll be able to track his moves as soon as he leaves. Your appointment at the dealership is at eleven, the same time Fielder is due there to sign the paperwork. When he arrives the dealership will tell him they were informed by the bank that his account has been frozen by the IRS. His check is rubbish. While he is on hold with his bank, he will get a phone call from his office saying the contractor at Riverwood Elementary wants to know why there is a trailer of rotting cabbage at the job site."

Annie could not help but howl in delight.

"Ten minutes afterward he will get another hysterical phone call from the New York office saying the U.S. Marshals service is confiscating all of their computers." Fergus paused to take in some air. "Approximately five minutes later he will receive a similar phone call from the REBAR plant in Santo Domingo. That phone call will be interrupted by the condominium association in South Beach informing him the U.S. Marshals have installed a padlock on his condo. If everything runs according to plan, his world will unravel within the timeframe of twenty minutes."

"And that's when I step in to save the day," Annie hooted.

"You'll invite him for a drink and offer to fly him to New York."

Annie jumped in. "Where I will slip something in his

drink to make him go nighty-night. Once we arrive in Nashville, Kathryn will meet us at the airport and we will shuttle Mr. Fielder to the motel where she will locate Mr. Walsh."

"Which is when you are going to do exactly what to them?" Fergus had been waiting for Annie to share her plans, but she wasn't ready just yet.

"Patience, my dear." Annie smiled.

The Aston Martin dealership was on Bird Road in Coral Gables, so Annie and Myra opted to stay at the Mr. C Miami hotel, less than a ten-minute drive away. Also close by was the Vizcaya Museums and Gardens. The women arrived at the hotel by one thirty and decided to visit the former estate of John Deering of the Deering-McCormick International Harvester fortune. Both had been before, but it never got boring.

Built during the Gilded Age, between 1914 and 1922, the main house with its Mediterranean architecture boasted over forty-five thousand square feet, with thirty-four decorated rooms open to the public. It was surrounded by ten acres of meticulous formal gardens and a mangrove shoreline on Biscayne Bay.

The two women marveled at the commitment to art, culture, and history that the magnificent historical landmark displayed. Myra turned to Annie as they passed one of the fountains. "One can easily forget we live in a different century and in a completely different world. It was only a hundred years ago. Mankind has done a lot of damage in a very short time."

"Makes one wonder how we got to this messy place in the world today."

"Because rarely has a woman been in charge." Myra chortled and linked her arm through Annie's.

Around four o'clock the guides discreetly advised the visitors that the gardens would be closing in a half hour. Annie sighed, reminding herself of the tasks ahead. "Back to reality," she muttered under her breath.

No stranger to the social trappings of wealth and society, Annie knew the best places to eat weren't necessarily the most expensive. She recalled a wonderful bistro in Little Havana where she and Myra decided to have dinner. Even though the mission wasn't complete, Myra had a very relaxed manner about her.

"Thinking about your getaway with Charles?" Annie inquired.

Myra gave her a whimsical smile. "Maybe you and Fergus should consider taking a holiday as well. But somewhere other than the Cayman Islands." She hooted.

"We wouldn't think of ruining all your fun and games." Annie knocked her knee into Myra's, giving her a raised eyebrow. "But first, we have a mission to complete."

When they returned to the hotel, Myra texted Pearl to confirm the arrangements. Pearl responded with: **All systems go.**

The women giggled at what was to come.

New York City

Zoe rode with Izzie to Penn Station. They stopped at a coffee kiosk before Izzie had to board her train. Zoe's eyes got misty. "I don't know how to thank you for everything you've done."

"It's not over yet," Izzie said. "We still have a lot of loose ends to tie up."

"For sure. But your boyfriendvention—my new name for boyfriend intervention—probably changed my life. I say *probably* because I don't know where it will lead, but at least I am going to take this one seriously."

"Zoe, you deserve to be with someone who treats you as if

they've won the lottery. Because having you in their life means they have been given a gift. Don't let your mind go astray. Think good thoughts."

Now the tears were falling. Zoe wiped her eyes.

"I don't recall ever seeing you cry this much in all the years I've known you," said Izzie.

"Ha. I don't think I have cried this much, ever!" Zoe smiled as her nose dripped.

Izzie handed Zoe a napkin from the coffee shop. "I am so happy you'll be going to visit Mason. It will do you a world of good."

"The big challenge will be coming back. I won't have a job."

"But you'll have Betty and Buster."

Zoe sniffled. "But they are so lazy. They refuse to go to work!"

Izzie chuckled. "I know. I have the same issue with Rufus. Lazy bum, that one."

An announcement for the Acela to Washington, D.C., came over the loudspeaker. They gave each other big bear hugs. "Ping me when you get home," Zoe called out as Izzie descended the escalator.

When Zoe got back to her apartment she sent Mason a text: **Making my travel plans. What's good for you?**

He wrote back: **As soon as you can get here.**

Zoe sat on the sofa and cuddled with Betty and Buster. "Listen, you guys, Mommy is going on a little holiday." She remembered what Sonya Fitzpatrick, the British pet psychic, once told her about letting your pets know you will be away. According to Ms. Fitzpatrick, animals don't know what a clock is. They measure time by daylight and night, so you must tell them you'll be gone for whatever amount of darks. You also must tell them who will be taking care of them. When Zoe first began traveling, Buster would climb into her suitcase and pee while Zoe was packing. She heard Fitz-patrick's television show, and out of desperation Zoe made a phone appointment with her. Zoe was astounded at what the woman told her about Zoe's personal life; things Ms. Fitz-patrick could not possibly know. It was worth a shot, and sure enough, Fitzpatrick's advice worked. Zoe hoped it would work again.

After her little cat-chat, Zoe called the airline company and made a reservation to Heathrow for the following Wednesday. Once she got her confirmation she sent Mason another text. He replied immediately:

Blinding!

Zoe remembered that meant "excellent."

Chapter Fifteen

Monday
D-Day

Brooklyn

Donald Walsh could barely sleep the night before. He couldn't remember the last time he was this excited. His only concern was being able to stay awake for the fifteen-hour drive. It would be close to midnight before he got to the motel. He arrived at the bank at eight forty-five and waited for it to open. They were expecting him, so the transaction wouldn't take very long. So he hoped. At the stroke of nine A.M. the security guard appeared and unlocked the double glass doors. Walsh grunted a good morning and scurried to the first available teller.

"Hello. Donald Walsh. I phoned Friday about closing my account."

The teller smiled. "Yes, Mr. Walsh. A manager will be with you shortly." He was not expecting that response. Did he think someone was just going to turn over a bag of money to him?

"Please have a seat." The teller gestured to a waiting area

outside a glass-enclosed office. An *empty* glass-enclosed office. Donald steadied himself. *There's no rush*, he told himself. But he couldn't help feeling panicked. He felt as if the
walls were closing in on him. Instead of sitting, he paced.
Then he realized he was drawing too much attention to himself. Maybe the security guard would think he was there to
rob the bank. *Sit down. Relax.* It was times like these when
he wished he hadn't given up smoking. But then again, if he
wanted to smoke he would have to do it fifteen feet away
from the entrance. He began tapping his foot. *Stop. Relax.*

"Mr. Walsh?" The voice almost sent him through the
ceiling.

"Yes. I'm Walsh."

"Please come in." The manager ushered him into the small
glass cube. "I'm sorry to hear you will no longer be banking
with us."

"Er, yeah. I have an opportunity to purchase some property down south."

"You know we offer a service—"

Walsh cut him off. "I know, but this transaction requires a
cash deposit." He was getting fidgety.

"I see. If you don't mind signing a few documents, we can
have you on your way." The manager slid a sheaf of paper
across his desk. Lots of words Walsh didn't have the time to
read. He signed the papers quickly and slid them back.

"Thank you. If you'll follow me, please." The manager
rose from his chair and walked to a door with a combination
lock and an electronic swipe device that recorded each entry
and exit to the vault room.

Walsh's palms were sweaty. He'd never handled this much
cash in his life. The manager and assistant manager counted
the packets twice before they handed them over to Walsh.

"Mr. Walsh, please sign this document stating you received

fifty thousand in cash, thereby closing your account," the manager said.

Walsh's hands were trembling while the manager looked the other way. He stacked the neatly banded bills in the nylon bag that once carried his good shoes. *Not a bad replacement*, he thought to himself. He thanked the managers and followed them back to the lobby, where he scooted out the door. When he got in his car, he sat for several minutes until his hands stopped shaking. He wiped the sweat from his brow, started the engine and began his journey to a new beginning.

Miami

Annie, Myra, Fergus, and Charles got on a group call first thing in the morning. Charles began to explain that in order to complete the plan someone from the Men of the Sisterhood would impersonate Fielder with a fake passport and an airline ticket to Montenegro. "We want it to appear he fled the country to a non-extradition destination."

"The passport will have Ted Espinosa's face and Malcolm's name. Should make it through security without any issues. Once Ted lands in Montenegro, he'll return using his own passport, which has been "updated" by our outside associates indicating he entered Montenegro earlier, thus avoiding any issues at customs and immigration," Fergus clarified, referencing one of the Sisterhood's other allies.

"Perfect," Annie said. "What about Walsh?"

"Someone with his likeness will cross the Mexican border, where it will be assumed he disappeared. He has no family and is a loner, so chances are no one is going to look for him except the feds, and they will have a photo of him crossing the border."

"Excellent," Myra chimed in. "Annie, you all set for your performance as Fielder's savior?"

"Indeed I am. I shall be heading over to the dealership shortly."

"What about Segundo?" Myra asked.

"We have that covered. He'll be alright," Annie assured her.

"I'm sure Alexis will be happy to hear that. She felt badly that he was an unwitting accomplice."

"We'll take care of that issue," Charles said firmly. "There is no evidence he had any knowledge of the corruption going on. He was never on the premises when the coal ash was delivered and did not know exactly what the load was or what was being shipped. It was always at night."

"What about the guard at REBAR?" Annie asked.

"His job was to check the drivers' credentials. If they passed, he let them in," Fergus answered.

"And the truck drivers?"

"Their job was to deliver a load. No one asks questions down there. They do as they're told."

"After reviewing all the transactions, thanks to Alexis, it appears that Fielder was the mastermind and everyone else just did his bidding. He was, in fact, the boss."

"Got it," Annie replied.

"So, we're good to go?" Myra said.

"Indeed we are," Charles answered. "See you soon." He gave Myra a devilish grin.

Santo Domingo

Alberto Segundo was on his way to the plant when his cell phone beeped. The text message read:

Please report to the school.

In a panic, Segundo pulled over on the side of the road and sent a text back:

Who is this?

The reply was the same:

Please report to the school.

He quickly turned the car around and drove toward his son's high school. He tried to maintain the speed limit, but he was alarmed by the vague instructions. Nothing like this had ever happened before.

When he arrived at the school, he dashed up the stairs and into the reception area. "¿Qué está mal?"

The secretary looked at him curiously. "Señor Segundo? I don't know what you're talking about."

"I received a text to come to the school immediately," he said, and showed her his phone.

She shook her head. "That did not come from the school."

Segundo was as perplexed as she was and said he didn't understand. The woman shrugged her shoulders and repeated that the message hadn't come from the school and perhaps it was a mistake. A wrong number. Segundo began to calm down and walked back to his car. As he was about to start the engine his phone rang. Again, an anonymous number. He answered. "Hello?"

"Mr. Segundo. This is Estelle Johnson," said Alexis.

"Yes, Miss Johnson." He cleared his throat. "I am running a little late. I received a text from my son's school, but it was a false alarm."

"Mr. Segundo, I am about to tell you something, and you must listen carefully and follow my instructions."

"Please explain what this is all about." His morning was getting much too peculiar.

"What I am about to tell you may sound like a work of fiction, but I am asking you to trust me."

"I am listening," he said, halfheartedly at best, but he hoped the conversation would lead to some clarity.

"The reason you were directed away from the plant is because it is about to be seized by the government."

"That is ridiculous!" Segundo was losing his patience. "I barely know you and I am supposed to believe you?"

"Mr. Segundo, I was sent there to check on certain things, which I am not at liberty to discuss. All I am asking is that you do not go to the plant but go straight home."

"And then what am I supposed to do?" Segundo's temper was starting to rise.

"There will be a letter waiting for you. It will have arrived by special messenger. Please follow the instructions."

"And if I don't?" Segundo was getting weary of this perplexing conversation.

"Please, Mr. Segundo. Just follow these instructions and you will be okay."

"What do you mean I will be okay? Are you threatening me?" His voice was at a much higher pitch at that point.

"No. I am trying to protect you."

"From whom?" By now his voice was at maximum volume.

"People at your company were involved in illegal transactions."

"Illegal? I have never done anything illegal in my life!" He was roaring at this point.

"Yes, we know, which is why I am trying to protect you. Please, Mr. Segundo, just go home." Alexis ended the call, hoping he would listen to what she said. There was no point in arguing any further, as she couldn't divulge any additional information.

Alexis looked at Maggie and Eileen. "I'm not sure he was buying it."

"You did your best," Maggie said sympathetically. "If he doesn't follow your instructions, it's on him now."

"You're right." Alexis sighed. "Let's hope for the best."

Alberto Segundo stared blankly at his phone. He felt as if he'd inadvertently stepped into an undercover spy novel. Little did he know he wasn't far from the truth. He decided to drive to the plant to see if there was any unusual activity, per the phone conversation he'd just had. As he made the turn on to Calle Nicolás de Ovando he spotted several police vehicles in the front parking lot along with several employees. He shuddered. Maybe that woman was telling him the truth. His phone rang again and he jumped. It was one of the secretaries, crying hysterically. He could barely understand what she was saying. What he was able to piece together was that the authorities had entered the building with search warrants and made everyone go outside. He told her to go home and be with her family, which was exactly what he planned to do.

When he pulled into his driveway, his wife was getting ready to leave for her job. She asked him why he'd come home so early and he told her he had a terrible headache, which also wasn't far from the truth. She gave him a kiss on the cheek and told him a package had arrived. She pointed to an envelope on the kitchen table. He waited until she had left the house before he sat down and opened the mysterious envelope. The letterhead was from Cayman National Bank, Office of the Manager. Alberto read on:

> *Dear Mr. Segundo,*
>
> *By now you are aware of the circumstances surrounding your previous employer. I say previous because the plant is in the process of being shut down. Your name was given to me by a close friend and associate who asked that I help you secure another position.*
>
> *Please report to Dominican Banco Nacional on Monday at eight thirty* A.M., *where you will begin your training as Office Manager. When you arrive please ask to speak to Louis Ottero, who will explain your duties. Your starting annual salary will be fifty-five thousand*

*plus benefits. I trust you will find that amenable to your
needs.*
   Yours truly,
   Mackenzie Stoddard

Alberto read and reread the letter. There was only one way
to find out if it was legitimate. He phoned the bank and
asked to speak with Mr. Ottero. When Ottero got on the
phone his first words were, "Good morning, Mr. Segundo. I
am delighted you will be joining our company. You have
come highly recommended."

Alberto stared at his phone. *Was he dreaming or was this
someone's work of fiction?* Alberto snapped out of his daze
and managed to say, "I . . . I am looking forward to working
with you."

"I understand you have a lot of management experience. I
believe you will be able to transfer your talents easily to a . . .
quieter environment."

Segundo almost laughed. "Yes, my background is office
management and it will be a good change of pace for me."

"Wonderful. I look forward to meeting you on Monday.
Enjoy the rest of your week and weekend."

Segundo pinched himself. Fifty-five thousand dollars was
fifteen thousand more than he was making at REBAR. Could
this really be happening? He poured what was left of the
lukewarm coffee sitting on the counter and switched on the
television. And there it was: the raid on REBAR. He watched
men in uniforms carry out boxes and boxes of documents,
while others wheeled computers out on dollies. He wondered
if they would come looking for him. But even if they did, he
had no idea why the company had been raided or who might
be involved. He clicked off the TV and walked out to the
patio. He sat down in a chair, smiled, and thanked God for
his good fortune as the sun warmed his face.

Miami

Annie and Myra strolled around the luxury cars in the Aston Martin showroom. Admittedly, they were works of art. The well-groomed salesman passionately described the features on the iconic DBS model, the same one Fielder had set his hopes on. Annie cooed. "Yummy. I'd also like to take a peek at the Vantage model."

"I see the Countess likes sleek and fast."

"My reputation precedes me." Annie gave a devilish smile. Little did he know how much she loved to speed. Myra gave her an elbow tap. Annie almost felt guilty wasting the salesman's time. If she ever wanted to buy herself a present, an Aston Martin would be hovering at the top of her list. It was too bad she was on a mission. She would have loved the opportunity to open up that baby on the Florida Turnpike.

The decibel level of the voices coming from the showroom manager's office was increasing. "I don't understand." Malcolm Fielder was cautiously haughty. He didn't want to appear overconfident, nor did he want to appear weak. "There has to be some mistake."

The manager turned his computer monitor around so Fielder could read the disappointing news from the financial department. The subject line on the email read: *Fielder: Bank Account Closed. Application Denied.*

The body of the email explained the details of the check number, amount, and status of his account—closed. Those words again. Fielder pulled out his cell and called the bank. He was told the manager was unavailable. He hadn't disconnected the call for more than a few seconds before his phone rang. It was the contractor who'd purchased the materials for the Riverwood Elementary School. Fielder could not fathom what the man was screaming about. *Cabbage? Rotting in a trailer?* "I'm sorry, but you must be confused. We did not ship you cabbage, or any other kind of produce." He was about to hang up on the raging lunatic when the call was interrupted by call waiting. It was his assistant in New York.

"Mr. Fielder . . . M-M-M . . ." she gasped.

"Victoria, calm down. Let me get rid of this ridiculous other caller. Hold on." Fielder was losing his patience. He returned to the other person, who insisted he had pallets of putrid vegetables on his premises.

The man was livid. "The bill of lading says concrete blocks. My nose says rancid. You better get someone on this pronto or I'll have a lawsuit slapped on your company quicker than you can say bok choy." He hung up.

Fielder had a stupefied look on his face. *Has the world gone mad?*

Annie slid closer to the office. "Oh, tell me about this one," she said to the salesman. It was the model closest to the office door where the men were. She could see their scheme was in play. She felt a rush of adrenaline and saw that Myra's face was also a bit flushed.

Fielder returned to his hysterical assistant. "Alright, Victoria, what seems to be the problem?"

The color rushed from his face as Victoria breathlessly explained that agents from the U.S. Marshals Service were on the premises with a search warrant and were removing all the electronic devices. "What on earth are you talking about?" *The woman must be having a meltdown*, he thought. Then the showroom manager cleared his throat, reminding Fielder there was other business that needed his attention. "Victoria, I will have to call you back. Take it easy." He gave a little shudder and turned to the man waiting semi-patiently beside him. "Sorry. Where were we?"

"The bank. Your account."

"Yes. Yes, of course." He scrolled through his contact list and redialed the bank's number. Again, the manager was unavailable. "Just give me a few minutes to figure this out," Fielder said and he walked into the main showroom to give himself a bit of privacy. He looked around and thought he was out of earshot. But Annie and Myra both had earrings with pin-sized short-range listening devices that allowed them to eavesdrop on conversations within fifty feet. They could barely contain their excitement when Fielder repeatedly told the person on the other end of the phone that it was imperative he speak to the manager now. His body language spoke volumes. He shook his head.

Fielder's phone rang again. It was an Ohio area code. *Probably that crazy produce guy*, he thought. He didn't answer it. Instead he decided it was time to check in with Walsh to see if there was any merit in the contractor's accusations. Walsh's phone went directly to voice mail. Fielder bounced the issue over to him. "Deal with it," was how he ended the message. As he walked toward the office his phone rang yet again. He thought he might scream. All he wanted to do was drive his car out of the lot. This call was from his condominium's association, informing him the building had been visited by the U.S. Marshals Service and they'd placed a padlock on Fielder's door. His world was turning into a major nightmare. Maybe that was it. He was having a nightmare. He took a detour into the men's room and splashed water on his face. As he stared into the mirror, he wondered how he was going to unravel this mess. Where to begin? Get to New York. Then he remembered his credit card had been canceled. That should have been his first clue something wasn't right. His phone vibrated in his pocket. It was the caterer. His check had been declined.

When he exited the men's room Annie and Myra were in his path. Annie stopped him. "Excuse me. Aren't you Malcolm Fielder?"

Now what? he thought to himself. "Yes, I am." He could barely choke out the words.

"I thought I recognized you. You're Andrea Watson's son. I mean Andrea Fielder. Your mother and I have been on a few charity committees together. I believe you and I met at one of them." Annie paused. "I'm Annie de Silva."

"Countess de Silva," Myra said proudly of her friend. "I'm Myra Rutledge."

Annie jerked a finger at Myra. "And she is the Candy Queen."

For a moment Malcolm thought he had started breathing normally again. "Nice to see you."

Annie jumped in immediately. "I couldn't help but over-hear that you are having some paperwork issues?"

Fielder let out a big sigh. "Yes. I don't know what is going on, but I need to get to New York immediately and my credit card isn't working either. I apologize. That is information you do not need to hear. I didn't mean to burden you with my problems."

Annie placed her hand on his arm. "Nonsense. I am going to be flying to New York this afternoon. You are welcome to join us. My Gulfstream is at the Miami Executive Airport."

"If it's not an inconvenience, I would greatly appreciate hitching a ride." Malcolm could not believe his luck.

"Of course. There's plenty of room." The hair on the back of Annie's neck was doing an excited happy dance.

"What time were you planning on leaving?" he asked, not that he had any place to go. The first order of business was to clear up this banking mess. Then he could deal with the condo mess, the car mess, and the yacht mess. He simply had to keep his wits about him.

"Actually, we were going there from here. We had a little time to waste so I thought I'd spend it here." She flinched, hoping the salesman hadn't heard her. She truly felt guilty. Time was precious and she had wasted his. If she could tell him why, perhaps he wouldn't have minded, but that was a nonstarter. She mollified herself knowing they had only spent about fifteen minutes of his time.

The car service had been waiting in the Aston Martin parking lot and was ready to bring them to the airport. Myra and Annie were like two schoolgirls getting ready for a prom. And Malcolm Fielder was their date.

An hour and a half later they were airborne. The pilot welcomed Annie and her guests and announced lunch would be served when they reached cruising altitude.

Myra had the exact dose of zolpidem ready to go. It was a long-term sleep aid, perfect for keeping Fielder unconscious for at least six hours. But first, he needed to relax.

Annie ordered a bourbon on the rocks for him. "That should soothe your nerves." He downed it lickety-split. The light on the FASTEN SEATBELT sign went off and Myra got up. Without asking, she fixed Fielder another drink, but this time it was laced with the sleeping drug; he would soon be down for the count. It was a good thing Kathryn would be waiting at the airport. Fielder was robust enough that an extra set of arms would be helpful getting him off the plane. Should there be any onlookers, the standard response would be "Drank too much."

Fielder began to yawn and blink his eyes rapidly. "Wow. I can't seem to keep my eyes open." Then he started to sway forward. Annie put her foot on his chest and nudged him back into his seat, where fell into a deep sleep. Annie and Myra watched in amusement at how his mouth was agape as he began to snore. "Time for the earphones." Annie placed her headset on and dialed to a channel that had nature sounds accompanied by piano music. Myra also donned a headset and chose Mozart.

Two hours later the pilot announced that they would be beginning their descent. Therefore, if they had to contact anyone using an electronic device, they had approximately fifteen minutes to do so.

Annie checked in with Kathryn. She was waiting at the terminal and Pearl was waiting at an abandoned junkyard on the outskirts of town. "Does she have the items I requested?" Annie asked.

"Yes, she does. All of it." Kathryn chuckled. "You are too much."

"Whatever it takes." Annie laughed.

When the jet landed, it taxied to the small terminal. There were only a few people milling about. The pilot, who had been with Annie for many years, knew she used her jet for a number of different purposes. He never asked questions and always looked the other way. This time he knew to taxi to the hangar and turn the jet so they could deplane without anyone observing. He lowered the airstairs and Kathryn climbed up, taking the steps two at a time. Annie and Myra guided her over to the still-sleeping Fielder.

"Come on, dude," Kathryn said as she slung one of his limp arms around her neck. Annie took his other arm around her neck and together they dragged him down the stairs to the waiting van. They heaved him in the back and Kathryn jumped in behind him. She began to zip-tie his hands and feet and tape his mouth. She looked over at Annie and Myra. "Just in case." High fives all around.

They had several hours to kill before Walsh would show up. So they went to a Chick-fil-A and bought almost everything on the menu, from a grilled cool wrap to a grilled spicy deluxe and, of course, the famous mac and cheese. "Four orders of that, please." Kathryn spoke into the drive-thru box to order their food.

"You'd think Maggie was here!" Annie laughed.

"In honor of her." Kathryn drove up to the next window, paid, and scooped up the bags of food. "Beer run is next." She knew to purchase Guinness. The flavor was so robust it could camouflage any additive.

When they arrived at the motel, Fielder was still out cold. "How long do you think he'll be like that?" Kathryn asked.

Annie counted on her fingers. Maybe another two, three hours. "We're going to have to pump him again."

"When he comes to, we'll poke a hole in the tape and give him something to drink. He might refuse at first, but he'll also be very thirsty," Myra said.

"If he tries to resist, I'll handle him." Kathryn smirked.

In the meantime, the women kept Fielder locked in the van, which was parked close enough so that they could keep an eye on it and check on him from time to time. Kathryn brought a blanket from her truck and spread it over one of the motel beds and they proceeded to have a chicken picnic. It had been a few hours and Kathryn went to check on Fielder. She brought a beverage in a paper cup with a straw to their guest. As expected, his eyes were rolling around as he was trying to focus. Before he could get much clarity, Kathryn poked a small hole in the tape that covered his mouth and slid the straw through the hole. "Here—drink this. It will make you feel better."

Fielder was so confused he readily accepted the drink. Within minutes he was out like a light once more.

It was almost eleven P.M. when the women received a message from Charles. Walsh was making good time on the interstate and should be arriving within the hour.

The rest of the evening was about to unfold. Kathryn would be sitting on one of the metal chairs outside her room. She would be drinking a beer. When Walsh showed up, she would make small talk and say, "You look like a feller who could use one of these." If he said yes, then it would be easy. More zolpidem. If he declined, she would have to use the sleeper hold Yoko had taught her. Then they would have to force-feed him the drug. "Let's pray for cooperation," Annie said.

"How about let's just pray anyway." Myra said. The three women held hands as Myra spoke. "Lord, give us the strength to help rid the world of evildoers and that these men should never have the opportunity to prey on innocent people again."

"Amen!" Annie said, followed by Kathryn.

Lights from an approaching vehicle swung past their windows.

"Alright! Places, everyone!" Annie clapped her hands and Myra cleaned up their picnic.

The car first stopped at the small motel office and then parked outside the room next to Kathryn's. She sat outside, rocking herself slowly in her chair and sipping beer out of the bottle. The taste almost made her wince, but it was for a good cause.

"Evenin'," she said with an exaggerated Southern drawl. She wanted to appear a bit in the bag, as if she might have had one too many. "Long drive?"

Walsh looked at the woman. He really wasn't in the mood for small talk. The six messages from Fielder had him unstrung, and he tried to put them out of his head. "Uh, yeah."

On cue, Kathryn said, "You look like a man who could use a beer right about now."

Walsh thought about it. If she was offering, why not? He knew he wasn't going to find anyplace open at that hour. "Sure. Let me put my things inside." He fumbled for his room key and opened the door. Kathryn quickly moved to get a cold beer for Walsh. She popped the top and poured in the ground-up sleeping pill.

After accepting the beer from Kathryn, Walsh took a swig and gave the bottle an odd look. Kathryn spoke up immediately. "Yeah, I always react that way on the first sip. After one or two, it's good going down."

"If you say so. I'm more of a Budweiser man."

"Well, sorry to say it's all that's available. So cheers!" She clinked her bottle against his. He took another swig and cringed. She thought he might decide not to finish it. "Have you eaten anything?"

He gave her an odd look.

"I've got some chicken nuggets left over if you're hungry. Got some mac and cheese, too, but it's kinda room temperature."

Walsh pursed his lips. "I think I'll take you up on that offer. A couple of nuggets and room-temp mac and cheese sounds good right about now."

"Y'all sit right there." Kathryn got up and sauntered into her room. Annie was already grinding up another pill. She smashed it with great vigor and then mixed it into the mac and cheese. "Maggie would cry if she saw that mac and cheese being used like this," Kathryn whispered.

"It's for a good cause," Annie whispered back and handed Kathryn the bowl.

When Kathryn returned to Walsh, she was surprised to see he was already halfway through the beer. "You're right. After a few sips, it's okay. Maybe it kills your tastebuds." He smirked.

Kathryn didn't know if she should bother giving him the mac and cheese. She didn't want him to overdose, but then he set the beer down and held out his hand for the food. She eyed him up and down. He could handle it. About halfway through the lukewarm, ooey-gooey stuff his eyes went around in a circle. "Must be too much driving in one day. Almost fifteen hours. I'm not used to it," he slurred.

"Yeah, if you don't do long hauls, it can wear you out. 'Road weary' is what I call it."

"That must be it." Then he collapsed. Kathryn checked his pulse. He was still breathing. She quickly dragged him into her room, where she zip-tied his hands and feet and taped his mouth just like Fielder. Kathryn ran out and pulled the van close to the motel room door. No one was in sight. The women dragged Walsh out and shoved him next to Fielder, who was still in la-la land. They rifled through Walsh's things and found the fifty thousand he'd stashed in the duffel bag. They took all of his belongings and removed all signs of him except for his rented car. One of the Men of the Sisterhood was on his way to drive the car to Mexico so it would look like Walsh went south of the border. They gathered all of their own personal items and got into the vehicle and were off to meet up with Pearl. Kathryn had also shoved the flatscreen TV Walsh had brought with him into the van. Along the way they dropped it off in front of a local senior community center.

Once the Sisters arrived at the junkyard, they found that the place was deserted, just as Pearl had promised. Annie jumped out and gave Pearl a big hug. "Got my stuff?"

"Here you go." Pearl handed Annie Viagra and Dulcolax. She pointed to the cement mix next to the oil barrels.

Kathryn could not contain herself. "I don't know what you're planning, but I can imagine something painful."

"You got that right." Annie mixed the Viagra and Dulcolax in a plastic cup. "Go force this down Fielder's throat." She handed the cup to Kathryn. Then she mixed another potion, but this time without the Viagra.

"How come you're not giving Walsh Viagra?" Kathryn asked.

"Because he isn't as big of a prick."

The four women laughed out loud. "Shall I begin to mix the cement?" Pearl asked Annie.

"Yes. Kathryn, make sure those guys finish their beverages."

"On it." Kathryn hopped back into the van and stirred the two men awake enough so that they could suck on the straws. It didn't take much convincing. Both men were bleary and terrified. Kathryn lifted Fielder and carried him over her shoulder like a firefighter would. She placed him in one of the oil barrels that came just above his waist. Then she handled Walsh the same way, placing him in the second barrel.

The cement mixture was reaching the right consistency and the women began shoveling it into the oil barrels. The cold cement brought both men to full consciousness. With their wrists and ankles tied, they could barely move. Their mouths were still taped so they couldn't scream. Only the whites of their eyes expressed the horror they were suffering. The women pulled an old sawhorse out from the nearby junk and placed it in front of the two men. Annie took out her tablet and dialed in the rest of the Sisters. They had front row seats to watch the cement hardening around the men while Fielder's erection was beginning to salute. As the cement hardened around his man-thing the laxative took hold. Unfortunately, there was nowhere for the excrement to go except backwards. Soon they would be choking on their own manure. It wouldn't kill them, but they might pray it would. Once the cement was completely stabilized they were in excruciating pain. There were no words to describe it and soon both men passed out from the misery.

Hoots, whistles, applause, and high fives were shared among

the jubilant group. "We may not have rid the world of evil, but we just got rid of two bad actors who will never be able to harm anyone again," Myra said proudly.

Pearl pulled out the hand truck and loaded the man-barrels into her van. She would deposit them in parts unknown, never to be seen or heard from again. They wouldn't be dead—but might wish they were.

Epilogue

Kyle took Zoe's advice and phoned Jack. Jack then phoned several of his contacts in New York. One of their previous missions involved a male strip club, and they had enlisted the services of a fashion design instructor who made the costumes. Within two weeks Kyle was working as an assistant administrator at FIT, the Fashion Institute of Technology. One of his duties was to coordinate student fashion shows. It was a dream job for Kyle.

Louise Phillips left the two-bit detective agency and started working for Avery doing background checks.

Fergus contacted one of his former colleagues at Scotland Yard and suggested that there should be an inquiry into the collapsed scaffolding that had injured Mason. As expected, it was revealed that someone had made a hole in one of the reinforcing rods, which caused the scaffolding to topple over. The perpetrator was never found, but Mason Chapman was cleared of any wrongdoing.

After two weeks of recuperation and spending time with Zoe in Cornwall, Mason decided to start a new chapter in his life. He invited Zoe to move to England. The only caveat was that they live in Cornwall together.

With no job and no real ties to New York, Zoe thought a change in scenery with someone she had grown deeply fond of was worth a shot. Annie helped Zoe get the cats to the U.K. and the three were off on a new adventure. Mason started a management company working with owners of bed-and-breakfasts and inns. Zoe got a job at a local dress shop and helped many of the women in town with fashion makeovers. Based on her recent extraordinary experiences, she also showed women how they could walk in their own power if they also felt fabulous about themselves.

And yes—Zoe and Mason got married.

Annie flew back to Miami and Fergus joined her. They went to the Aston Martin dealership and bought that beautiful car Fielder had so much wished was his. As soon as the papers were signed and the insurance company faxed over the paperwork, they hopped in the car and headed to Key West.

Myra returned to Grand Cayman, where Charles met up with her. They spent a glorious week rekindling their passion like two young lovers. Myra was very happy there was no one to hear their moans and groans, but she would ultimately recount some of the highlights with Annie. That's what girls do with their besties.

Eight months later

The day had finally come when the Village Square Project was ready to open. It was hard to believe that the project had been the impetus of the Sisterhood's recent adventure, which led to changes in so many people's lives. Izzie and Yoko were surrounded by the mayor, the local shopkeepers, and the city council members for a grand ribbon-cutting ceremony. Among the spectators were all of the Sisters, including their newest member: Zoe Chapman.

Please read on for an excerpt from SANTA & COMPANY, coming soon!

In this sparkling new Christmas novel by #1 *New York Times* bestselling author Fern Michaels, four close friends get together for a skiing vacation filled with a few unexpected bumps—and lots of laughter . . .

When longtime friends Amy, Frankie, Rachael, and Nina reunited for a holiday singles cruise, it not only deepened their bond, it changed their lives. Now they're getting together for another adventure, and what better winter setting than a fabulous ski lodge? Crisp snow and fresh air by day, cozy fires and delicious food by night, capped off by meeting up with their significant others for a New Year's Eve celebration—it's perfect.

At least, it's perfect until Frankie decides to go snowshoeing alone. When she twists her ankle right after losing her phone in the snow, Frankie wonders how she'll be able to summon help— only to be rescued by a reclusive Grizzly Adams look-alike who lives nearby and introduces himself as Troy Manchester.

Troy saves the day by helping the injured Frankie back to the ski lodge, but in the process, encounters a part of the L.A. life he's tried to leave behind. Nina, visiting the gift shop to buy magazines for a recuperating Frankie, is similarly shocked to glimpse someone to whom she was once connected.

Even in this unlikely spot, it seems there's no way to avoid their pasts. And as the mischievous Rachael and her sidekick Amy go to great lengths to patch up old friendships and spread the spirit of the season, the New Year may contain all kinds of new beginnings . . .

Prologue

It had been two years since the class reunion of Ridgewood High School, when four friends reunited and made a pact to go on a singles cruise if they hadn't secured a date for New Year's Eve. The anxiety-producing holiday was six months away so each of them thought they might be saved from the dreaded ship of lonely, desperate fools. Fortunately, the cruise wasn't the disaster they had thought it could be and each of them began new chapters in their lives.

What all four women had in common, besides graduating from the same high school, was their passion for their work. Most men found it intimidating to be with a woman who was smart, successful, and attractive; leaving a handful of eligible men who didn't feel threatened or overshadowed by their partner.

They approached these high jinks on the high seas as potentially entertaining if nothing else. Yet each of them had experiences that would change the course of their lives. Maybe not forever, but at least up until now.

Chapter One

Two years earlier

The instigator of the cruise, Francesca (Frankie) Capella, discovered romance right around the corner from her Manhattan apartment. Giovanni Caserta, a partner at Marco's Restaurant, offered to look after her cat Bandit while she was on the cruise. Across the sea and thousands of miles away, the universe was working behind the scenes to bring Frankie and Giovanni together upon her return. For Frankie it was an extremely comfortable relationship. Giovanni was as married to the restaurant as Frankie was to her publishing career. Both appreciated the affection and attention they received from the other without the insecurities and demands. Frankie knew the elephant in the room was the word "marriage." Neither broached the subject, and their friends and family had the good sense to keep their lips zipped.

Rachael Newmark had the reputation of being a major flirt. "Boy crazy" was often used to describe her, much to her dismay. She was coming out of a messy divorce followed by a string of unfortunate relationships. But it was her passion for dancing that recharged her self-worth when she opened a dance studio in Ridgewood, New Jersey. Her talent was her introduction to Henry Dugan, a dance virtuoso who spent every year on the cruise ship raising money for his organization, Let's Dance, a program to enrich the lives of underprivileged children. He was more than a decade older than Rachael, but that seemed to be working for her.

Nina Hunter was the star of an immensely popular sitcom. She was told the series was canceled while she was aboard the ship. Fortunately, her writing talent caught the eye of a colleague, which opened a new and exciting opportunity for her. The stipulation was she had to move from L.A. to New York. It took two blinks, and she was ordering packing materials. She was ready for a big change. She had convinced herself she wasn't ready for romance, but it too presented itself. What began with snarky banter at the cruise's opening cocktail party became the basis for interesting, deep, intellectual, and often hilarious conversations. They say the way to get into a woman's pants is through her brain. Make her laugh. Seal the deal.

Nina and Richard shared similar interests in the arts, theatre, books, and music. He was an attorney in Philadelphia, which made their arrangement feasible. He was only an hour's drive or train ride away.

Amy Blanchard was indeed a brainiac. She worked as a bioengineer at a firm in Silicon Valley, but academia was her true love. She applied for a position at MIT as an associate professor. This, too, would mean a major move across the country. There was also the downside of a decrease in her salary, but it was her dream job. Eventually she would figure out her finances with the help of Peter Sullivan, an accountant she met on the cruise. He lived in Connecticut, a much shorter commute from Boston than Northern California. In Peter, Amy found someone who loved solving math puzzles, whether they were business related or for sheer entertainment. It was true nerd love.

Nina, Frankie, and Amy agreed they had almost perfect situations. No one was smothering them, yet it was comforting to know there was that one special person out there. As for Rachael? The jury was still out. No pun intended. Richard once referred to Rachael's relationships as "one mistrial after another." Sure, it sounded cruel. But Richard was a pragmatist. It was remarkably close to the truth.

Amy's father, William Blanchard, had not been part of the friends' original plan, but after his golfing buddies canceled their weekend in Florida, he decided as long as he was already there, he might as well take advantage of the opportunity to see a few sights, eat, drink, and be around people. A cruise sounded like the perfect solution. His daughter was off with some friends, and his ex-wife? Well, who cared? He booked his ticket to the ocean air and relaxation.

The day the women boarded the ship, Amy thought she was having "Dad Sightings" but Frankie convinced her it was just her guilt about leaving her father alone for the holidays. While on the ship the four gal-pals became acquainted with a slightly older woman named Marilyn. One evening Marilyn canceled their dinner plans, saying she was meeting someone. The women were concerned she might be seduced by a charming lothario looking for a rich widow, so Amy and

Frankie stalked Marilyn, only to discover the "someone" was Amy's father. Surprise!

A year after the cruise, the five couples, including William and Marilyn, met for New Year's Eve at the Ridgewood Country Club. As they reminisced, they agreed the trip had been a magical adventure and promised never to do it again. But "never say never" was always one of Frankie's favorite expressions.